More Than I Can Bear:

Always Divas Series Book Two

More Than I Can Bear:

Always Divas Series Book Two

E.N. Joy

URBAN CHRISTIAN

www.urbanchristianonline.com

Urban Books, LLC
97 N18th Street
Wyandanch, NY 11798

More Than I Can Bear: Always Divas Series Book Two
Copyright © 2014 E.N. Joy

ISBN 13: 978-1-60162-669-1
ISBN 10: 1-60162-669-X

First Trade Paperback Printing May 2014
Printed in the United States of America

10 9 8 7 6 5 4 3 2 1

*This is a work of fiction. Any references or similarities
to actual events, real people, living or dead, or to real
locales are intended to give the novel a sense of reality.
Any similarity in other names, characters, places, and
incidents is entirely coincidental.*

Distributed by Kensington Corp.
Submit Wholesale Orders to:
Kensington Publishing Corp.
C/O Penguin Group (USA) Inc.
Attention: Order Processing
405 Murray Hill Parkway
East Rutherford, NJ 07073-2316
Phone: 1-800-526-0275
Fax: 1-800-227-9604

More Than I
Can Bear:

Always Divas Series Book Two

E.N. Joy

Other Books by E.N. JOY:

Me, Myself and Him
She Who Finds a Husband
Been There, Prayed That
Love, Honor or Stray
Trying to Stay Saved
I Can Do Better All By Myself
And You Call Yourself a Christian
The Perfect Christian
The Sunday Only Christian
Ordained by the Streets
"A Woman's Revenge" (Anthology: *Best Served Cold*)
I Ain't Me No More
Flower In My Hair
Even Sinners Have Souls (Edited by E.N. Joy)
Even Sinners Have Souls Too (Edited by E.N. Joy)
Even Sinners Still Have Souls (Edited by E.N. Joy)
The Secret Olivia Told Me (N. Joy)
Operation Get Rid of Mom's New Boyfriend (N. Joy)
Sabella and the Castle Belonging to the Troll (N. Joy)

Dedication:

This book is dedicated to my most dedicated readers. Because you picked up this book, you have invested in me with either your time, money, or both. Without that investment, there would be no divas series. There would be no BLESSEDselling author E.N. Joy. Because of you, I am. Thank you!

Acknowledgment

Natalie Weber of Urban Books; Girl, I don't even know what title to give you. You wear so many hats with the company. But what I do know is that you are the wind beneath so many of the authors' wings. Unfortunately, just like the wind, you sometimes might feel invisible. So I just wanted to take this time to let you know that I know you are there. I see you!!!!!!! Thanks for everything.

Chapter One

"I hate you! I hate you! I hate you!" With a piece of paper crushed inside each one of Paige's fists, she looked up to the heavens and cried out. Tears streamed down her face like a flowing river that had no ending place. If her eyes could shoot darts, she'd aim them at God's heart . . . if He even had one. As far as Paige was concerned, if God had a heart for her and He loved her as much as the Bible had professed, then why would He do something like this to her heart? Why would God tear it up into a million little pieces and serve it up to Satan on a silver platter?

Paige pulled her fists from the sky slowly and rested them under her chin, still clutching the two separate documents that each played a starring role in her real-life drama. Her mouth opened to ask God, for the thousandth time, "Why?" This time, though, nothing came out. Her query was stuck in her throat. Perhaps the word knew, like all those that had managed to escape Paige's throat within the past hour, it was useless to try to free itself. No answer had come as of yet. What would have made the exception this time around?

Paige melted down into what metaphorically resembled a pile of extra-dark chocolate that had lost its previous form of a nice sturdy bar. The mascara on her thick, long eyelashes had not run, but instead caked up on her lashes like dirt does once mixed with the wetness of rain. Although the sun was beaming through her living room window, she could barely see through the thick, black, blurry clouds her eye makeup was creating, not to mention the rain that kept pouring down from her eyes as well.

Right there on her living room floor, where she'd opened the piece of mail that was ultimately the straw that broke the camel's back, Paige could not stop the tears. She could not stop the pain. Hadn't she endured enough pain in her almost twenty-nine years of life? She'd dealt with the pain of being the blackest berry on the vine as a result of her dark skin complexion. She'd dealt with the pain of feeling as if her own mother had been ashamed of her, therefore not spending any quality mother-daughter time while Paige was growing up. She'd dealt with the pain of being a plus-size girl and pretending she was happy and comfortable with the skin she was in. She'd dealt with the pain of being in an abusive marriage. She'd dealt with the pain of finding out that her best friend, Tamarra, had slept with her abusive husband. She'd dealt with the pain of ultimately choosing to divorce both her husband and her best friend.

For the first time since she could remember, Paige was on the verge of true happiness. Forget true happiness; she'd been on the verge of joy. Of peace. For once in her life, true freedom from the grip it seemed the devil had had on her all her life had been within her reach. It was in plain view. She could have almost reached out and touched it. And now, just like that, it had been snatched away from her.

"I don't want Satan to consider me anymore," Paige pleaded to God in reference to the Book of Job, where Satan had been roaming the earth seeking whom he could devour. Then out of nowhere God asks if Satan had considered His servant Job. From that point on, Satan made Job's life a living hell. "Enough! Enough!" Paige began to pound her fist on the floor like a terrible two having a tantrum because her mother had refused her a lollipop in the supermarket checkout line.

Not even the ringing of Paige's cell phone tore her from her fit. As far as she was concerned, unless Jesus really was on the main line, no one on the other end of that phone could comfort her right now. She was certain no one else had the answers to the questions she'd been crying out. No one could possibly understand how she felt at this very moment. So to voicemail the caller went as Paige spread her body across the living room floor, finally releasing the papers from her grip. After a couple minutes she pulled herself into a fetal position and bawled. After a few minutes of that she lay on her back staring up at the ceiling, shaking her head, still in disbelief. Next she rolled onto her stomach again. Onto her side, pulling her knees to her chest with one arm across her stomach, as if the pain were something tangible she could scoop up like a baby. And like a baby, she ultimately fell off into a sleep.

By the time Paige opened her eyes again, the sun had taken cover for the night. Opening her eyes to complete darkness, Paige managed to pick up all 165 pounds of herself off the floor and walk her size-fourteen frame over to the lamp that sat on the end table next to her couch. She flopped down on the couch and washed her hands down her face. She'd almost felt like she was awakening from a bad nightmare until she spotted the balled-up pieces of paper at her feet. There lay the evidence that today's findings had been oh so real.

Living on the hope and a prayer of the possibility that this all still could have been a nightmare, Paige slowly bent down and picked up one of the balled-up documents. Back in a sitting position she unwrinkled it, flattening it out in her lap. After taking a deep breath and then exhaling, she allowed her eyes to roam the document in hand. There it was; she'd been granted her divorce from her now ex-husband, Blake. He hadn't contested any of the judge's orders. Thanks to the assistance of legal aid, it had been a rather quick and smooth process. The house: hers. Fifty percent of Blake's assets: all hers with the agreement that she would waive any type of alimony or seek any other type of support or civil damages from him whatsoever. Blake had also slid in a clause that Paige would forfeit and have to pay back all funds if she was ever found to have been unfaithful in the marriage. Blake had been adamantly convinced that Paige had cheated on him with her coworker-turned-best-friend, Norman. He could never prove it though, probably because it wasn't true. But it was obviously something Blake felt in his spirit was in fact true and would one day come to light. Knowing that wasn't the case, Paige didn't dispute the clause.

"The nerve!" Paige had spat upon reviewing the clause. "How dare the cheater have a clause about cheating?"

Overall, Paige had been just fine with her divorce arrangements. She couldn't have cared less about receiving alimony from Blake. She wanted no ties to the man. Besides, she'd been an independent sister taking care of herself before she'd met Blake. She would continue to do the same post-Blake. Under ordinary circumstances she wouldn't have even considered taking 50 percent of his assets, but he'd abused her mentally, physically, sexually, and spiritually. Yes, Paige had been certain vengeance was the Lord's and God would make Blake pay . . . eventually. But having no idea how long God would take to get him and get him good, Paige wanted to make Blake pay now—literally. So she hit him in his pockets, knowing money meant the world to Blake.

The next step Paige had planned on taking once the divorce was final was restoring her last name to Robinson: her birth name. Dickenson was her ex-husband's last name. The woman so unlucky enough to ever marry that man was the one who deserved to bear his last name, not her. The last thing she wanted to do was walk around being Paige Dickenson. That was not who she was anymore. Carrying a man's family name was serious business as far as she was concerned, and she was no longer part of Blake's family. What's in a name? Obviously a lot; otherwise, God wouldn't have renamed so many people in the Bible. And even though the last thing she was concerned with at the moment was remarrying, how did she expect her future husband to find her, the real her, Paige Renea Robinson, if she was still running around connected to and disguised as her last husband's wife? She did not want to present herself to the next man while bearing the name of the last man.

Paige looked down at the other document that lay balled at her feet. This paper just might have been the thing to have her reconsider this whole business of changing her last name back to Robinson. She picked it up, laid it on top of the divorce decree, and unwrinkled it. She blinked as she read the doctor's notes from her visit just a couple hours ago. She blinked again, hoping and praying the words would unscramble to read something else. They didn't.

"Pregnant." The word wrestled its way out of Paige's mouth. She wasn't just pregnant, but right at the peak of her second trimester. With the criminal trial against her husband for abusing and raping her, the filing of the divorce from Blake and the emotional divorce of her friendship with Tamarra, Paige had neglected her body to the point where she didn't even acknowledge her MIA monthly cycle.

"Stupid, stupid, stupid." Paige directed the insult at herself. "How could I have been so stupid as to not realize I hadn't been having a period?" The only reason why Paige had even gone to the doctor was because it was time for her annual Pap smear; otherwise, she probably wouldn't have even known she was pregnant until her dang water broke!

"This can't be happening." She continuously shook her head. "I don't even want his last name, let alone his baby. Please, God, don't do this to me. It's too much." Paige began to breathe in and out so deeply she just about hyperventilated. Scared that she would have an anxiety attack, she stood to her feet and began pacing her breaths until her breathing pattern was normal as well as her heart rate. She swallowed hard and then sat back down on the couch.

She rested her forehead in her hand as she tried to keep from throwing up just thinking about why she had ever willingly lain down with Blake and made a baby with him. That's when it hit her, the god-awful truth. She hadn't willingly lain down with Blake and made a baby. He'd raped her.

No sooner had Paige sat down on the couch than she jumped back to her feet. "The product of rape. You place a baby in my womb that's the product of the most awful experience of my life: my husband raping me? Really, God. I mean for real? You hate me that much?"

Paige refrained from using cuss words at God, as if technically she hadn't already been cursing him. There was so much more within her that she wanted to spew out, but she knew God knew her heart so her words were falling on deaf ears. Deep inside she loved God, but right now she was so frickin' mad that the last thing she wanted to do was tell Him how much she loved Him. Even though that's exactly what she knew she needed to do in order to get through this ordeal. She needed God. No matter how angry and upset she was with Him, she needed Him right now: this hour, this second. So without further delay, Paige kneeled down, looked upward, clasped her hands together at her chin, her fingers intertwining, and then closed her eyes.

"Dear God, first and foremost, I repent for my negative and hateful words I've spoken in this time of sorrow," Paige prayed. "I know you are a kind and loving God, but I'm so mad right now that I had to just get that off. And, well, you were the only one around for me to lash out at . . . besides myself. And believe me, I know I'm the only one to blame for this."

Tears fell down Paige's dimpled cheeks as she continued to pray. "I should have known Blake was a wolf in sheep's clothing. I knew He wasn't my soul mate when I married him. But I wanted him. I wanted him whether he was the one you had for me or not, which is why I didn't even ask for your permission before I walked down the aisle with him. Which is probably why I turned a blind eye to all the signs you placed before me telling me he was not the one you had for me. So I can't help but wonder, God, if being pregnant with his child is my punishment for not seeking you first. If it is, please let me off punishment, God. I know I might be asking a lot, but with you, I know I'm never asking the impossible. In Jesus' name I pray. Amen."

Paige found the strength to get back on her feet. Next she just had to find the strength to take a step. Not literally, but she had to find the strength to take a step toward resolving the dilemma she now found herself in. She had to do something and she was going to do something . . . with or without God's help, or His blessing.

Chapter Two

It was ten o'clock at night. Paige had wasted away that entire day, weeping on her living room floor. Finding out first she was pregnant and then returning home to find her divorce decree in her mailbox had been a gift and a curse, overwhelming her. The divorce decree would have been cause for a celebration had it not meant that in about five months she'd be an unwed mother. She'd give birth to a baby out of wedlock. She almost wished she never would have . . .

"Girl, don't you even think like that," Paige kept telling herself every time the notion popped in her head that had she known she was pregnant, she would have never filed for divorce. It was bad enough that God hated divorce and she'd have to bear that cross among her Christian peers. What would they think of her now as a divorcée running around pregnant? The thought was more than Paige could bear. That thought alone kept her weak.

Just when she thought she'd found the strength to pull herself together, she'd burst out crying. Now, after taking a shower and putting on her pajamas, she lay in her bed, practically turning it into a waterbed with all her tears. She'd ignored the many calls to her cell phone until the phone had gone dead. When her landline started ringing, she was quick to take it off the hook. She wanted to be alone and wallow in her own tears. Misery didn't want company today and neither did she. But evidently someone didn't get the memo as Paige heard her doorbell ring.

"Who in the world . . . ?" Paige asked, lifting up on her elbows and looking toward her doorway. Paige contemplated answering the door but, knowing she'd been crying all day, was certain she looked a mess. Her eyes were probably as swollen as Kim Kardashian's feet during her pregnancy and as red as Kim's cheeks the day she realized her and Ray J's sex tape had leaked.

Refusing to be seen as such a complete mess and not yet ready to talk about her situation to anyone, Paige decided against answering the door and lay back down. The doorbell rang again and once again Paige ignored it. When the ringing bell turned into a pounding knock, Paige placed the pillow over her head in an attempt to drown out the annoying sound. There were a few seconds of silence and Paige was almost sure the caller had gotten the hint and left her to lick her wounds in peace. That was until she heard a rapping on her bedroom window.

"You've got to be kidding me." Paige's emotions had done a 180 and gone from pity to pissed. She stomped over to her window and ripped the curtains back like she was imitating Norman Bates during the shower curtain scene in the movie *Psycho*. "Norman?" Paige said in surprise. She wasn't referring to Norman Bates either, but instead the Norman who had seemed to take over the role of her best friend.

"What's going on?" Norman's voice was barely audible through the window glass. "I've been calling you and texting you all day. I tried your cell phone. I tried your house phone. I knew you had to go to the doctor's today, so I've been scared to death," Norman spat, his tone a mixture of being perturbed and worried. "I hate to say this, but if you weren't already diagnosed with a terminal illness today at the doctor's office, then I'm going to kill you, woman."

Paige just stood there looking at Norman through the glass only wishing she'd been lucky enough to have a terminal illness. That way she wouldn't have to live with her current diagnosis . . . if that made any sense.

"Well, if you're not going to talk to me, can you at least let me in?" Norman pleaded.

"I don't feel like talking. Not tonight, Norman."

Norman knew it had to be something serious for Paige to refuse talking to him. Paige always talked to Norman, and he to her. They were like BFFs, if guys could be considered BFFs. They had worked at the movie theatre, where Paige was his boss, over the years. Here, recently, they even attended church together. Norman and Paige had been living proof that a male and female could be friends and comingle without hooking up. In spite of Blake's accusations, Paige had never been unfaithful to him with Norman. Norman had never played any other role than that of a friend.

Paige couldn't 100 percent say there wasn't a time when she had entertained the idea of being with Norman while married to Blake. It was the first few months of her marriage when Blake was so engrossed in his job and making money that he barely had time for Paige. He'd cancel dinner dates with Paige and even fun outings. It got to the point where Blake would even suggest Paige hang out with Norman; of course that was before he started suspecting something was going on between the two. When Blake cancelled last minute on their dinner reservations at Fondue Restaurant, reservations that weren't easy to get, it was Norman who filled in. When Blake couldn't attend the Cleveland Cavaliers game with Paige, back when the King himself was still playing for the team, it was Norman who filled in.

Because Paige had felt so neglected by her husband, she was in a vulnerable state around that time. She was starting to enjoy the company of Norman a little more than a married woman should. Mentally, she was allowing herself to cross the line of just coworker/ friend. It only made things worse when she and Norman shared an accidental kiss. Then of course there was the time when they did attend the game in Cleveland, had car trouble, and ended up having to share the last available room at a hotel. Feeling neglected by Blake, Paige enjoyed being with Norman. Being next to Norman. Even being accidentally kissed by Norman. Truth be told, it could have been any man. Paige just needed confirmation that she was a woman worthy of a man's attention . . . since her own husband wasn't showing her any.

Eventually Paige pulled herself out of la-la land and realized she was treading dangerous waters with the thoughts she was having about Norman. They were able to resume their close friendship without any awkwardness. Norman had been there for Paige ever since. He was there when she ended her friendship with Tamarra. He was there the day Blake came up to their job threatening Paige. He was even there to support Paige the day in the courtroom during her hearing against Blake assaulting her. It shouldn't have surprised Paige that he'd be there for her now.

"I'm not leaving until you let me in and talk to me, Paige," Norman warned.

"Go home, Norman, please," Paige pleaded right back.

Norman shook his head. "I'm a white guy standing outside of a black chick's bedroom window in the hood in the middle of the night. We've probably got about ten more seconds before one of your neighbors dial nine-one-one. So either you let me in or you take that money you've been saving up for years for that Louis Vuitton luggage set and bail me out of jail."

Norman knew just what buttons to push to open Paige's doors, literally. She sucked her teeth, threw the curtains back closed, and then marched to her front door. She unlocked it and sharply flung it open. "There. Happy?" she snapped at Norman as he stepped up onto her porch.

"Not yet," he replied, entering her house, closing the door, and locking it behind him. "Not until you tell me what's going on with you." He eyeballed the room for any telltale signs of what had Paige in such a funk that she'd barricaded herself in her home, avoiding all phone calls. That's when he spotted two crumpled pieces of paper on her couch. He looked to Paige then back to the couch. He did this a couple of times before Paige caught on and followed his eyes to the papers.

Paige hurriedly rushed over and retrieved the papers just in case her friend had any ideas about snooping.

"I take it those have something to do with the way you are acting," Norman surmised.

"No," Paige was quick to say. "They have everything to do with the way I'm acting." Just like clockwork, the tears filled Paige's eyes and flowed down her cheeks.

"Paige, honey, what is it?" Norman asked as he approached her, resting his hands on her heaving shoulders.

Paige took in Norman's comforting hands, resting her face on one of them while closing her eyes. Norman allowed her all the time she needed to gather her thoughts. After a few seconds, Paige finally opened her eyes to find Norman's, filled with sympathy, staring into hers. Right now he was more than just her friend. He was her superman, willing and ready to take the world off of her shoulders and place it upon his. Paige knew that couldn't be done, but it touched her soul to know that if Norman could, he would. He'd proven he'd place himself in harm's way if it meant protecting her the day Blake came up to her job in an evil fit. The gelled, dirty blond–haired, tall, slinky white guy didn't stand a chance against the tall, muscular-built, 230-pound black guy he found himself nose to nose with. Still, he didn't back down until Blake was out of there. Norman was indeed that genuine friend she thought she'd never have after being betrayed by Tamarra. He was her sign that God did, in fact, have a heart after all.

"Want me to get you something to drink? A glass of water?" Norman offered.

"Only if you're going to do a Nikki Newman and put vodka in it." Paige chuckled at her own reference to one of her favorite soap operas, *The Young and the Restless*. There were plenty of times during her lunch break she would sit and talk to Norman about the characters like they were real people. The storyline of Nikki Newman being an alcoholic and pretending her vodka was water was one of them.

"Here, sit down." Norman escorted Paige over to the couch.

Paige sat and then stared at the documents she knew Norman was patiently waiting to be clued in on. She figured there was no need to torture her friend any longer, or herself, as she really needed to talk to someone about her situation. She picked the papers up, then handed one to Norman.

Norman took the paper and then briefly scanned it. "Your divorce decree." A look of confusion accompanied Norman's statement. "I guess I kind of thought you would have called me over to celebrate, not be sitting here moping." With paper in hand, Norman sat next to Paige. "I thought this is what you wanted."

"It was," Paige said. "I mean it is. I mean, it would have been if it weren't for this." She handed Norman the other document.

He skimmed the second document. "Holy—"

"Didn't you just walk down the altar and get saved last Sunday?" Paige reminded Norman.

When Paige first started working with Norman at the movie theatre a few years ago, neither one of them had been into church. Paige was the first to join the Kingdom. Once she did, it kind of put a dent in her and Norman's friendship. Prior to Paige getting saved, her conversation was different and more compatible with Norman's, as the two often enjoyed conversations about dating experiences and sex. Paige getting saved came along right around the time she got promoted to Norman's supervisor. Paige began to distance herself from Norman, as the conversations he'd been used to having with her became uncomfortable to Paige in her newfound Christianity. The two ended up exchanging words when Norman accused Paige of acting "too good" to associate with him anymore.

Once Paige explained her walk with Christ to Norman, not only did he accept it and the new "trying to stay saved" Paige, he even agreed to visit her church. One visit turned into a couple more here and there. Those couple turned into a few before Norman ended up, just last week, both joining the church and the Kingdom. Paige liked to think she'd led the horse to the water on that one.

"I got saved last week, not last year. It's going to take me a minute to get rid of some of the words my vocabulary has been accustomed to," Norman explained, still staring down at the paper regarding Paige's pregnancy. "You're pregnant. But how?" He looked at Paige.

She tilted her head and twisted her lips as if to say, "Really?"

"I mean, I had no idea you two were still . . . after he came up to the job and all. The court hearing . . . I just thought . . ." Norman threw his hands in the air and then let them drop. "Heck, I don't know what I thought." He shook his head, stared at the paper one more time and then looked to Paige. "Please don't take this the wrong way, but what are you going to do? Are you going to go visit him in jail and tell him? Are you going to give him visitation of the baby when he gets out of jail? Joint custody?" There were dozens of other questions Norman had, but he decided to pause to allow Paige to answer the ones he'd already posed.

"I have no idea," Paige said. "The reality of it all still hasn't set in." She placed her hands on her stomach. "There is a frickin' baby growing inside here. A baby by a man who raped me, Norman." Paige tightened her lips to fight off the emotion that she couldn't quite put words to. "A baby by a man who I divorced, who I never want to see again for as long as I stay black."

Norman scrunched up his nose.

"Oh, that's just a saying some of us black folk use every now and again."

He straightened his face out in understanding.

"Anyway, what do I do?" Paige asked Norman with all sincerity as if he were the master of her fate and whatever door he suggested she walk through, she'd do just that. She wanted to be free from the burden of decision making. She had a saying that you only have to deal with the consequences of the choices you make in life, not the ones someone else makes for you. She figured if she let Norman make her choice, she'd be off the hook in the consequence department. "Just tell me what to do, Norman, because I can't even think straight."

Norman was silent for a moment as he put the words together in a decent order in his head before they left his mouth in any ol' fashion. "Do you want to be a mommy?"

"Of course, just not right now, and not with the seed of Satan."

"Paige!" Norman was appalled that a mother would refer to her child as a seed of Satan, no matter how it was conceived.

"I'm sorry. I know that sounds cold, but, Norman, that's how I feel." Paige looked down at her stomach as tears filled her eyes. "I don't want any part of Blake and it sickens me to know a part of him is growing inside of me."

"But it's a part of you too."

"But I don't want it to be and I don't look at it that way. To me, it's my rapist's baby. Because my baby, the one I'm going to call my child, will be made in love with a person I am in love with and who is in love with me. Now I've read the books and I've seen the movies where a woman finds herself pregnant by a rapist and she still considers the baby a gift from God. Well my life is not scripted. This is the way I feel and being a Christian does not protect those kinds of feelings from infiltrating my heart. I'm still a Christian."

"I hear you. I get it and I'm not judging you. I believe you absolutely feel that way right now, but once you have—"

Paige threw her hand up in Norman's face, coming a mere inch from accidentally mushing him. "Unh, unh. Don't you say it. Don't even think about saying it." Paige stood to her feet and began to pace the floor.

"So if you don't even want me to make a mere mention of you having the baby, then obviously your mind is already made up. So what the hel . . . what the heck are you asking me my advice for?"

"Because you're my friend," Paige said in a tone begging for her best friend's sympathy.

"No, because you wanted me to say it so that you wouldn't have to. You wanted me to give you marching orders so that you wouldn't feel like it was all your idea. Well it ain't happening."

"Tah, and since when did it become such an issue with you?" Paige spat. "It wasn't an issue with that trifling Britney Spears lookalike you dated three years ago who told you she was knocked up and ganked you for five hundred dollars to get rid of the baby."

"Well you know like I know that it turns out she was never really pregnant. She just wanted money so that she could go to Cancun with her girlfriends."

"Yeah, but you didn't know that at the time you were laying five Benjis in her grimy little paws. You didn't have a conscience about your own poor little unborn baby then, so why have one with mine now?"

"Because yours is real," Norman countered.

"You thought yours was at the time you laid money for the procedure in her hand."

"But I wasn't saved then. I didn't know then what I know now. Do you not think for one minute there are not any Christian women today who had abortions back before they knew the Word and were saved? God's not holding that against them. When you know better you do better. Well I know better now, and you can't throw in my face now what I didn't know then. That's not how this Christian thing works. I've only been saved a week and even I know that. That's not how God works."

"What's God got to do with it?" Paige roared. "This is about me and my inability to love this child the way it would need to be loved. I don't have it in me."

The word "revelation" might as well have appeared on Norman's forehead as he digested and dissected Paige's words. "Oh, I get it now. This whole 'you not wanting to have this baby' thing goes beyond the rape and this being Blake's child. You're afraid that the same way you and your mother didn't have the loving mother-daughter relationship you desired, you won't be able to have that with your child either. You're afraid that you won't be able to give your child what you feel your mother didn't give you when you were a child."

"No, it's not . . ." Paige started, but then decided against lying. "Okay, so maybe you're right. Maybe it's all of those things. And all of those issues equal three strikes. I'm already out of the game before the national anthem is even sung. I can't do this, Norman. I won't. And I haven't even mentioned the challenge of raising a child without a father. I was raised in a two-parent home and I half made it out sane. I can't bring a baby into the world knowing its father isn't going to be in its life because he'll be in jail the next four years for raping and beating his mother, and then on top of that assaulting a court officer during the trial. And what if it's a boy? I can't teach a boy how to be a man. I'm not having this baby."

"Are you not having this baby or are you not keeping this baby? There is a difference. And not once have I heard you say either 'A' word. So which is it, Paige. What are you going to do? Which 'A' word is it going to be?"

Paige paused for a moment and then spoke. "I'm not having this baby, Norman."

"Then what are you going to do?"

"Not have this baby."

"We can dance around the word all you want, but if you're big and bold enough to do it, then surely you're big and bold enough to say it. So say it. What are you going to do, Paige?"

Paige shook her head and turned away in shame. "You know what I'm talking about."

"Say it," Norman demanded.

"I won't."

"You can't."

"It's not that I can't—"

"Then say it. You mean you can trot out here to some clinic to have the procedure done but you can't even fix your lips to say the technical term for it. Wow," Norman pressed.

"Why are you doing this?"

"Because I need you to listen to yourself. I really want to hear you put that out in the universe if that is truly what you are hell bent on doing. Because I'm not going to stand here and try to talk you out of something your mind is made up on doing. Now if your heart is still on the fence, that is a different story. But if you're all in, then just say it and do what you need to do."

Paige looked into Norman's eyes that silently pleaded with her to please consider other options. The other 'A' word might not be so bad, especially if the child landed with a family who could do all the things for the child that Paige couldn't. But did she really want to sacrifice her body for something she felt no connection to?

"Well, what's it going to be?" Norman said.

Paige swallowed hard and then forced herself to say what deep within she'd made up her mind to do from the moment she got her pregnancy results. "Abortion. I'm getting an abortion." Hearing herself say it almost brought Paige to her knees. As a matter of fact, she would have fallen to her knees if Norman hadn't been there to catch her fall and take her over to the couch.

The two just sat on the couch while Paige buried her face in Norman's chest and cried. "Please don't hate me for my decision, Norman. It doesn't make me a bad person. I'm still a Christian." Paige tried to convince herself more so than Norman.

Kissing Paige on the forehead Norman replied, "And I'm still your friend."

Chapter Three

When Paige first opened her eyes, she had no idea where she was, as they were greeted with darkness. She jumped up, the cover that had been pulled up to her neck dropping to her waist. She frantically looked around until her eyes became familiar with her surroundings. She exhaled once she realized she was in her living room on her couch.

"What time is it?" she mumbled. She pulled the covers off of her and placed her legs on the floor. She wiped her eyes and then that's when something else familiar caught her eye. "Norman?"

He stirred upon hearing his name, but he didn't wake up. He was curled up on the living room chair. Seeing how uncomfortable he looked made Paige wish she hadn't been so cheap and splurged for the matching loveseat instead. No, his six-feet self wouldn't have stretched out comfortably on that either, but it would have been better than that chair.

Paige sat there for a moment trying to recall how her night had ended with Norman before she lost consciousness into a sleep. "Ahh." She recalled having finally confessed her plans of an abortion, then burying her shameful face in Norman's chest, where she cried shameful tears. That's how she must have fallen asleep. Of course Norman being the caring friend to her he was must have gotten her a cover and let her sleep. Too bad she couldn't sleep off shame like one could a hangover.

Paige stood and stretched. She followed the moonlight into her kitchen, where she turned on the light and went to the cabinet to get a glass. She went to the freezer and got ice, then filled her glass with tap water.

Paige wasn't a bottled water type of chick. Tap water hadn't been too good for the generations before her, so it wasn't too good for her either. She placed the glass to her lips as she turned away from the sink. "Holy . . ." Her glass went crashing down onto the floor, shattering into pieces, with water splashing.

"And you've been saved how long?" Norman scolded her the same way Paige had scolded him earlier in the evening for almost slipping up and cussing.

"Yeah, but you scared the . . . You scared me, man," Paige said, rolling her eyes. "You don't know how to announce yourself when you enter a room, a quiet room, in the middle of the night?" She made her way over to the utility closet to retrieve the broom, dustpan, and some rags.

"Here, I got it." Norman took the items from Paige's hand. "Sorry. I'm a bachelor. I'm used to just getting up in the middle of the night and entering a room without announcing myself. At least I'm not in my boxers. Or even worse." He winked at Paige.

"Ugh," she said at just imagining Norman in the buff. She shook her head and went to fix herself another glass of ice water. "You want a glass?"

"Sure." Norman accepted her offer as he cleaned up the mess. By the time he was finished cleaning, Paige was finished preparing their drinks and had sat down at the kitchen table.

Norman joined her after putting the cleaning supplies back into the closet and then washing his hands. "So, how do you feel?" Norman took a sip of his water as he awaited Paige's response.

"Honestly?"

"Since when have I known you to bite your tongue and not be honest?"

"I feel like killing myself." Paige took a sip of her water as if she'd simply told Norman her favorite color was blue and not that she had thoughts of suicide.

"What?" Norman gave Paige the "come again" look.

"In the short amount of time it took me to get from that couch" —she pointed—"to this kitchen, I truly thought about coming in here to get a knife to cut my wrist instead of a drink to quench my thirst." Paige took in the look of horror on Norman's face and let it die down before she continued. "What can I say? That's just how quickly the devil can work on someone's mind." She took a drink of water.

Cupping his hands around his glass, Norman thought for a second and then spoke. "Paige, honey, if you feel like that now, imagine how you are going to feel after, you know . . ."

"After I kill my baby?" There was a sharpness to Paige's tone.

"I didn't say that, Paige. Don't put words in my mouth."

"I'm not putting words in your mouth. I'm taking the words out of your eyes. I see it in your eyes, Norman. Just say it. You think I'm a killer."

"I don't think you are a killer. I don't agree with what you are doing, but heck, over the years I'm sure there are a lot of things you've done that I haven't agreed with. I'm sure there are a lot of things I've done that you haven't agreed with." Norman exhaled. "Heck, I know for a fact there are because you don't hesitate to let me know. Still, just because I don't agree with some of your choices doesn't mean I'm not going to be there for you. Like I said, Paige, I'm your friend. Friends don't abandon friends in their time of need. I was called to be your friend, not your judge. What don't you get about that?"

Paige could tell from Norman's tone that he was almost offended that she perhaps doubted his friendship to her. "I'm sorry, Norman." She shook her head as if her scrambled thoughts might happen to fall into order with a shake or two of the head. "I don't mean to question your friendship. But right now I'm questioning life. Not just the life of this baby, but my own life." Paige pounded her flat hand against her chest. "For a split second"—she snapped her finger—"I thought about taking my own life. That's serious." Her eyes watered.

"This is all serious. I get that," Norman assured her.

"And you know what changed my mind about taking a knife and cutting my wrist? The fact that I'd guarantee myself a ticket to hell for committing suicide. But see, if I just take out this baby, I reasoned with myself, I could repent, receive God's forgiveness and have some kind of chance at getting into heaven. Is that sick or what?"

"No, it's actually valid reasoning. And at the same time, it's selfish."

"Of course it's selfish, but don't I have the right to be selfish for once in my life? All the crap I've been through? I was in an abusive relationship, my so-called best friend sl—"

"Slept with my husband," Norman cut her off and began mocking her. "You were raped. Your mother didn't give you the attention and love you deserved growing up," Norman said. "Is that your story? Is that who you are going to be for the rest of your life? Is that what is going to define you? If so, I don't know, Paige. Maybe I'm not the friend you need in your life."

"Well, maybe you're not!" Paige spat as she stood to her feet. "A friend understands and sympathizes when—"

"And that's just what you're looking for isn't it? Sympathy. Well, if you don't mind, I'd like the pleasure of being honest for once. Or 'keeping it real.'" Norman used quotation marks for his last statement. "Paige, I truly understand all that you have been through in your life and you don't deserve not one ounce of the pain you've endured either physically or mentally. But what I don't want to see you do is use that pain as an excuse or as an attention seeker."

"What, come again?" Paige's bottom lip began to tremble in anger at Norman's words.

"So many people use their pain as a means to get people to feel sorry for them because when someone feels sorry for you it's a form of attention. I can think of so many other things about you that are attention getters. Positive things. Don't let the negative things that have happened to you in your life be who you are. That's not a person I would want to be friends with, Paige. And neither would you if the shoe were on the other foot."

"If the shoe were on the other foot I'd . . . I'd . . ." This was the moment of truth for Paige. Either she was going to face her truth or get mad at Norman for telling the truth. "I'd want a friend like you to tell me the truth and not just what I want to hear." There; she'd relented. "If the shoe were on the other foot, I wouldn't bite my tongue not for one second. But the shoe is not on the other foot. I'm wearing it and everything in me wants to kick it off and go running away barefoot."

"You can't run from this." Norman walked over to Paige and put an arm around her. "Well, maybe you can run, but you can't hide."

"And I can't have this baby either, Norman. I just can't. I don't want it. I don't want it. I don't want it." Paige burst out into tears. "Someone who is meant to be a mother would never say that about her child. And if I'm saying that now, if I'm feeling that much disdain about the baby now, I can only imagine how I'll feel if I have to look into its eyes and see . . . and see . . ."

"And see what, Paige? And see who?" Norman prodded.

"I can't." Paige shook her head.

"You can. Just say it. It's a time for truth, remember? The whole truth. That's what's going to make you free." Norman grabbed Paige gently by the shoulders to face him. "You don't want to look into your baby's eyes and have to see who?"

Paige allowed the flow of her tears to lighten before she spoke. "Me. I don't want to have to look into my baby's eyes and see me. Not Blake, but me, my life. I'm so afraid I won't be able to save my baby from all the hurt and pain that I'm filled with, all the hurt and pain that led up to its conception. I don't want to see that every time I look at my child. I can truly understand now why Tamarra did what she did."

A puzzled look scurried across Norman's face.

"Nothing. Never mind," Paige said, realizing Norman was clueless of her former best friend's past that Tamarra had shared with Paige.

Whether Paige was no longer friends with Tamarra or not, it wasn't her place to reveal to anyone that Tamarra had been raped repeatedly by her blood brother when she was growing up. As a result of the rape she became pregnant and gave birth to a child that her parents ended up raising as their own. Tamarra couldn't bear to nurture the seed of her pain. So she packed up and moved from Maryland here to Malvonia, Ohio, leaving her past behind . . . and her child. A child whom she never raised as her own a day in her life.

Paige had never judged Tamarra for that. She was so glad she hadn't either, because now she found herself in a similar circumstance. Only she wasn't even going to give her child the opportunity to be born, let alone abandon it. She didn't even want to weigh the worst of the two evils.

"Like I said, Paige, change your story. Change who you are. Choose to see something different in yourself, in your child."

"Norman, don't. You don't have to agree with what I'm doing, but please don't try to talk me out of it. My luggage is already overweight for this guilt trip and I can't afford to pay any extra fees." Paige sharply removed herself from the kitchen, and headed back to the living room where she turned on a lamp.

Norman followed on Paige's heels with what appeared to be excitement. "No, no, I'm not trying to talk you out of anything. I'm just trying to get you to understand your true reasons for wanting to abort your child. Maybe if you can confront and deal with your reasons—"

"I know my reasons. As selfish as they are, I'm well aware of them." Paige sat down on the couch on top of the blanket that had once covered her. "I'm damaged right now. I never even got a chance to heal from the last wound before I got inflicted with something else. I'm bitter, I'm mad, and it's poison. It's not fair to bring a child into this mess. Besides, I'm divorced. I'm pregnant. I ain't been saved but a few years. That ain't long enough to restrain myself from kickin' some church folk butt if anybody says the wrong thing to me about my situation."

"I'm sure Sister Unique felt the same way when she got pregnant with the twins knowing she already had three children by three different fathers," Norman was quick to remind Paige.

"But . . ." Paige's words trailed off when she realized that there was no but.

"If God did it for Unique, if He pulled her through, what in the world makes you think He won't do it for you?"

"But . . ." Again, Paige knew there was no but. Norman was speaking the truth right now, and it was actually starting to soften Paige's heart toward the matter.

"But God," Norman said, sitting down next to Paige and taking her hands into his.

"I know it sounds weak and shallow, but I do care about what people think of me. I hear people say all the time that they don't care what people think of them, but they are lying. Half the things we do in life we do because of other people. We don't buy that nice pair of pants not because we don't like how we look in them, but we are concerned with how other people will think we look in them. 'Does my butt look big?'" Paige mocked. "As long as you like how your behind looks in it, buy the dang pants! But no, we concern ourselves with what others think we will look like. The things we do, the things we say, even the decisions we make somehow are always influenced by what other people will think."

"Then if what people think, about you running around as a divorced woman pregnant, is a big part of the reason why you want an abortion, that and the fact that you don't want to raise your child alone without a father, then I think I have the perfect solution." A smile crept across Norman's lips and Paige braced herself for his bright idea that had already lit up his face.

Chapter Four

Paige gripped her stomach as she slid off the couch. She couldn't control her laughter. Just moments ago she felt as if she may never laugh again, and now here she was feeling as if she may never stop laughing. "Ahhhh, haaaaaaa, ahhhhhh," Paige roared as tears of laughter fell from her eyes.

"Come on, what's so funny?" Norman said, feigning a smile to hide the agitation he was feeling from Paige's reaction to his suggestion.

"You. You're what's so funny." Paige continued to laugh. She twisted and rolled from left to right as she laughed uncontrollably. "Oh my goodness, Norman. You are a good friend," she said as she attempted to get her laughter under control. "Thank you so much for cheering me up. I really needed that laugh." Her laughter subsided as she looked to Norman, who wore a dead serious look on his face. "Wait," Paige said as she ceased her laughter all together. "You weren't . . . you weren't serious were you?" The stoic look on Norman's face let her know that he very much had been. "You were. You were serious." Paige couldn't help but to holler out laughing again.

"It wasn't that farfetched of a suggestion," Norman said with an attitude, displaying his disdain at Paige's reaction.

"I'm sorry. I'm sorry," Paige said, trying her best to stop laughing, but little chuckles still made their way out.

"Just forget it. Never mind. I was simply trying to help is all."

Paige stood as she managed to stop laughing completely. "Really, I know you are only trying to help and I appreciate your offer to make an honest woman out of me, but seriously, Norman, I know that was just a desperate effort to keep me from getting an abortion." She looked at Norman. "Me marry you?" She pointed from herself to Norman and cried out, "Jesus, take the wheel!" And before she knew it, Paige found herself laughing in Norman's face yet again.

"Look, do what you want." Norman stood. "I was only trying to help. I'm out of here. Call me if you need me."

"Whoa, whoa, wait." Paige stepped into Norman's path, stopping him in his tracks by placing her hand on his chest. She, with a serious face, looked at Norman, whose eyes were cast downward. It was as if he was too embarrassed to even look at his friend. "Norman, you . . . you actually truly are serious aren't you?"

He turned his entire face away.

"Norman." Paige was so moved she threw her hands around his neck and pulled him in for a hug. "I'm sorry, I honestly didn't . . . I truly didn't . . . I . . ." She couldn't even express the words that described how moved she was that Norman would be practically willing to give up his life to save the life that was growing inside her. To save her reputation as a Christian woman.

"Like I said, just forget it. It's all good." He wobbled his head as if shaking it all off. He removed Paige's hands from his shoulders and stepped aside and around her, heading for the door.

"No, Norman, please don't go," Paige pitifully called out to him. "Stay. Let's . . . let's talk about . . . it."

Norman slowly turned to face Paige. He was looking for any sign of laughter. Her appeal to him had almost sounded genuine. He wanted to make sure her expression matched her tone. It did. Without saying a word, Norman went and sat back down on the couch. Paige followed suit, sitting down next to Norman. It would be several seconds before either spoke.

"I just . . ." both started. "I was just . . ." They did it again. "I . . ." It kept happening. "You go first." And happening.

"Ladies first," Norman finally squeezed in before Paige could speak over him.

Paige cleared her throat. "I was just thinking that, I don't know . . . maybe you've got something here. You know, the whole 'you and me getting married' thing."

"Just a moment ago you were laughing hysterically. Now you're actually sitting here telling me with a straight face it might be a good idea after all. What gives?"

"It's just that nobody has ever been willing to sacrifice their entire life for me. Nobody outside of Jesus anyway. And you're serious. You're one hundred percent serious. I mean, sure we've been friends for some years, but I've never even met your parents before, nor you mine. As far as they are concerned, we're just coworkers. They'd think we were crazy."

"There you go worried about what other people think again. That's going to prevent you from making any decisions at all, let alone the right decision."

Paige ran her hand down her slicked-back ponytail. "I know, which is why the abortion is so much easier. No one will ever know. Just the three of us: you, me, and God."

"Lord knows I've fantasized about it before, but that's not really the threesome I had in mind."

Paige play punched Norman in the shoulder. He smiled. She returned the smile. It was official: they were on good terms again.

"You wanted my advice," Norman reminded Paige. "You practically wanted me to make your decision for you, hoping it would be the one you'd had in mind. And even though it wasn't, I'm asking you to trust me enough and believe in me enough to still want my advice . . . and follow it."

So many thoughts ran through Paige's mind she started to get dizzy. "Oh, God, this is too much." She held her head in her hands. "Way too much."

"It's not." Norman turned and removed Paige's hands from her head and nestled them inside of his. "The Word says that God will never give you more than you can bear. Never. So even if you don't trust me, don't you trust God and His Word?"

Paige stared at Norman for a moment. "Uggghhhh. Why did I have to go and invite you to church? Had I not, you might just be the devil's advocate agreeing to go to the clinic with me. But no, you gotta keep bringing up God and His Word, convicting me for an action I haven't even committed yet. Uggggghhhh," she yelped again, mad that Norman's words were seeping into her spirit, into her mind, slowly but surely changing its course.

"Hey, you created this Frankenstein," he told her.

She nodded. "Yeah, I did, didn't I? And you know what? I'm glad I did." Paige smiled. Inviting a friend to church and introducing them to Jesus was the most priceless thing a friend could ever do for another friend.

"So what are you saying? Are you going to be a mommy in a few months?"

Paige looked down at her stomach. For the first time she allowed herself to imagine a beautiful life, a gift from God, snuggled up inside of her. For the first time, the thought of being chosen by God to bear life made her smile. Even if bearing life was more than she could bear.

Chapter Five

"Okay, so rule number seven is no—"

"This is stupid," Norman cut Paige off as the two of them sat at the kitchen table with a composition notebook before them.

Norman had slept on the couch that night while Paige tossed and turned in her own bed. She was anxious to put on paper all the thoughts and ideas that were running through her head about her and Norman's little plan. As soon as the sun poked the tip of its head from behind a cloud, she felt it was okay to go wake Norman up from his sound sleep to get to work. With pen and notebook in hand, Paige had excitedly awakened Norman from the couch and led him to the kitchen, which was soaked with the scent of the fresh pot of brewing coffee.

"How do you know it's stupid? I haven't even told you what it is yet," Paige said with her coffee mug in one hand and a pen in the other.

"I mean this whole thing is stupid. Who makes up rules to follow in a marriage?"

"Two people who make up a whole marriage in the first place," Paige reasoned. "It's not like you and I have been friends with benefits or friends who had been hiding a love and passion for one another. Norman, you and I have almost been like brother and sister." Paige thought about that comment for a moment and then scrunched her nose up. "Yuck, I take that back. Makes this whole marriage thing between the two of us sound kind of sick.

But anyway, if this is going to work, we have to lay some ground rules. And so far, I don't think any rule I've listed so far is unreasonable."

Norman yanked the notebook in his direction and scanned over the six rules Paige had already taken it upon herself to list. "Okay, what about sex then? I don't see any rules about sex on here."

Paige spurted out the sip of coffee she'd just taken, soaking and ruining the page of rules. She quickly stood with her hand under her chin to catch the coffee dripping out of her mouth. She rushed over to the counter and retrieved a paper towel and wiped her face. She then grabbed a couple more and went to sop up the spill. She wiped the table and dabbed at the notebook as if Norman weren't even there and she was simply engaged in her daily chores.

"You can grab as many paper towels as you'd like, but you're never going to be able to wipe away the big elephant that's standing right in the middle of the table." Norman chuckled. "Since when did the word 'sex' get you all choked up?" Norman decided to keep teasing Paige. He leaned back and massaged his chin. "Although I'm sure the visual of you having your way with a fine stud like me can cause you to get a little choked up."

Paige immediately stopped wiping. "Don't flatter yourself. That is not what got me choked up. The fact that you'd think for one moment that this marriage will include sex is what has me choked up." Paige went and threw the soiled paper towels into the trashcan.

"What kind of marriage doesn't involve sex?" Norman asked before biting his bottom lip and saying, "Hmmm, I guess let my buddies tell it, pretty much all of them." He let out a laugh.

"This is not a laughing matter." Paige returned to her chair. "Seriously, we're only doing this for the sake of the baby. So that it's not being raised by some divorcée single mother, but, instead, two loving people."

"And don't forget we're doing it for you as well." Norman reminded Paige about her insecurity of what people would think of her as a single, divorced, pregnant woman.

Paige snatched up the notebook and went and threw it in the garbage as well. "This is an awful idea. I can't even believe I considered it for one moment. What were we thinking?" Paige leaned against the kitchen counter.

"I was thinking about my friend." Norman stood and walked over to Paige. "And the baby growing inside her belly." He pointed, placing his index finger on her stomach. "A baby that, no matter how hard and tough she tries to act, if she gets rid of will hurt her more than anything else in her life." Suddenly Norman felt little droplets of water hitting his hand. He looked up to see tears falling from Paige's eyes. He wiped her tears away. "I'm just trying to make this as easy as possible for you. I'm putting my own self aside for the sake of the baby. I don't want any sex from you. I was just messing with you. I just wanted you to see how ridiculous it is to go into something so unconventional with rules. We have to let God be in control of this."

"But this is a mess. And you know the saying: God don't bless no mess."

"No, but God can take your mess and make it a blessing."

Paige placed her hand on Norman's cheek and stared into his eyes. "I'm so tired of you making sense."

"I'm just trying to make you happy." Norman returned the stare and for one second, just one second, he envisioned that Paige could be his wife and the two could raise a family together . . . for real.

Chapter Six

"Will you please stop biting your nails? That's one of my pet peeves. It makes my skin crawl to see a woman biting her nails," Norman said to Paige as he turned onto his parents' street.

"I can't help it," Paige said, sitting over in the passenger seat, staring out of the window. "I'm nervous. I'm about to meet your parents for crying out loud."

"Well, find some other nervous habit. The whole nail-biting thing is just disgusting. Do you know your hands, fingers, fingertips are the dirtiest part of your body? I mean they touch everything. They touched the door handle to this car, which sits outside and gets covered with all type of debris and whatnot. And now you have them in your mouth." Norman made a face to show his disgust.

"Then don't look, then. I can't help it. It was a habit I had as a child. For years I managed to overcome it, but now, today, it's back with vengeance. See?" Paige put her hands in Norman's face so that he could witness where she'd bitten her middle fingernail down to the skin.

"Yuck, no!" He swerved and then regained control of the vehicle. "We've only been married four hours and already you're trying to kill a brother." He looked to Paige and then back to the road. "Was this all a setup so you could marry me, kill me, and then live off my social security? You're probably not even pregnant. Don't think I don't watch the ID channel. You women are a trip."

"For one, no, it's not a scam. Sorry, I didn't mean to make you almost drive off the road. For two, look at yourself in the rearview mirror and you will see for yourself that you are no brother, so no; I'm not trying to kill a brotha." They both laughed.

Glad that the tension had turned to laughter Norman said, "You know what, I think we kind of just had our first fight as husband and wife."

The couple had taken a trip down to the courthouse just a few hours ago. Their plan was officially in motion now that they had officially said their "I do's." There was really no need to wait. Paige would be showing soon and before she changed her mind about the whole crazy idea of theirs, she figured there was no better time than the present to etch their vows in stone. So just one week after Norman's so-called proposal, the two were now husband and wife.

Paige thought for a moment. "You know, you're right. That was our first argument as husband and wife. Guess that makes it official."

"Oh, no. Only one thing makes it official." Norman looked to Paige and raised his eyebrows up and down.

"Do I have to remind you that our marriage is just like the rest of America's? Sexless?" Once again the two laughed as they pulled up into a long, hidden drive.

They passed lovely trees and beautiful landscaping. "Hey, what street is this? I've never seen it before. Where are we anyway?" Paige had been too busy biting her nails and playing out in her head what a disaster this introduction could be to pay attention.

"We're in New Albany. And this is no street. It's my parents' private drive to their house."

Paige perked up in awe. "This is just the driveway?" Once again she admired the surroundings that looked like she was riding down a country road and not someone's driveway. "Wow. I'm going to have to come visit my in-laws quite often." Paige relaxed back in her seat, some of the excitement fading away. "If they'll have me that is."

"Of course they'll have you. My parents are going to love you. I told you, they're happy for me."

Paige had to admit that when she sat next to Norman while he told his parents over the phone of his nuptials just hours ago, she was surprised of their excitement and invitation for the newlyweds to join them for dinner that night. "I can't believe you told your parents you got married, not only without them being in attendance, but with them never even having met your wife . . . and they didn't get the least bit upset." Paige shook her head. "No way am I breaking this kind of news to my parents over the phone. That would be salt in the wound."

"Well, your parents will find out soon enough since we plan on going to their house for breakfast," Norman said. "So it seems like I'm the one who should be biting my nails. At least my parents already know . . . and they're happy for me."

"Which, still, I can't help but to find as strange."

"Well, don't." Norman took a deep breath. "Between me and you, my parents have always had this underlying suspicion that I was gay."

"What?" Paige asked in shock, not even trying to hold in her laugh. "With all the tail you done chased and caught, how could they possibly think that? Had they seen you in action in the Lion's Den flirting with every woman who came and purchased a movie ticket, they'd know for sure you were anything but gay." The Lion's Den was the nickname Paige and Norman gave the ticket booth at the theatre.

"Well, I'm not one to kiss and tell with my parents you know. The things I used to converse with you about I'd never share with my parents in a million years. That and the fact that I've never brought a girl home before."

"Never?" Once again Paige was shocked.

"Never," Norman confirmed.

"I'm the first?"

Norman turned and looked at Paige. She wore a dark pink crinkled linen dress with black lacy trim around the neckline and puffy short sleeves, looking like the blushing bride that she technically was. "You are indeed the first, wifey."

Instantly, Paige felt all warm and fuzzy inside. She felt special as a huge grin formed on her lips. Then she caught herself feeling a certain kind of way and immediately wiped the smile off her face. Reality had slapped that smug little grin right off her face. The reality was there was no need to feel special. This wasn't about her. This was about the baby. She had to keep that in perspective so that she didn't get caught up in a fairytale that had absolutely no chance at coming to pass. There was nothing between her and Norman besides a friendship. Yes, they loved each other. That was nothing new to either one of them. They'd declared their love for each other as friends, and it was only as friends. But they weren't in love with each other as far as the other one knew.

"Well, here we are," Norman announced as they drove into a circular drive, parking behind a white convertible BMW. "Ahhh, and I see they've invited my spoiled, bratty little sister and her twenty-fifth birthday present." He nodded toward the car.

"Wow, those are the kind of presents your parents give," Paige said. "Then, on second thought, we should have invited them to the wedding. I can only imagine what the gift might have been."

Norman exited his vehicle, a nice reliable Honda Accord, and went around and opened the door for Paige. He took Paige by the hand and helped her out of the car. Hand in hand, he led her up to the door as she admired the house like she was a hungry, fat kid approaching a real, live gingerbread house. Once they hit the doorstep, Norman rang the bell and then followed it with a knock.

Within a few seconds, the door swung open. "Norman, now, child, you know darn well you don't need to ring the doorbell," the round-faced, slightly chubby older black woman who answered the door said. "This here is your home more than it is mine. Get yourself on in here. Your mother has been expecting you for dinner." She pulled Norman in and gave him a long, warm hug. She then released him and stared at him. "And you look like you need a good meal. It's only been a couple months since I last seen ya, but I swear you look like you've lost weight. Nothing but skin and bones. Ain't that new wife of yours been feeding you? Speaking of which, where is this fine gal your mother has been calling up all her friends to brag about?"

Norman reached out the door for Paige, who had stayed placed to the side out of the view of the doorway . . . biting her nails. "Why she's right here." Norman had to somewhat struggle to pull Paige to the doorway. "Miss Nettie, this is Paige, my wife. Paige, this is the woman who practically raised me, Miss Nettie, our housekeeper of almost twenty years."

"Very pleased to meet you, Miss Nettie." Paige extended her hand. She waited patiently for Miss Nettie to extend her hand as well, but it never happened. Instead, Miss Nettie just stood there for a moment all bug-eyed, staring at Paige at if she'd seen a ghost.

"Miss Nettie, are you okay?" Norman asked. "Miss Nettie," he said again after not getting a response the first time.

"Hunh, what?" Miss Nettie finally snapped out of her gaze.

"I said are you okay?" Norman asked with concern.

"Oh, me, uh, yes, of course." She set her eyes on Paige, eyeballing her up and down. She finally spoke, while Paige's arm remained extended. "So you're the new Mrs. Vanderdale?"

Paige didn't know how to take this woman's reaction. "Well, uh, yes, I am."

Miss Nettie stared at Paige stone-faced for a few more seconds before the stone shattered and resting under that expression was a huge Kool-Aid grin. "There is a God!" She clasped her hands together and let out the biggest yelp of laughter. "Hot dang!" She clapped again. "Child, put that arm away. You's family now." Miss Nettie pulled Paige in for a hug and shook her like she was her toy teddy bear. "Whoa whooo. Yes, there is a God indeed, and if we wait on Him long enough, He'll show up and pay folks back on our behalf greater than we ever could."

"I have no idea what she's talking about," Norman said to Paige. "She's always talked in riddles since I can remember," he added. "No offense to you, Miss Nettie."

"None taken. You call it riddles," Miss Nettie said as she released Paige, "but I call it God having a sense of humor. And with that being said"—she grabbed Paige by the hand—"it would be a true blessing from God Himself for me to have the honor of presenting you to your mother-in-law." Miss Nettie practically dragged Paige by the hand while Norman closed and locked the door.

Paige looked over her shoulder at Norman with her eyes pleading for help. In less than ten seconds she'd need help all right. But her help would definitely have to cometh from the Lord.

Chapter Seven

"Was that my boy I heard?" The singsong voice coming from the dining room was heard prior to Norman, Paige, or Miss Nettie ever even making their way into the room.

"Oh, he's here all right, Mrs. Vanderdale," Miss Nettie called out as she looked back over her shoulder at Paige while pushing the swinging dining room door at the same time. "My oh my is he here." Miss Nettie hustled her way through that door with Paige in tow as if there were a three-alarm fire they were trying to escape. There may not have been a fire, but Miss Nettie knew one thing for certain: there was at least about to be some smoke blown. And where there's smoke . . .

"Son! My only son. Come give Mumsy some love."

Paige watched as a pale-skinned woman with blond hair, and a house coat that would have given both Maude and Mrs. Roper a run for their money, brushed by her and embraced Norman.

"Mom, please," Norman said as his mother began planting kisses all over his face as if he were a five-year-old child. "Come on, Mom," he pleaded to no avail, finally just dropping his arms down to his sides like dead weight and giving in. He rolled his eyes up in his head while his mother smothered him with kisses.

"You don't come visit as often as I'd like, so I have to make up for times missed," his mother said, planting one more smuckerroo right on his nose.

"Come on, Mother, let's not start with the whole 'you never come by to see me' routine. You know I make it by as often as I can."

"Oh, hogwash. You're too busy at that ridiculous peasant-collar job of yours." His mother shooed her hand.

"It's blue collar," Norman corrected his mother, not noticing the offended look on Paige's face, seeing how she worked at the same place of employment. "And don't say it with your nose up in the air so. Miss Nettie here's job is blue collar. I'm sure she might find that offensive."

"Oh please." She shooed her hand again, never taking her eyes off of Norman as she straightened his already-straightened collar. "Nettie is family. I don't even consider her part of the hired help anymore. It's just like having a dog. Once it's been around for so long, it's like part of the family." She chuckled, planting an unforeseen peck on her son's lips.

"What the . . . ?" Paige started under her breath, lightweight lunging toward her mother-in-law until Miss Nettie's grip on her hand tightened and pulled her back.

Paige's words reminded Mrs. Vanderdale that someone other than her and her son were in the room. She turned and addressed Miss Nettie. That's when, for the first time, she noticed Paige. "Why, Miss Nettie, you didn't tell me one of your kinfolk was in town again." She lowered her voice but with a stern tone and wagging finger in Miss Nettie's face she said, "I thought we had this talk before. Now I don't mind your people coming for a visit every now and again and sharing your quarters, but you must give Mr. Vanderdale and me a heads-up. Is that understood?"

"Yes, ma'am, but I—" Miss Nettie started before Mrs. Vanderdale cut her off.

"Now I hope you saw to it that the kitchen staff made extra for your guest. You know we are already going to start having an extra mouth to feed whenever my Norman comes around now that he's a married man." She sharply turned to Norman. "Speaking of which, son, where is that lovely bride of yours? Why, I can't wait to welcome her to the family." Mrs. Vanderdale began looking over Norman's shoulder toward the swinging door leading to the living room.

"She's right there, Mother." Norman nodded toward Paige.

His mother turned around only to find Miss Nettie and her supposed kinfolk standing there. She continued looking at the doorway. "Where, son?"

"Right here, Mother. Standing right here in your face." Norman walked around his mother and went and stood next to Paige. "Mumsy, this is my wife, Paige. Paige, this is—"

"Mrs. Vanderdale!" Miss Nettie shouted as she quickly went to her boss's aid.

Norman joined Nettie in keeping his mother on her feet as she appeared faint and weak, as if her knees had given out.

"Mom, are you okay?" Norman asked worriedly. "Miss Nettie, help get Mother over to the chair. And please have Stuart fetch her some water."

Miss Nettie just stood there, torn, not moving a muscle.

"Please, Miss Nettie, why are you just standing there?" Norman asked.

How could Miss Nettie tell the young lad that she didn't want to leave that room for even a second? She didn't want to miss what she felt was a long time coming and overdue. "Oh shucks," she said under her breath and then scurried over to the swinging door that separated the dining room from the kitchen. "Stuart, Mrs. Vanderdale needs a glass of water, quickly." Miss Nettie hurried back to her employer's side. Under ordinary circumstance she would have gotten the water herself. But to her this was a long-awaited extraordinary circumstance.

Within seconds, Paige stood to the side and watched as a black man with salt-and-pepper hair dressed in a long-tail tux took over a glass of water to Mrs. Vanderdale. Norman took it from his hand.

"Thank you, Stuart," Norman said with a nod, then turned and placed the glass to his mother's lips.

She took a few sips and after a moment or two, she seemed to regain her strength.

"Mom, what's going on?" Norman questioned. "Have you been feeling okay? Are you sick again and haven't told me?" He looked to Miss Nettie for an answer.

"No, no, not as far as I know. She's been just fine," Miss Nettie assured him.

Norman felt his mother's forehead. "She doesn't seem to have a fever."

"I think it's your fever that's got her feeling a certain kind of way," Miss Nettie said between her teeth with a knowing look on her face.

"Huh, what?" Norman was confused by Miss Nettie's statement. He looked to Paige to see if perhaps she had any idea what the older woman was talking about. He always did have the hardest time deciphering what he referred to as Miss Nettie's riddles.

Miss Nettie looked to Paige as well, whose expression told the older woman that the new Mrs. Vanderdale knew exactly what the punch line was. Paige decided to translate to her husband.

"She's talking about you having jungle fever, Norman. Your mother is in shock that your new wife is black," Paige said.

"Please, my mother doesn't care about what color you are." Norman turned to face his mother. "Do you, Mother?"

His mother couldn't speak. She was still trying to catch her breath. But her dilating pupils begged her son to realize that he'd hit the nail on the head.

"Mother, is that what has you acting this way? The fact that Paige is black?"

Realizing his mother was still trying to catch her breath, Norman offered his mother another sip of water, which she gulped down. She wiped the dripping water from her chin and was finally able to speak and the only words she could manage to force out were, "Who on earth names their African American daughter Paige?"

"Mom!" Norman said, embarrassment peeking around his tone.

"Well, I'm sorry, son, but I thought I raised you better than that."

"What?" Paige had held her tongue long enough.

No one noticed Miss Nettie standing off to the side with a satisfied grin across her mouth and her nose in the air as if she were sniffing roses instead of smoke.

"Oh, my, and I see she even has the attitude that comes along with it," Mrs. Vanderdale said, grabbing her chest.

"That comes along with what?" Paige asked verbally while Norman asked with his eyes.

"With . . ." His mother motioned her index finger up and down the length of Paige's body. "With that."

Paige took another step toward her mother-in-law.

"Hold on just a minute." Norman put his arm out, stopping Paige from getting any closer to his dear mother. "Mother, I'm not clear on what you're trying to say here, but if it's what I think it is, disappointment in you would be describing how I feel without crossing the line of respect."

"Norman, it's totally clear what your mother is implying," Paige said. "But just in case you really don't understand, let me break it down for you."

"Oh, gosh, and there she goes ready to start breaking things," Mrs. Vanderdale panicked. "Nettie, put away all the china and crystal. I've caught glimpses of those reality shows and know how they like to throw glasses and stuff at each other."

Paige's mouth fell to the floor. She wanted so badly to go off on her mother-in-law for stereotyping Paige, but then she realized she'd be going off on the wrong person. It was those trifling basketball and housewives she'd have needed to speak her piece with. She couldn't blame Mrs. Vanderdale for believing what her eyes showed her to be true on all these cable networks. Not only that, but Paige had to remember that she herself had lost control to the point where her hands had to be pried from another woman's head full of weave . . . a couple of times. She didn't categorize that as a "black thing" though. She categorized that as a woman out of control. And from the looks of things, if his mother kept it up, Norman was about to be out of control as well.

"Enough, Mother!" Norman spat. By now Miss Nettie had an arm full of dishes after starting the task her employer had instructed her to do. Stuart, who had remained silent off to the side waiting for Mrs. Vanderdale to finish her water so that he could take the glass back into the kitchen, began helping.

"Miss Nettie, Stuart, please leave the settings and excuse yourselves." Norman looked to Paige. "Paige, can you go with them, grab a drink, appetizer, or something? I'd like to have a word with my mother." He turned and shot his mother a condemning look. "Alone."

"But . . ." Paige started. No way did she want to excuse herself from the room. She wanted to give her mother-in-law a piece of her mind. Or at least bear witness to her husband giving her a piece of his mind in her defense.

"Come on, honey." Miss Nettie took Paige by her elbow after placing the dishes back on the table. "I make the sweetest tea mixed with lemonade that you'd ever want to taste."

Paige didn't budge.

"Come on now." Miss Nettie nudged her. "Trust me, God's got this."

Paige finally gave in and allowed Miss Nettie to lead her off to the swinging door that led to the kitchen.

"Believe you me," Miss Nettie said, "I don't want to miss it either. But don't worry, as long as I get to witness her finding out about that bun you got cooking in the oven, it'll make up for whatever I miss right here."

Paige stopped in her tracks and stared at Miss Nettie, wondering how on God's green earth she knew she was pregnant. Because she was plus size and her dress was a little big, no way could that woman have realized she was showing.

Miss Nettie simply winked and said, "Child, you'd be surprised at what God shows me in my head before it ever manifest before my eyes. Now come on and get some of this sweet tea and lemonade. You need a break before we's get to round two." Miss Nettie chuckled as they disappeared into the kitchen.

Chapter Eight

Paige sat at the nook in the enormous gourmet kitchen, sipping on the tea and lemonade concoction Miss Nettie had prepared for her. "Yummy, this is good," Paige said after taking a sip. "What's in this besides lemonade and tea?" She held the glass to her eyes as if the ingredients to the magic potion would appear in writing on the glass.

"Family secret recipe," Miss Nettie said as she moved about the kitchen among three other staff members, including Stuart.

Paige noticed how the staff were all African American. "That boss of yours is really something." Paige spoke as if she and Miss Nettie were the only ones in the room.

"You mean your mother-in-law?" Miss Nettie chuckled. "You better go ahead and start claiming that woman for who she is. You done took vows with her only precious son." Miss Nettie shook her head. "Like I be trying to tell them young girls at church: y'all think y'all just marrying the man, but honey, y'all marrying the wholeeeeee family." Miss Nettie spread her arms out wide and grinned.

Paige found nothing funny as she took another sip of her drink.

Realizing she might be going a little too far, Miss Nettie exhaled and walked over to Paige. "I'm sorry, baby. I don't mean to make fun of the situation. It's just that I'm used to the ol' missus."

"But she's demeaning and degrading. How do you get used to something like that?"

"Through prayer. When you see the person ain't gon' change, then you ask God to change you in order to deal with the person. But at the same time, you don't give up hope. You just keep praying for the person. Maybe one day after all is said and prayed, they just might change."

"Humph, ain't that much praying in the world." Paige twisted in the seat while rolling her eyes.

"Come on, now you know better. You's a God-fearing woman. Norman done told that much about you."

"He has?" Paige was surprised. She never thought twice about whether Norman had ever spoken of her to his parents over the years of them knowing one another.

"Sure he has. Although he doesn't make it over here as much as his mother would like him to, when he did come, he dropped your name on more than a few occasions. Paige this and Paige that. I'd see how his eyes would light up whenever he'd say your name. Then when he had that attitude about you running off and finding Jesus, thinking you was better than everybody . . ." Miss Nettie laughed. "I knew right then and there why God had put you in his path. And I knew it would only be a matter of time before you showed up at this dinner table."

Paige brushed off her blushing and her flattering chuckle. "Oh, Miss Nettie, I'm sure God shows you a lot, but trust me when I say Norman and me . . . it's not what you think."

Miss Nettie let out a knowing laugh. "Oh, my dear. It's not what you think." Miss Nettie walked off like she was taking a secret with her that only God and she knew.

Paige couldn't let her off the hook just that easy, though. She wanted in on the secret too. "Miss Nettie, what do you mean by—"

"Daddy, next time I'm riding Sunrise and you're riding Champagne. Just like you, Champagne is getting a little rusty in his older years. I don't think you can keep up with Sunrise anymore," a bouncing blonde said, entering the kitchen through the back patio sliding doors. Paige instantly noticed the resemblance, realizing she was the spitting image of Mrs. Vanderdale, minus about twenty-five years.

"Ahhh, watch it with the insults, young lady," an older man following the young blonde said with a smile. "I'm still your father and I still hold the key to your trust fund."

"Oh, Daddy, you know money doesn't mean everything to me."

"Fine, then I guess I'll leave it to charity."

"Now I didn't say all that. Money doesn't mean everything to me, but it means something."

"It means enough, huh?" the older gentleman groaned.

"Like father, like daughter." She laughed, removing the riding hat she'd donned. She shook her long blond hair before noticing Paige sitting at the table. "Hi." She bounced over to Paige like Buffy the high school cheerleading captain. "You must be my brother's girl." She raised her eyebrows up and down several times. She then put her arms on Paige's shoulders and pulled her up. "Let me get a look at who my brother chose to be a pest to and nag until death do them part." She turned Paige around as she gave her the once-over. "Ooooooh, and baby got back." She swatted Paige on the rear end, which surprised the heck out of Paige, catching her off-guard.

"Oh, Samantha, stop it before you frighten the poor girl off," the older gentleman stepped over and said, moving his daughter away from Paige. "You must forgive my daughter. In spite of her last name, she was raised by wolves; we just adopted her." He laughed and pulled Paige in for a hug. "Paige, I take it?" He pulled back, awaiting confirmation.

"Uh, yes," Paige said. She was completely dumbfounded. Based on the reaction of her mother-in-law discovering that Norman had married outside of his race, she'd expected the same thing from the rest of the family. She remained reserved with her guard slightly up. She looked to Miss Nettie who gave her a smile and a nod, letting her know it was safe to let the sister-in-law and the father-in-law in.

"It's a delight to meet you. I'm Norman Senior, but you can call me Dad, of course. Welcome to the family, daughter. "He brought Paige in for another hug, kissed her on the cheek, and released her. "Oh, forgive me. I didn't mean to dirty you up. Samantha and I have been out riding. I must go get cleaned up and changed. If you'll excuse me, I'll see you at the dinner table. Yes?"

"Uh, yes," Paige said and watched Mr. Vanderdale go walking up a back set of stairs off the kitchen.

"Guess I better go get cleaned up too," Samantha said. "Sorry we're late." She put her hand to her mouth as if whispering. "The old man doesn't realize he's getting up in age and can't keep up like he used to. I had to fall back several times."

"No need to apologize." Paige smiled.

"Then I, too, shall see you at the dinner table," Samantha said and then turned to Miss Nettie. "Miss Nettie, where's Mumsy? Somewhere having a heart attack at the news of having a black daughter?" She'd said it with such a straight face, Paige couldn't believe it.

"What do you think?" Miss Nettie said with a knowing look on her face. "Your brother's out there giving her a talking-to now."

"Hmmm." Samantha turned to face Paige. "Don't take it personal. Miss Nettie here doesn't. Nobody does. It's just how Mother is. As a matter of fact, she has no idea that that is how she is. Kind of like the ugly duckling that is clueless of the fact that it's not a swan. We all just let her be, hoping one day she'll walk past a mirror and see her true reflection." Samantha winked, shrugged her shoulders, and moseyed up the same staircase her father just had.

Paige exhaled and sat back down. "Lord, what did I get myself into?"

Miss Nettie walked over to Paige with the pitcher of sweet tea and lemonade. "I don't know, missy." She refilled Paige's glass. "But either one of two things God's gonna do for you."

"Oh yeah, what's that?" Paige asked curiously.

Miss Nettie leaned in real close and said, "He's either gonna get you out of it, or bring you through it."

Paige shrugged her misunderstanding.

"Oh you'll see," Miss Nettie assured her. "You'll see."

Chapter Nine

"Dinner was delicious, wasn't it?" Norman asked, making conversation as he drove Paige to her house. For the past five minutes not a solitary word had been spoken. "Miss Nettie and most of the staff have been with the family for years. I grew up on that cooking. It's the best, huh?"

"Huh?" Paige said mockingly. "So now you're back to the Norman I know."

"What are you talking about?"

"Now you're using words I'm used to you using."

"I still have no idea what you're talking about."

"I'm talking about that guy back there who was using words like Mumsy and fetch. What was that about?" Paige didn't even wait for him to respond. "Oh, my bad. That was the trust fund Norman with a filthy-rich family I had no idea about. I mean, I've talked to you about my parents before over the years. You know who I am and what type of family I was raised in."

"Yeah, but I don't know what your family filed on their 1040s last year. How much your family has or doesn't have has never made a difference in our friendship. Forgive me for thinking the same went for my family as well."

"Oh, stop it!"

"Stop what?"

"Trying to downplay all this. Your dad is frickin' Daddy Warbucks for crying out loud."

"And I still have no idea what that has to do with anything, why you are so upset."

"I'm upset because you never told me you were a trust fund baby. It's like you've been living a double life. Like that one time we went to the Fondue Restaurant; you wore a bib because you didn't want to get chocolate on your Versace shirt. You said you'd never be able to afford another one. That was a lie."

"If I recall correctly, I said I'd never be able to afford one on my salary. And that was the truth."

Paige gritted her teeth. "You work at a movie theatre when, all the while, your family owns a chain of theatres that happens to be our company's competition. And the thing is you don't even have to work! Your sister doesn't." Samantha had made this fact known during their dinner conversation.

"Yeah, that's because Samantha is a spoiled brat who thinks my parents owe her in money what they couldn't give her in time. Her saying is that since they were so busy out making all this money that they deemed so important, the least she can do is spend it. So she gets a new car almost every other birthday and has one of those ridiculously priced penthouses in downtown Columbus overlooking the riverfront, but comes home to my parents' house weekly and stays just long enough to go riding with my father, have dinner, and collect her allowance. That's not who I am."

"And I can't believe you didn't trust me to understand that. I told you all about my father's construction business that my brother took over and how I just wanted to do me and get my own. I would have understood, Norman."

"I know you would have," Norman said gently. "Because that's just who you are."

Paige let out a harrumph. "Well, guess what? I don't know who you are, or why you chose to hide who you are."

"I am who I am, Paige. I mean, what's really going on here? Is this about my mother? Then just say so. You have every right to be upset at the way she acted, but be upset with her, not me. I had your back. I stood up for you. When I spoke to my mother alone, I told her how disrespectful and shameful her behavior was."

"And racist."

"Whoa, hold on now. A bit caught up in the past when it comes to race relations, sure, but racist is a pretty harsh word to call my mother. My mother doesn't have anything against black people. If I thought she did, I would have never dreamed of subjecting you to that."

"Your mother doesn't have a thing against black people? Tuh!" Paige said, folding her arms. "I'll be surprised that if the next time we show up for dinner, she doesn't hide all the good silverware. That is if I even get invited over for dinner again. The woman couldn't even stand to break bread with me. She feigned ill and excused herself from the table before we even made it through the first course."

"My mother has no problem breaking bread with black people, Paige. Now you just sound ridiculous. I can recount many times she and Miss Nettie have enjoyed meals together. Why, I've even watched her prepare holiday meals with the entire staff."

"An entire staff that happens to be black!" Paige spat then turned and said under her breath, "Great, a real, live Paula Deen."

"Now that is enough!" Norman hit the brakes and said. He heard tires skid behind him and the driver in his rear laid on the horn. He pulled over to the side of the road. He threw the car in park and then turned his body to face Paige. "The way I told my mother that any disrespect toward you was not going to be tolerated is the same way I'm telling you that any disrespect toward my mother is not going to be tolerated."

"Well, you should have told me that she had the tendencies of Archie Bunker." Paige's comparison of Norman's mother to the scripted bigot of the seventies' sitcom *All in the Family* might have been crossing the line.

When Norman's eyes filled with hurt, he put the car in drive, and then drove off without saying a word, Paige knew that, without a doubt, she'd crossed the line. "I'm sorry, Norman," she said within seconds. She looked upward. "I repent, Lord." She then turned her attention back to Norman. "Will you forgive me? I'm wrong. The whole Paula Deen–Archie Bunker thing . . . I'm wrong. But I hope you won't ask me to endure that type of treatment again."

Norman chuckled. It was a sarcastic kind of chuckle.

"What? What's so funny?"

"Christians, that's what. Or maybe I shouldn't dump them all into a single category, just the ones who are glad that Jesus hung, bled, and died on the cross for them, but can't deal with a proverbial thorn in the side."

"Are you saying that because I'm a Christian I should have to endure prejudice?"

"No, not at all, but I'm saying that when you are subjected to it why shoot back? Why not try to take all that Christianity and heal the offender, or at least diplomatically relay to them their offenses? Once a person knows better and doesn't do better, then that's on them. Then you just ask Jesus to work on you in how you deal with those types of people. Imagine if Martin Luther King Jr. ran around talking about, 'Oh, well, I'm not going to stand for this type of treatment. I'm out of here.' What would have become of the Civil Rights Movement?"

"Are you really comparing your mother's prejudice and ways to the Civil Rights Movement? It ain't that serious."

"Bam! My point exactly."

Paige stared at Norman for a moment, trying to figure out exactly what his point was. It was to no avail. "You've obviously been hanging around Miss Nettie too long. You're starting to talk in riddles like her."

"Look, forget it. I don't want to fight," Norman conceded. "I apologize for my mother's behavior. She's kind of old school in her ways."

Paige snapped her head and twisted her lips. "Kind of old school?"

"Okay, way old school." Norman smiled a little, letting Paige know things were somewhat cooling down. That made her smile.

"I don't like fighting with my best friend," Paige confessed. "Outside of Jesus and my parents, you're the only person in the world who has ever sacrificed so much for me. I don't take this lightly. I don't take what you are doing lightly. As a matter of fact, I want to try the whole 'dinner with your family' thing, namely your mother, all over again. I will be on my best behavior." Paige lifted her left hand and placed her right hand over her heart. "Nothing but the God in me. Saint's honor."

"Hmmmm. Can I trust you?" Norman teased.

"Why you married me, Mr. Vanderdale," Paige said in an exaggerated, over-the-top Southern drawl. "You wouldn't marry a woman you couldn't trust now would you?"

"No, and you wouldn't marry a man who you couldn't trust would you?"

"Not on purpose." Paige smiled.

"Then trust me. Everything is going to work out just fine. I'm going to drop you off at your place, head back to mine, and then we'll do it all over again tomorrow morning with your family."

"By the way, what are we going to do about us being man and wife, yet living in two different places? I think

I had something about that as rule number ten, but you never let me get that far," Paige chided.

"Ha-ha. No, but seriously. I don't know. I guess we'll just have to cross that bridge when we get to it."

"Uh, hello, we're like standing in the middle of the bridge." Paige waved her hand that don the wedding band that matched the one Norman wore. The rings were something they had just picked up for show at the mall yesterday.

"Ahh, decisions, decisions," Norman moaned. "Let's just get breaking the news to your family out of the way tomorrow and we'll take it from there."

"Yeah, this is probably a moot conversation anyway considering my dad is probably going to kill you for marrying his daughter without asking for her hand in marriage." When Paige saw Norman turn beet red, she broke out in laughter. "Calm down, I'm just joking with you. My dad is great and very understanding. He just wants his little girl to be happy. So as long as I'm happy, he'll be happy."

"And are you happy?" Norman pulled into Paige's driveway and then waited for her response.

Paige turned, looked at Norman, took his hand, and then said, "In all honesty, happier than I've been in a long time and happier than, just last week, I could have ever imagined myself being. And I thank you for that, Norman. Thank you for saving me." Paige patted Norman's hand with her free hand and then released it so that he could walk around and open her car door for her.

The minute Norman got out of the car she began fanning herself. For some reason, it had just gotten hot in there . . .

Chapter Ten

"On the phone you were ecstatic to hear about my nuptials," Norman said to his mother as the two of them sat in the family dining room alone. "You couldn't wait to meet your new daughter-in-law. So what's changed?"

"Nothing has changed. I'm still happy for you. I'm just a little taken aback that you married someone who is . . . you know." Mrs. Vanderdale leaned in closer to her son and said in a whisper, "Colored."

"Mother, no one uses that word anymore in reference to African Americans. You are just trying to be disrespectful and I will not tolerate it. I won't tolerate it toward my wife or any person of color."

"See, you said it yourself." Mrs. Vanderdale pointed accusingly at her son. "You said colored."

"Mom, don't try to misconstrue my words. I didn't mean it like that; not how you meant it. Blacks haven't been referred to as colored in ages. And since I can remember, I can't ever recall you referring to a black person as colored. Please don't start now."

"Okay, then, black. African American, or whatever they're calling themselves these days. Heck, some of them are still calling each other the N word, and I can't say colored. How hypocritical."

"This is bigger than what you choose to call a black person. This is about how you choose to treat Black people. My wife is black and she will not be mistreated or disrespected by you or anyone else because of it—not under my watch."

"Are you getting fresh with me?" Her cheeks turned red. She and her son had had their differences in the past, but he'd always spoken to her with the proper tongue. As far as she was concerned, he was sadly mistaken if he thought he was going to start getting fresh in the mouth with her now. It was time she reminded him that she carried the ace. "Don't forget your inheritance isn't engraved in stone. I can call up the family lawyers right now and—"

"Mother, please." Norman shooed his hand. "You know me better than that. The whole 'waving the trust fund over our heads like a carrot' thing works with Samantha, not me. And that's the exact reason why I chose to be my own man and never got comfortable with your and Father's money. I won't be manipulated. I'm no one's puppet. Like I told you guys the day I left here on my eighteenth birthday and never looked back: I will do whatever I want, when, where, and however I want to do it in spite of what you think about it. And that includes marrying a black woman."

"So is that why you married a color . . . I mean, black girl? To spite me? If that's the case, you win." She threw her hands up in the air. "I believe you now; you're your own man. Guess you told me. Now run, get an annulment, and we'll forget it ever happened. Joke's over. Ha-ha."

Norman shook his head. "Unfortunately for you, Mother, this is no joke. My marriage to Paige is very real."

Mrs. Vanderdale let out a deep breath and then took her son's hands into her own. She used her thumbs to massage the backs of his hands. "So you love this . . . this Paige woman?"

Norman didn't even hesitate. "If I didn't love her, I would have never married her."

Mrs. Vanderdale, not one to easily be satisfied, dug deeper. "Fair enough. But are you in love with this woman?"

Norman's ringing cell phone brought him out of his thoughts of yesterday's private conversation he'd had with his mother in the family dining room after asking everyone else in the room to give him a minute alone with her. "Hello," he answered into the receiver.

"I'm pulling into your driveway now. You ready?"

"Yep. Give me a second," he answered.

"Okay. I'm waiting."

Norman ended the call, locked up his apartment, and went and met Paige outside in her car.

"Ooooh, you looking dapper!" Paige exclaimed, checking out Norman in his nice crisp Sean John shirt and slacks.

"Thank you," Norman replied. He put on his seat belt, and then looked straight ahead, waiting for Paige to back out of his driveway. After a few seconds, when the car didn't move, Norman looked over to find Paige staring at him. "What?"

"Oh, nothing really. Just wondering why you didn't grab you a pair of Fubu tennis shoes and a red, black, and green kufi cap while you were at it." Paige began digging in her purse. "And you know what? I just might have an afro pick in my purse you can borrow to top off the ensemble."

Norman still didn't get what Paige was saying and his puzzled face stated as much.

Paige pulled her hands out of her purse and placed them on her hips as best she could in a sitting position. "Sean John; really? Since when do you wear designs by Puff Daddy? Where's your usual Ralph Lauren polo?"

Norman was so busted. "I uh, well, uh. I happened to be in Macy's at Easton's the other day. This shirt was

hanging on a mannequin and caught my eye. I really
didn't pay much attention to the designer. I just thought
it would look nice on me as well, so I . . . I bought it." He
shrugged it off.

Paige continued to stare at him in disbelief. "And the
pants." She nodded.

He looked down at his Sean John jeans. "Oh, these."
He brushed off invisible lint. "The uh . . . the sales clerk
suggested them since they were twenty-five percent off."
He saw that Paige was still looking at him, not buying it.
"That's my story and I'm sticking to it," he said before
she could continue her interrogation. "Now let's go." He
stared straight ahead again.

"Norman, my dear husband, you are a true piece of
work." Paige put the car in reverse. "Like I told you,
though, with my parents all you have to be is yourself, not
a Caucasian Sean Puffy Combs."

"I guess we'll find out soon enough."

After a fifteen-minute drive, Norman and Paige stood
in her parents' living room.

"Daddy," Paige said, jumping into her father's arms
as if she were a little girl. Paige was more of a daddy's
girl now than she was when she was little. She felt that
growing up, as much as she loved and as close as she was
to her brother, Brandon, he'd had the spotlight on him.
Now that Brandon was grown and out of the house with a
family of his own, Paige felt it was now her time to shine
in the eyes of her parents.

She had to admit, though, that once upon a time she
had envied the whole father-son relationship thing. And
then even once Brandon got older, working for the family
business, he and her father still spent a great deal of time
together. Paige eventually got over that whole spirit of
selfishness and instead of dwelling on past times she felt
she was missing with her father, she decided to make up
for it now. That went for her mother as well.

"Hey, Paige, baby. How have you been doing?" Her father held her in a warm hug. He knew his daughter had had a rough past few months. He was glad to see what looked like a genuine smile on her face.

Paige appreciated the acknowledgment from her father. The days of her feeling invisible and like her father felt women were beneath him were no more. Things looked so much clearer without that little girl hurt and pain Paige had carried around for years. "Things have been rough, as you know, but I'm just trusting in God to see me through."

Mr. Robinson admired his daughter. "Well, you look better than ever."

"Thanks, Dad, but you're my daddy. You're biased. You're supposed to say that."

"Maybe so, but it's still the truth." He smiled at his daughter.

"Where's Mom?"

Mr. Robinson looked over his shoulder. "She's finishing up breakfast for you and your guest here." Mr. Robinson turned his attention to Norman. "Sorry to have been so rude, but I get distracted whenever my baby girl is around." Mr. Robinson extended his hand. "I'm Samuel Robinson, Paige's father."

"Pleasure to meet you, Mr. Robinson," Norman said, shaking his hand.

"Oh, you don't have to be so formal. Samuel is fine," Mr. Robinson said. "Norman, right? You work with Paige? You and her are friends? Although I've never had the opportunity of a formal introduction, I've heard quite a lot about you." Mr. Robinson gave Norman one last strong shake. "Thank you for being there for my baby girl. You've been a good friend."

"Uh, yeah," Norman agreed, knowing that as of yesterday, legally he and Paige had become way more than just friends.

"There she is." Paige's mother came sailing out of the kitchen, wiping her hands down her autumn leaf–covered apron. "I knew I heard voices." Mrs. Robinson went over to Paige, grabbed her hands, and kissed her on each cheek. "You holding up okay?"

"Yes, Mother," Paige replied.

"Good, because I worry about you so sometimes." Mrs. Robinson took each one of Paige's hands and kissed them.

"Don't be rude like me and ignore Paige's guest," Mr. Robinson said.

Norman smiled and extended his hand to Mrs. Robinson while Mr. Robinson continued the introductions. "Honey, this is Norman," Mr. Robinson started. "He's Paige's—"

"Husband!" Mrs. Robinson shouted as she threw Paige's hands out of hers and snatched up Norman's left one, holding it up to her face.

"Coworker," Mr. Robinson corrected her with a chuckle. "Our daughter is barely out of one marriage, so don't go trying to put her in another."

"Paige, you're married?" Mrs. Robinson asked. "To this man?" She shook Norman's hand like a ragdoll.

"Honey, stop that." Mr. Robinson could see that this wasn't a joke. His wife was serious. Dead serious. He looked to Norman. "I'm sorry. I apologize for my wife's behavior. I don't know what's gotten into her."

"Don't go apologizing for me," Mrs. Robinson spat. "I'm not blind. I know what I see." She snatched Paige's left hand into hers while she still held on to Norman's. "These are matching wedding bands." She stared at Paige. "I know for a fact you got rid of the wedding set Blake gave you because you didn't want the memories. So unless you two lucked on the prizes in a box of Cracker Jacks, young lady, you've got some explaining to do." Mrs. Robinson was almost trembling she was so emotional.

Paige and Norman looked at each other full of guilt.

"Paige, is what your mother saying true?" Mr. Robinson asked, almost heartbroken.

This really wasn't how Paige wanted her parents to find out about her marriage to Norman. She wanted them to hear it from her own mouth. She never thought in a million years her mother would notice the rings and put two and two together.

"Yes, Dad, it's true." This was hard enough. Paige didn't find a need to delay the inevitable truth by beating around the bush or trying to explain their action before confirming it. "Norman and I were married yesterday."

Mrs. Robinson threw both Paige's and Norman's hands away like they were trash. She then stormed back off into the kitchen.

Paige threw her hand on her forehead. "No, no, no. This isn't how this was supposed to happen." Paige shook her head as her eyes filled with tears. She'd shed more tears in the last month than she had her entire life. She was surprised the well hadn't run dry. "My relationship with Mom was going so well after years of being so dysfunctional."

"Come on, baby girl." Mr. Robinson took Paige into his arms.

"Oh, Daddy." Paige began to cry.

"Now, now. It's not that serious. Sure your mother is a little shocked right now. But she'll get over it. Don't look at this as a setback, but just something else you and your mother can get through together. Probably just God testing y'all's relationship again." He took Paige by her arms and looked at her in the eyes. "Now why don't you go mosey off into the kitchen and pass that test?"

Paige sniffed and nodded.

"And I'll stay out here and have a little chat with my . . . son-in-law." Mr. Robinson gave Norman the side eye.

Norman gave off a nervous grin that only lasted about two seconds before his face went straight again.

"Yeah, you're right," Paige said with confidence as she straightened herself up, wiping the tears from her eyes. She turned to face Norman. "I'll be right back. I need to go talk with my mom. Do you mind?"

"Oh, not at all," Norman assured her. "I'll be waiting right here when you get back." He then hinted at Mr. Robinson, "Alive and well."

"Okay," Paige said as she walked away and into the kitchen, leaving Norman and her father alone.

There was awkward silence for a moment as the two men watched Paige disappear into the kitchen. Then finally Norman looked over to his father-in-law and said, "Nice Ralph Lauren polo you're wearing there, Mr. Robinson." No verbal response was received. Just a look that let Norman know this conversation didn't appear as if it was going to be any easier than the one Paige was about to engage in with her mother.

Chapter Eleven

When Paige entered the kitchen she saw her mother setting the table. Back and forth her mother went as if Paige weren't even standing there right in front of her.

"Are you going to pretend that I'm not here?" Paige finally asked her mother.

"No, just waiting on you to say something. Unless you don't think you owe me an explanation." Mrs. Robinson stood still with her hands on her hips. "What were you thinking running off and getting married before the ink on your divorce papers is even dry?" She let out a tsk, shook her head, and walked over to the stove, where she proceeded to take pots and pans of food over to the table.

Paige began to help and allow her mother to continue her rant. She owed her that much as to let her voice her discontent.

"Then you marry someone who your parents haven't even met. People hide things and people for a reason." Her mother paused and her jaw dropped. "Oh my Lord. Was Blake's accusations more than accusations? Have you been having an affair with that man all this time?"

"Mother! How could you think such a thing? I thought you knew me better than that."

"I did too, but today, with you showing up with this new husband of yours who, I repeat, I'd never been formally introduced to, is proof that I don't know you as well as I thought I did. I never imagined you'd do something so . . . so . . . stupid!"

"Mom, I had to. It was either that or . . ." Paige caught herself before she told her mother the complete truth. *One shocker at a time.*

"Either that or what?"

"Please, Mom. Just trust me. Marrying Norman is not a mistake, but not marrying him could have led to one . . . one I might not have been able to live with. And no, you may have never formally been introduced to him, but it's not like you've never heard me talk about him before. You know what a good friend he's been to me."

"Oh, obviously he's been more than just a good friend." Her mother rolled her eyes and began putting condiments on the table.

"Mother, please, we haven't even . . ." Once again Paige caught herself before giving too much information. Her mother didn't need to know that she and her husband had never had sex before . . . at least not with each other.

"I know what it is. That boy knows how much money you've got coming to you in that divorce settlement. He ain't stupid. He's looking to cash in. He's probably never seen that much money in his life and never will. He's got him a sugar mama."

Paige chuckled. "Oh, Mother, you couldn't be more wrong."

"Do you think this is funny?" Mrs. Robinson slammed down a potholder she'd been using to transport some of the dishes of food.

Paige stood at attention, her mother's sharp gesture knocking the grin right off of her face. "No, Mother, I'm sorry. It's just that . . ." Paige didn't really know what to say next. How could she explain the full details behind her reasoning for marrying Norman without dumping the entire boatload of the situation on her? One dose at a time or her mother could possibly disown her for life. Paige threw her hands up. "What's the big deal? Why are you so angry? It's my life. It's not hurting you any whether I'm married or not."

"But it is," her mother snapped. Her eyes filled with water and her bottom lip began to tremble.

"Mom." Paige hurried over to her mother and put her arms around her. "Mom, you're crying." That was a rare sight for Paige. Her mother had this hard exterior shell, always taking care of business and never letting 'em see her sweat . . . or cry. "What is it, Mom?"

"When you hurt, I hurt," Mrs. Robinson explained. "And I just don't want to see you hurt anymore. Blake scarred you. You haven't even let the wounds heal. You've just got them all exposed for the next man to go picking at the scabs, causing even more pain."

"Mom, it's not like that. Trust me."

"Sure it is. You just want somebody to love you. To make you happy. To make you feel happy, loved, and wanted. I get that. I'm sure that Norman is a nice guy, but even nice guys can change when they're dealing with someone who's still hurting. Who's still bleeding. Who's still wounded. It's okay to be alone. Date yourself for a while. Get to know who you are and who you want to be. Because if you just go from one man to the next, you'll find yourself always being who someone else wants you to be. You'll die maybe never knowing who you really were. Who you could have been." Mrs. Robinson released herself from Paige and turned away quickly.

Paige gave her a moment. "Mom, you sound like you're speaking from experience."

She wiped her tears away and shrugged. "Maybe I am. Maybe I'm not." She turned and faced Paige. "All I know is that if I am, hypothetically, if I am speaking from experience"—she began shaking her head as tears welled up again—"I wouldn't want no daughter of mine being me."

From behind, Paige wrapped her arms around her mother. She kissed her on the back of her head. "Mom, trust me, believe me, and I promise you when I say I'm not you . . . I'm not that girl. I'll never be her. I've fought too hard for finally loving myself—loving who I know I am—for me to ever allow anyone to not allow me to be me. It will never happen."

A tearful Mrs. Robinson nodded her belief in her daughter's words. "I hear you. And I believe you." She turned and faced Paige. "And now that we've got that out of the way . . ." She grabbed a dish towel, twisted it up, and whacked Paige a stinging good one on her behind. "That's for not inviting me to the wedding!"

Paige grabbed her rear end. Once she got over the initial pain, she and her mother laughed it up before inviting the men in to join them to eat.

The women had no idea what the men had talked about and the men had no idea what the women had talked about. But considering everyone used their knives to cut their French toast and Polish sausage and not each other, it was a good sign that all was well.

After eating, the four conversed for another half hour before Paige and Norman said their farewells.

"Well, we got through telling our parents about the marriage." Paige exhaled loudly as she and Norman sat in the car about to pull out of her parents' driveway.

"Yeah," Norman said, exhaling just as loudly. "Next mission: operation telling our parents you're pregnant."

"Ah, not so fast." Paige wagged a finger between the two of them. "We still have that one small task that we need to decide."

"Oh yeah." Norman was reminded. "Do we or do we not tell them that I'm not the father?"

Chapter Twelve

"You're the only one we felt we could trust with the whole truth."

Pastor Margie, the pastor of New Day Temple of Faith, the church to which both Paige and Norman belonged, sat speechless. She was more than caught off-guard when reading the paper and learning that Norman and Paige had secured a marriage license and had actually gotten married. For three days, since reading the announcement, she'd had to reprimand her flesh each time it picked up the phone to call Paige. Pastor or not, she was human. Her human side wanted the scoop, the dish, and the 411. Her spirit man knew better than to pry and go fishing. As the shepherd of the lambs, if she was doing her job right as a trusting and faithful leader, she knew God would send them her way; she wouldn't have to go to them. But then again, even if she was doing her job right, that didn't always mean the folks would be obedient and seek counsel from whom God drops in their spirit to seek it. She'd been in ministry long enough to know that people not always sought out God, let alone His chosen vessels.

Nonetheless, in spite of the fact that Pastor Margie's flesh had been dying to call Paige, instead, for the past three days she waited . . . and prayed. She'd felt in her spirit that there was more to this marriage than just a young couple in love. Today, all had been revealed. Paige and Norman had spent the last half hour telling their pastor the truth, the whole truth, and nothing but.

Paige and Norman sat in chairs side by side, waiting in anticipation for their pastor's response to what they'd just shared with her. They not only shared with her their secret, spur-of-the-moment marriage, but the entire reasoning for them deciding to get married in the first place—the pregnancy and all.

After a few seconds, Pastor Margie stood from her desk and walked over to her huge picture window, from ceiling to floor, in her office. She used her index and thumb to move a couple of the vertical blind panels out of her way. She stared out for a while and then finally turned to her congregants and spoke.

"I think I might already know the answer to this, but here it goes anyway." Pastor Margie walked over to her desk and sat back down. "Did God instruct you two to get married? Was this the answer He provided when you went to Him in prayer about the situation?"

One would have thought that both Norman and Paige had seen a ghost. One looked to the other for an answer to give their pastor. All either of them could give her was what they'd agreed they were coming there to give her in the first place: the truth.

"Pastor, I honestly don't think either of us sought the Lord on this one," Paige admitted.

"The idea just popped in my head," Norman interjected. "I'd like to think it was the Holy Spirit planting something within me, but I don't think it was. I think it was that whole voice thing that man talks about in that one book, *Untethered Soul*."

"But then again," Paige added, "maybe it was the Holy Spirit, because I know whenever God agrees or prompts a decision, there is nothing but peace in it. And, Pastor, I think I can speak for the both of us when I say there was nothing but peace about my decision to marry Norman. I mean, sure, at first I thought Norman was joking when he suggested such a thing. When I realized he wasn't joking, that he was wholeheartedly serious about sacrificing the single life he could be off having in order for mine and my baby's . . . Not trying to be funny, but my baby leaped. My spirit leaped." Paige's eyes leaked tears.

Norman grabbed his wife's hand and held it in his. They each looked at each other, smiled, and nodded in agreement that they had both stood by their decision to marry.

"I know you two have been friends for quite some time," Pastor said. "I know you two truly care and love one another. But what you have committed to under God requires more than care and love."

"But God is love, Pastor," Paige interjected. "That's what you've always taught and that's what the Bible teaches. So if we have love in our marriage, then we have God. And with God for us, who can be against us?"

"I hear what you're saying, spiritual daughter. And what you are saying is true beyond a doubt. But God being in the midst of something is all the more reason for the devil to get ticked off and try to get you to forget about God altogether. And you know what comes about from doing things without God."

"Nothing good," both Paige and Norman said in unison. That was one of their pastor's regular sayings.

"With that being said, what's done is done," Pastor Margie said. "I'm not going to tell you what you did is wrong and try to talk you into running down to the court-house to get an annulment. I'm not even going to tell you whether I agree or disagree. Absolutely none of that matters now. It's like when people ask me what I think about abortion or homosexuality. It's not about what I think. It's about what God says. I will never tell a person what I think, but I will tell them what God says. Now what they do with that information is between them and God."

"That's good, Pastor, because we didn't come here to get your opinion on it," Paige said. "Like you said, what's done is done. And like I said, we have peace with our choice and are not considering undoing it." She looked to Norman. "Right, Norman?"

"Definitely," he agreed, squeezing Paige's hand even tighter for confirmation.

"Fine," Pastor Margie said. "Then might I ask why you wanted to meet with me today?"

"Well, because now that we've gotten past the whole letting our families know we are married, we know we need to tell them about my being pregnant. Our issue is whether we wait to tell them that the baby isn't Norman's, do we just tell them everything at once, or if we just leave out the fact that Norman isn't the baby's biological father altogether and just live as one big, happy family forever."

"You mean you just live a lie forever," Pastor Margie corrected.

Paige swallowed at her pastor's bluntness. "A lie by omission, sure," Paige agreed. "But people adopt children all of the time and never tell them they are adopted. Wouldn't that be considered living a lie . . . by omission?"

"Sure, it could be." Pastor Margie shrugged. "It's clear that you think it is. And again, that's okay. You are entitled to feel how you want about a situation. But prior to you being in the situation you are in, would you have felt that way?"

"Ye . . . Well . . ." Paige had to pause and think about it.

"Sometimes man has a tendency to look at someone else's situation in order to find some type of justification or validation with his own," Pastor Margie said.

"I suppose I might be guilty of that, Pastor. But at the end of the day, I just want to do what's right for the baby," Paige said.

"Oh, I see, and do you mind telling me at what point this became about the baby . . . and not you?"

Sticking with the truth Paige said, "Now. At first, it was all about me—what my situation would look like to other people, heck, what it would look and feel like to me. I'll tell the truth and shame the devil; I was never really torn about getting an abortion if it meant getting the desired outcome that I wanted."

"Which was?" Pastor Margie asked.

"Which was me not having to deal with the fact that I was pregnant with my ex-husband's baby, which was a result of an act of nonconsensual sex between us. I felt dirty just thinking about it."

"And how do you feel now?"

"Truthfully?"

"That's the theme of today's meeting, right?"

Paige took a deep breath. "I've convinced myself that the child I'm carrying is my husband's." She looked at Norman, let a smile appear on her lips momentarily and then turned back to her pastor. "I've envisioned this whole life we're going to live, and it doesn't include Blake. It doesn't include that monster."

"So again, it sounds like you've pretty much made up your mind. The only way it seems like you're going to be able to mother this child is in the make-believe world you've already created in your mind."

Paige had never looked at it that way before now. "I guess you're right."

"Then, Paige honey, it still ain't about that baby," Pastor Margie didn't bite her tongue to say. "As cold as this may sound, I know you came here with every intention of us operating in the truth. I will pray for you both, and that precious seed. But I won't invest time in providing guidance to live a lie or fix a lie, as the only way to repair that is with the truth. But you, my friend, have to be willing to operate in the full truth, regardless of the consequences. The truth is that is not Norman's baby. The truth is Blake is the father of that child. Whether it was conceived during consensual sex or not, Blake is the father. Either way it goes, whether you decide to face the truth or hide it, there will be consequences. But believe me, as scared as you may be of the consequences of the truth, it don't hold a candle to the consequences of a lie. Because guess what? When you lie, not only will you have to deal with the consequences of the lie, all the stress and worry of hiding the lie, but then when and if the lie is uncovered you still have to end up dealing with the truth anyway. So I always ask folks, 'Why not just go ahead and deal with the consequences of the truth in the first place and just get it over with?'" Pastor Margie raised her hands in the air and then let them drop as if it was a no-brainer.

Pastor Margie's last comment put a fear over both Norman and Paige. If they'd never experienced the fear of the Lord before, they had now. Sure God would forgive them for any sins and lies they committed, but Pastor Margie had just reminded them that consequences of their sins and lies would still be theirs to face and deal with. What would those consequences be? Jesus was the truth and the truth had made them free. Freedom was priceless, therefore they wanted to maintain that freedom and they wanted the baby Paige was carrying to inherit it as well. So before leaving that office, they thanked Pastor Margie, prayed with Pastor Margie, and then left, knowing exactly what their next move had to be . . . at least when it came to their parents.

Chapter Thirteen

"A baby! Jesus Christ, Son of God! Oh, Mary, mother of God." Mrs. Vanderdale placed her hand over her forehead and fell backward, knowing her husband would catch her fall before she could hit the floor.

And even though this was one of Mrs. Vanderdale's normal practices whenever she was faced with so-called devastating news, everyone still rushed to her aid. Miss Nettie fanned her while Stuart fetched her a glass of water. Norman, well, for the first time almost ever, this time Norman just stood there and watched everyone else make a fuss over his mother. She never even gave him the chance to tell her that the baby wasn't his before she went off into her antics. Perhaps if she had they could have avoided this huge production.

The longer Norman just stood there doing nothing, the more his mother felt she needed to do more of something, anything, to get a sympathetic reaction from her son. After all, he was the one responsible for this reaction of hers. How dare he within a week's time bring more shocking news to her doorstep?

Norman's father walked his wife over to the couch where he laid her down. She took sips of the water Stuart had brought her. All the while Norman kept telling himself he'd made the right decision by not bringing Paige with him to break the news of her pregnancy to his mother. He had a feeling she was going to put on a show worthy of a high-priced Vegas show ticket.

"Honey, please, pull yourself together," Mr. Vanderdale pleaded with his wife.

"Oh, Norm," Mrs. Vanderdale said to her husband, Norman Senior, "that son of yours is going to be the death of me yet. I swear to you!"

Norman Senior looked at his son and shook his head. "You know your mother," he mouthed, suggesting she didn't mean the words that were coming out of her mouth. She was just being her dramatic, usual self.

Yes, Norman did know his mother. He knew her very well. She'd always been a drama queen. It had kept things quite interesting in the Vanderdale household when he was coming up. But there had never been drama or issues when it came to skin color, creed, or race. Sure, Norman's mother had come from the South and a long line of ancestors who'd done their share of slave trading, but that wasn't how his household had been run. Everyone was equal. It had always been that way. Norman had never seen any signs of his mother having a prejudice against Black people. So he was baffled at her behavior this past week. Had there been any indication his mother would play the role of Fred Sanford and fake having a heart attack every other day, he would have never knowingly subjected Paige to that type of behavior, or himself for that matter.

"Mother, where is all this coming from, seriously?" Norman said, sounding as unsympathetic as ever.

"Oh, don't play stupid with me, young man," his mother replied. "You knew what this would do to me. This is just some kind of payback for all the years we wouldn't allow you to dance to the beat of your own drum."

"Nonsense, and you should be ashamed to even insinuate that me marrying Paige, a black woman, is a punishment to you and Dad. Do you hear yourself? Do you know what you sound like, Mother?" Mrs. Vanderdale remained silent. "It sounds like something a racist would say."

There, the elephant in the room had been addressed.

"What? Well I . . ." Mrs. Vanderdale placed her hand on her chest and began taking in heavy, deep breaths.

"Do you think we might need to call a doctor?" Stuart asked once he saw that it seemed as if Mrs. Vanderdale wasn't doing any better.

"The only doctor she needs is the one standing right over there," Norman said sarcastically, pointing to his father, who was a psychiatrist by trade.

That comment seemed to jar his mother back to her healthy composure. She sat up straight and stiff on the couch, her feet slamming onto the floor and her eyes shooting a look of disbelief at Norman. "Well, I've never."

"And I never thought you'd act this way either, otherwise I never would have even introduced you to my wife," Norman said. "She and I, and our baby, would live happy and in peace without ever stepping foot into this madness. This whole sick act, it's all in your head. And since you married a head doctor, hopefully we can get you cured quick, fast, and in a hurry."

"Son, I think you've crossed a line," his father warned.

"No disrespect, Father, but I think she crossed the line a long time ago." Norman gave his father an intense, serious look. "We just always excuse her behavior by saying 'That's how she is,' or 'You know your mother.' Well how much longer are we going to continue to give her a pass?"

"Son, we're not giving your mother a pass. You know she doesn't mean any harm. It's just . . ." Mr. Vanderdale allowed his words to trail off when he realized his only defense was about to be what it had always been over the years.

Norman exhaled. "Dad, you would truly be okay with someone who felt this way about another race? Like the family is being contaminated because I brought a black woman into the home?"

"How many times do I have to say it's not about a black woman being in the home?" Mrs. Vanderdale said. "Have you noticed that Nettie is a black woman and she's been in the house for years? And will you two stop speaking about me as if I'm not sitting right here?"

Norman ignored his mother's last request and continued talking with his father, who, he hoped, would be the voice of reason. "I can't imagine that you would be okay with that, Dad, not with where you come from. Not with you being who you are."

Prior to joining the family business he had married into, Mr. Vanderdale had been referred to as the underground Dr. Phil of the Midwest. Mr. Vanderdale had been known as Dr. Vanderdale to most. He'd received his doctorate in psychiatry and had practiced mainly in the prison systems. He felt that if an effort was truly put forth, then the inmates could actually receive what they'd been placed in the prisons to receive: rehabilitation.

Initially Mr. Vanderdale had been a business major, but one evening after leaving a college bar and heading back to his dorm on campus, it had started to rain so he began a light jog back to his dorm. The next thing he knew, a cop car had come out of nowhere and pulled up onto the sidewalk, cutting him off. Within seconds he was face down on the pavement with a gun to his head. He was placed in the back of a police car and waited there for a few minutes in fear, wondering what in the world was going on.

Eventually another police vehicle pulled up. A young, disheveled-looking female, who Norman had seen around campus, was brought over to the car he was in. The officer who led her there pointed at him. The girl then nodded while going into hysterics. Shortly thereafter, Norman was driven downtown and booked on rape charges.

It was a long, drawn-out ordeal that took a couple of months to be cleared up. Mr. Vanderdale was released from jail when the girl later said that she wasn't sure if she'd fingered Mr. Vanderdale because he was the actual rapist, or if she'd just recognized him from around campus. Then there was some DNA testing that didn't match up with Mr. Vanderdale. But before his release, he'd been jailed for two months and in those two months he'd witnessed things he'd never even imagined animals doing. But then he realized why. The inmates were being treated like animals. You can only treat someone like a dog for so long before they start barking and biting like a dog.

Mr. Vanderdale, although two years into his business major and paying for college out of his own pocket, changed majors and vowed to do what many thought couldn't be done in the prison system: rehabilitation. He'd succeeded greatly, receiving all types of awards, accolades, and honors. He became sought after for counseling services in jails and prisons all over the country. He finally began to focus on the youth in the juvenile system, figuring if he could get them while they were young, he'd never have to meet up with them in the prison system.

He'd met his wife during this time in one of his travels to a Southern prison. She'd been the clerk at the theatre he'd decided to catch a movie at during some of his down time. They quickly fell in love and when Mr. Vanderdale moved back north, he had his new bride in tow, who he had found out upon marrying was the daughter of the owner of the theatre chain. Mrs. Vanderdale had kept her relationship to the owners of the chain a secret. Many men had tried to court her simply for her money. But Norman Senior had been different.

From day one his wife's family had pressured Mr.
Vanderdale into joining the family business so that their
children could continue the family legacy. It took five
years of pressure and Mr. Vanderdale almost losing his
life after being attacked with a knife during one of his
counseling sessions for him to give in and join his wife's
family business.

During his days of counseling, Mr. Vanderdale had met,
stayed connected with, and continued to counsel pro bono
some of the inmates. He did this mainly through letters
and phone calls. This was the reason the Vanderdale family
currently had and had always had an almost all-black staff.
Most of them were rehabilitated convicts. It hadn't gone
unnoticed by Mr. Vanderdale the African American ratio
of inmates versus the other races. Even when he agreed to
join in on the family business, it was under the strict and
unwavering stipulation that he'd be allowed to hire some of
his past rehabilitated clients to work for him.

"Son," his father-in-law had spoken to him all those
years ago, "you are the best at what you do. If you were a
car repairman, and my car broke down and I sent it to you
for repairs, if you had the reputation as a car mechanic as
you do a mind mechanic, I'd trust driving that vehicle one
hundred percent. Therefore, I'd trust anyone you chose
to hire."

Even when Mr. Vanderdale informed his wife that he
wanted some of his past clients, who were mainly African
American, to work for them in and around their home,
her words mirrored those of her father. She didn't put up
a fight.

"I believe in you, Norm," she'd told him. "Anything you
fixed isn't broken anymore. You've made a well-earned
name for yourself in your field. Besides, I think it's about
time that family of mine show some reparation for how
they treated those people in the past. It might not be forty
acres and a mule, but, my God, it's something."

Mrs. Vanderdale had shared childhood stories and the history of her family with her husband and children over several evenings throughout Norman's years of coming up. Some were disturbing while others were intriguing. But his mother had always expressed remorse in how her ancestors had treated those outside of their race. But here now, Norman couldn't help but wonder if in all actuality the apple hadn't fallen too far from the family tree.

Norman threw his hands up. "Look, I'm sorry." He apologized to both his parents. "I'm just really going to need Mother to explain to me what's going on in that head of hers."

Mrs. Vanderdale swallowed and then looked toward Miss Nettie and Stuart, who'd been standing there taking everything in as if they'd been watching a game of Ping-Pong. "Nettie, Stuart, could you excuse my family and me please?"

"Yes, ma'am," they said in unison before exiting the room. Once they'd exited the room, Mrs. Vanderdale spoke her piece.

"Son, first off, I'd like for you to forgive me for the way I've been acting."

Norman nodded his forgiveness, but knew better than to take his mother's apologies at face value. There was always something more lying beneath the surface.

"I guess I should have just come out and said it. Or as you might better relate to now"—she used her fingers to make quotation marks—"I should have kept it real."

"Mother," Norman warned her not to go there.

"Okay, okay, I'm sorry," she apologized again and then continued. "I don't have a problem with Black people. I just have a problem with my son marrying a black person; there I said it."

Norman was silent at first. "I appreciate you for sharing how you feel. Thank you, Mother, for owning it. But now can you please explain why you feel that way? I mean, you don't mind them cooking for you, and cleaning for you, and—"

"Son," his father interrupted when he saw that Norman was getting heated, "let your mother finish."

Norman took a breath and then sat down in a chair while his mother explained herself.

"Son, I have a guilty pleasure I need to confess with you," Mrs. Vanderdale said as she began to wring her hands.

"Yes, go ahead."

She turned to her husband. "You too, Norm." She then talked directly at Norman. "Nettie records all those wives this and wives that reality shows. Then every Saturday afternoon, when your father sometimes thinks I'm off having tea with the ladies, Nettie and I sit and watch them all back to back over some of her sweet tea with lemonade." Mrs. Vanderdale then mumbled under her breath almost as if she was embarrassed, "With a bucket of popcorn and hot sauce."

"Honey," her husband said. "You've said a million times that is trash TV and you'd never let it into your ear gates and eye gates."

"I know, I know," she admitted. "It's just that that stuff is so addictive and entertaining. I mean watching those people act like ani . . ." Her words trailed off and she looked to her husband.

"Like animals," he finished her sentence. It was obvious he was hurt by his wife's actions and comments and that it had struck a chord on that old guitar called the past.

"I'm sorry, Norm, I know how you dedicated your life to make sure, whether a human was caged up behind bars or not, that they were never looked at as animals." Her eyes watered. "Please forgive me."

"Honey," Mr. Vanderdale started, "you told us inhumane stories that were passed down to you of how your ancestors used to treat the male slaves like animals, matching them up against one another, putting them in fights, betting on them and whatnot while everyone sat around and watched for entertainment. You've basically just said you're getting a kick out of the modern-day version of it."

"I know, and it won't happen again."

"I guess I'm lost, because I still have no idea what this has to do with me marrying Paige," Norman said.

"Because she looks like those women on the television. I don't want to have to worry every night that that's what my son is dealing with. Those women are damaged goods. They carry so much baggage with them. They're hurt and full of pain and misery. Lots of them don't have fathers who stuck around and some of them have never even laid eyes on their fathers. Wouldn't know him if he was standing in front of them in the grocery store. Then there is their health. They deal with that sugar diabetes, high blood pressure, and all that weight they tend to end up carrying. Have you noticed how thick most of 'em are? Or just outright overweight? I don't want that for you; not my son. Maybe somebody else's, but not mine."

"Mother, you're being—" Norman started.

"Wait, let me finish." She put her hand up, cutting Norman off. "Every mother under the sun wants what is only the best for their child. Well, you are my child and I want only what is the best for you. And you have to admit it, son, Blacks aren't always granted the best treatment and opportunities. I don't want you to have to bear witness to that. All it will cause you is hurt and pain. I don't want my son having to deal with unnecessary hurt or pain, or my grandchild. Because no matter how you dice it, a mixed child is usually deemed black by society.

My son, my only son," Mrs. Vanderdale said, heartfelt, "you wouldn't have to deal with all that drama if you had a white wife. I'm sorry if this sounds racist, prejudiced, or whatever else. You know me; I've never discriminated or said a bad word about Black people. And I repeat, I don't have anything against Black people. I just have something against my children marrying Black people." And with that, Mrs. Vanderdale sat on the couch, her eyes darting from her son to her husband as if waiting to see who would cast the first stone.

Norman's father spoke first. "Like our son, I appreciate you being honest and voicing how you feel. That took courage. But allow me to let you know that, under no uncertain terms, do I mirror your thoughts, opinion, and/or concerns. I still love you dearly. I will continue to love you, but I'll also start doing something I've never done before when it comes to you. And that's to pray." He kissed his wife on the forehead and then exited the room, patting his son on the shoulder to show support as he left.

There was dead silence as Norman and his mother sat in the living room alone. The silence became agonizing torture to Mrs. Vanderdale. "So are you going to disown me now? Are you and your wife never going to return again? Am I never going to see my grandchild?"

Norman waited a moment before replying. "I, my wife, and our child will always return to the place I call home. Whatever that spirit is that has a hold of you will not get rid of us, but we will get rid of it. Especially now that we have Dad on our side as well. The Bible says that when two or more gather in His name, touch and agree—"

Mrs. Vanderdale put her hand up to halt Norman's words as tears fell from her eyes. "You don't have to finish. I've heard Nettie say it a million times before when I walk by her room and hear her praying." Tears continued to spill from her eyes. "Do you know she prays for me?" She swallowed. "I guess this right here is that moment Miss Nettie's been praying about for years. I think she calls it deliverance. And here I thought she was praying my designer gowns would be delivered on time for my affairs." Mrs. Vanderdale chuckled and Norman joined her. She looked up at him. "I'm sorry, son. I must apologize to Paige as well."

Sensing it was genuine pain, hurt, and remorse his mother was demonstrating, Norman felt he no longer needed to make this about his feelings, but make it about his mother. He went and sat next to her on the couch.

"Mom, please." Norman didn't want to see his mother so torn like this. "I forgive you. Please don't cry."

"I just feel no better than my ancestors right now. Because when you mentioned the fact that Paige was pregnant, my skin just . . ."

"Well, Mom, if you'd let me finish, you would have learned that the baby Paige is carrying isn't my baby."

"What!"

Norman couldn't tell if it was shock or relief in his mother's eyes. Nonetheless he continued to tell her the entire truth about his marriage to Paige, including the situation with her being pregnant by her abusive ex-husband.

"Can I ask you something, Norman? And please don't take this the wrong way," Mrs. Vanderdale said. "It's not your baby, but you and Paige have decided you are going to play the role of the baby's father by signing the birth certificate and everything. This child is going to be one hundred percent African American. God forbid anything ever happens to Paige, but if it did, how on God's green earth are you going to raise a black child?"

Norman opened his mouth, but nothing came out, as that thought had never crossed his mind. And for the first time ever his mother planted a seed in Norman's mind that made him question whether he'd bitten off more than he could chew.

Chapter Fourteen

"Whoa, this is a lot of stuff!" Norman looked around his decent-sized two-bedroom apartment that now looked like the overflow of Babies"R"Us. Between the baby shower her mother and church had given Paige, and the one her job had just hosted today, neither of which his mother attended, he was rethinking their choice of moving into his apartment together versus Paige's house. But Paige said if she didn't want to keep the man's last name, she certainly didn't want to live in his house, so just last month, when Paige was nearing her eighth month of pregnancy, the house sold. She'd moved into Norman's place a month prior to that though. It was as if everything was lining up in divine order. Maybe the old scripture, indeed, was correct about God not putting on a person more than they could bear. What Paige initially thought was going to be way too much, God had managed to lighten the load.

"Tell me about it," Paige huffed as she struggled to sit down comfortably on the couch. "But we got some awfully nice stuff though. And expensive. Like that stroller your sister bought—"

"No, my parents bought it. Samantha just brought it over since my mother couldn't make it."

"Oh, yeah, that's right; her standing tea social with the ladies," Paige said, not buying her mother-in-law's excuse for one minute. "When my mom and the church had theirs it was her standing hair appointment that kept her from coming."

"Hey, at least she sent a gift. Let's give her some credit. Baby steps. She's trying here. Okay?"

"Yeah, you're right," Paige agreed with a shrug. Norman had shared with Paige the conversation he'd had with his parents when breaking the news about Paige's pregnancy. Paige figured with that many folks now praying for her mother-in-law, the chains were bound to be broken eventually. Hopefully before Paige exploded and let that mother-in-law of hers know how she really felt. As far as Paige was concerned, God needed to hear their prayers and answer them quickly before she was left alone in a room with that woman.

"So do you want me to start hauling these things off to your and the baby's room?"

"Ummm, I don't know. It's already tight in there with my double bed and the crib," Paige said.

"I told you I felt we should have just set up the bassinette for now." He gave her an "I told you so" look.

"Husband, I think you might have been right." When Paige referred to Norman as husband, it wasn't in a romantic way or anything like that. It was just basically his title in her life. And even though they agreed that it only made sense to live as husband and wife, who, legally, they were, they didn't share the same bed. Norman had given Paige and the baby his master bedroom and taken the guest bedroom for himself.

They'd talked of maybe getting a place together but decided to table that notion and revisit it later. A couple months before the two got married, Norman had just signed a two-year lease to receive a discount on his rent, so it wouldn't have made sense to lose all that money he'd have to pay out to his landlord for terminating his lease early. And again, Paige couldn't get out of that house she and Blake had shared as husband and wife soon enough.

"What? Should we mark this as a milestone in our marriage?" Norman said. "You saying I'm right?"

"Oh please. I've always been woman enough to admit when I'm wrong . . . eventually." Paige and Norman shared a laugh. "Owee." Paige grabbed her stomach.

"You okay?" Norman rushed over to her side.

"Yeah, I'm fine." Paige lay back on the couch.

Norman sat down and lifted her legs onto his lap, removed the slippers she'd been wearing, and began to massage her feet. "Is that better?"

"Yeah, I just think I overdid it a little today is all. This baby is not due for two more weeks and I need all fourteen of those days to get ready for it."

"I hate referring to the baby as 'it.' I wish you'd just gone on and let the doctor tell you the sex during your last ultrasound."

"No, I wanted it to be a surprise," Paige said. "As if life hasn't given me enough surprises."

"Well, this is a good surprise," Norman said while patting her feet. "Let me go make you some tea, then I'll get to putting away all this stuff." Norman exited the living room and went and put on a pot of water to boil.

"Ouch. There it goes again." Paige hunched over.

"What is it?" Norman came racing back out of the kitchen. "Do you think you could be going into labor?" Norman was concerned.

"No. I'm not sure what labor pains feel like, but from the way my mother described them, it would feel far worse than this." Upon telling her parents that she was pregnant, Paige was relieved not to have to deal with the same reaction from her mother as she'd had to deal with upon telling her about the marriage. Surprisingly, Mrs. Robinson had been ecstatic that she was about to become a grandmother. Since then she'd kept Paige on the phone for at least an hour daily sharing with her the joys of motherhood. She'd made it a point to share the pains as well—labor pains, which was how Paige knew that if she was in labor, the pain would be much more severe, according to what her mother had told her.

"Well, maybe I should at least call the doctor just to make sure," Norman suggested.

"Norman, it's Saturday. Let that doctor be. Besides, I'm feeling better already." She got up from the couch. "I'll come to the kitchen with you to get that tea."

Norman and Paige went into the kitchen. Paige leaned against the counter while Norman stood over the pot of water, waiting for it to come to a good boil.

"You know what?" Paige said. "Why don't we play around with some baby names? I'll list five girl names and you list five boy names. We'll both agree on the top three from each of our lists. But if it's a girl, I get to pick the name from the top three girl names and vice versa for you if it's a boy."

"What? Really?" Norman was astonished as he placed tea bags into the two cups he'd set on the countertop. "You're going to give me that much power?"

"If it's a boy. And I'll have all the power if it's a girl. Talk about girl power." Paige held up a fist to the sky. "Got any boy names you've been thinking of?"

"Well, Norman III of course." He poured the boiling hot water into their cups.

"Okay." Paige didn't dismiss it, but the fact she just nodded and couldn't look Norman in the eyes were signs of dismissal enough.

"Just kidding." Norman decided to let her off the hook.

"You little . . ." Paige began laughing and playfully swatted Norman. "Oh my!" She grabbed her stomach.

"What is it? Is the pain back?"

"Well, no. It's just that I just now laughed so hard that I think I peed my pants."

Both Norman and Paige looked down at the liquid streaming down her legs to form a puddle at her bare feet.

"Paige, I don't think you peed your pants. I think your water just broke. I don't care what you say." Norman rushed over to the phone on the kitchen wall. "I'm calling the doctor." He found the refrigerator magnet the doctor's office had given them with all the doctor's contact information on it and began to dial. "Where are you going?" he called out as he saw Paige shuffling out of the kitchen.

"I'm going to call my mama." She looked down at the liquid still slightly flowing down her legs. "And to see if one of those packs of diapers we got as a gift is big enough to fit me!"

"It's a girl!" Norman ran into the waiting area and yelled. "The most beautiful, head full of curly hair, brown little ball of joy I've ever seen in my life." Tears poured from Norman's eyes. It was evident that watching life come into the world had been something that had moved him beyond his wildest imagination. "She's just beautiful."

When Norman's tears of joy started to include weeping, Mrs. Robinson went and embraced her son-in-law. "Now, now, son, it's all right. I know."

Norman wrapped his arms around his mother-in-law, wishing that his own mother could have been there to celebrate with him. He hadn't even wasted his time phoning her. He had phoned his sister though, who had just arrived at the hospital about twenty minutes ago.

"I'm an auntie," Samantha said. "Good job, big brother." Samantha walked over and patted her brother on the back. Mrs. Robinson stepped away and allowed the siblings to share this moment.

"I love you, sis," Norman told his sister. "Thank you for being here for me."

"I'm not here for you." Samantha pulled back and looked her brother in the eyes. "I've hated you ever since I was seven and you flushed my goldfish down the toilet to get back at me for setting that stupid hamster of yours free when you wouldn't let me feed it. You think I'm here for your ugly mug? I'm here for my beautiful niece and don't you ever forget." A smile cracked across Samantha's lips.

"Thank you, sis. This means the world to me. You've always accepted and supported me. But this, right now, your support means more to me than anything in the wor . . ." Norman broke down and there wasn't a dry eye in the room.

Mr. and Mrs. Robinson embraced one another as they were touched by Norman's exchange with his sister. Pastor Margie and a couple other church members huddled with tears streaming down their face. Samantha fought hard to keep the tears filling her eyes from falling. When she saw it was a losing battle, she excused herself from the room, claiming she needed to go to the ladies' room.

"Son, can I talk to you for a moment?" Mr. Robinson approached Norman and asked.

"Sure," Norman agreed, wiping the moisture from his face.

The two men stepped off to the side of the room for some privacy.

"I just wanted to let you know that I see right through you," were Mr. Robinson's words to his son-in-law.

Norman was a little stumped by Mr. Robinson's words. "Excuse me, sir?"

"You may have everyone else fooled as to why you married my daughter, but, son, you ain't fooled me one bit."

"Mr. Robinson, I . . . I . . ."

"And don't call me Mr. Robinson."

Norman remembered upon meeting Mr. Robinson months ago he'd told him to call him by his first name. "I'm sorry."

"You claimed you married my daughter because of that baby." He pointed toward the doors where the delivery rooms were. "But that's a lie. Mr. Vanderdale, I ain't too fond of liars."

The stern look Mr. Robinson initially had on his face did not let up, not one bit. Norman had no idea where this attitude was coming from nor why Mr. Robinson would try to steal the joy of the moment.

"Mr. Robinson—I mean, Samuel—I don't know what you're talking about."

Mr. Robinson put his hand on Norman's shoulder. "Don't call me Samuel either. You don't have to pretend with me anymore, son. I'm on to you. This marriage to Paige wasn't all about Paige and that baby. No matter how much you deny it, there was some selfishness involved as well. I see it in your eyes. Son," Mr. Robinson said, "you love my daughter."

"Of course I do," Norman said, swallowing hard.

"No, I mean you looooovvve my daughter." He looked Norman dead in his eyes. "You are in love with my daughter." The corners of his mouth just slightly curved up into a smile.

Norman exhaled. He was relieved. One, because he thought he was about to get beat down by his father-in-law, and two, finally, someone had taken notice and was now forcing him to confess the feelings he'd been harboring for Paige for some time now, even prior to her divorce. The look of relief that rushed across his face said it all.

"Ah, ha ha. I knew it." Mr. Robinson clapped his hands. "But don't worry, son, your secret is safe with me. I think that's something she needs to hear from you for the first time."

"Tha . . . thank you, Samuel."

"Didn't I tell you don't call me that?" Mr. Robinson's voice was stern again.

"Well, sir, you said not to call you Mr. Robinson, and I can't call you by your first name. I'm, uh, not sure what I should call you."

"Son," Mr. Robinson said proudly, placing his arm around Norman's neck and bringing him in for a hug, "call me Dad."

Chapter Fifteen

"Isn't she just so precious?" Paige said as both she and Norman stared down over three-week-old Adele Monique Vanderdale. The baby girl was sleeping soundly in her bassinette, the one Norman had substituted her crib for.

"That she is," Norman agreed, taking his thumb and rubbing it down the baby's soft brown skin. "She looks just like you, Paige, even though she's this tiny. All your features are just so prominent that it's eerie."

"Yep, eerie," Paige said out loud, but thought, *or a prayer answered.* From the minute she decided she was going to give birth to the baby, she prayed to God every day that the baby would look nothing like its biological father. She just didn't know if she'd be able to handle looking into Blake's eyes every day. That might have been just a tad too much to bear, and God must have known it. God must have known Paige wouldn't have been able to handle that. Maybe some other mother, but not her.

"I'm going to go change out of my work clothes." Norman had rushed right in from work to do what he did all the time: lay eyes on his new bundle of joy.

During her pregnancy, Paige had often wondered if, once reality hit, if once her little black baby by another man was born, Norman would be able to deal with it. His conjuring up the idea for the two to live in holy matrimony for the sake of the baby had been a good deed indeed. But no good deed goes unpunished. Would he be tortured by looking at the reminder that Adele was not his, yet he was claiming her as his own? This could hinder him from moving forward in future relationships. There was really no turning back. Norman had signed the birth certificate. Besides, in the state of Ohio, the husband is automatically considered the father unless tests prove otherwise. As far as Paige was concerned though, there would be no test. Blake, due to the restraining order, was not allowed to make any contact with her whatsoever. With that being so, she'd never have the opportunity to tell him about Adele. Not any time in the near future anyway.

Sure Paige knew that one day she'd have to tell Adele the truth, but it would be on her timing and terms. And of course Adele would have the free will of seeking out her biological father if she so chose. But Paige had a feeling that after hearing the full details about her father and what kind of man he was, that would be something Adele would have to think long and hard about. Paige didn't plan on bad-mouthing and running Blake into the ground to his daughter, but for safety reasons, she owed it to her daughter to let her know what type of man she'd be dealing with, which was violent.

"I'll get your plate ready and warmed up," Paige said to Norman as he left her bedroom and headed to his own. Paige made her way into the kitchen where she warmed up Norman some fried chicken, macaroni and cheese, greens seasoned with ham hocks, and a slice of cornbread. Soul food wasn't anything new to Norman's palate, having grown up with Miss Nettie in his house.

About ten minutes later, showered and wearing only his plaid pajama bottoms, Norman entered the kitchen just as Paige was turning around from the microwave with his plate in hand.

"Oh, God!" Paige said as his plate came crashing down to the ground.

"What's wrong? Paige, are you okay?" Norman raced over to Paige and put his arm around her.

"No, no, don't touch me. Don't do that." Paige appeared nervous and her forehead began to sweat. She couldn't even make contact with Norman—eye contact or physical. She wriggled out from under his arm and took a few steps away from him.

"What did I do? What's wrong?" Norman questioned, confused. He thought back to the night he'd found out she was pregnant and how he'd startled her by walking into the kitchen in the middle of the night without announcing himself. But now that the two shared the same space, did he really have to announce himself?

"You came out here with no shirt on, that's what's wrong. Boy, go get some clothes on," Paige demanded.

Norman looked down at his bare chest. He wasn't a cut-up built dude who spent hours in the gym, but he had a nice body with some pretty scrumptious definition. This was a part of him Paige had never seen before. "It's August, the heat of summer, and it's hot in here."

"I thought I heard Adele sniffing today. I turned the air off."

"Maybe you should have turned it down, but off? It's an oven in here, especially after getting out of that hot shower."

"Then you should have taken a cold one," Paige snapped. *Kind of like what I need to do right about now.* Paige began to fan herself. That same heat she'd felt that day Norman dropped her off at her house after having breakfast with her parents was making another cameo.

"You're hot," Norman said, standing there, looking at Paige.

Paige looked down at her sky blue furry slide-in slippers that matched her nice little summery cotton housecoat. "Am I?" She began to blush at Norman's compliment.

"Yes, it's obvious." Norman slowly approached Paige. He lifted his hand to her face. "See, you're sweating." He rubbed her forehead then showed her the moisture on his hand. "Means you're hot."

A frown covered Paige's face. "Oh, that's what you mean?" She couldn't hide the disappointment in her tone. She turned away in embarrassment.

"What else could I have meant?" Norman shrugged his shoulders until his mind thought just long enough to reach the intersection of where Paige's thoughts had parked. "Oooooohhhhh. You thought that when I said you're hot, that I was saying you are *hot* hot." Norman bent over in laughter. "You are so crazy."

Paige didn't say a word; she just stomped over to the counter, snatched off a wad of paper towels, and began picking up the food from the dropped plate off the floor. Stomping and a-slamming and a-seething, Paige cleaned up the mess. Norman was in too many hysterics to even notice her attitude. By the time Norman was able to get himself together, Paige was picking up the broken glass from the plate with tear-filled eyes.

"Paige, why aren't you laughing?" Norman asked, finally taking notice of his wife's disposition. "That was funny, right?" Norman had noticed that Paige had been more emotional than usual since getting pregnant and giving birth to Adele, but he was certain he hadn't said or done anything to make her cry.

"No, it wasn't," Paige replied, carrying the broken glass over to the trashcan. With hands on hips Paige sharply turned around to face Norman. "And I don't think you thought it was funny either. Not that dang on funny." Paige shot Norman a suspicious eye.

"What? What are you talking about?" Now it was Norman who couldn't look Paige in the eyes. His eyes looked downward at the few remnants left of the spilled plate.

"Umm, hmmm, just what I thought." Paige lowered herself, trying to get within Norman's eyesight. The closer she walked to him, she raised herself, until she was smack dead in his face, forcing him to make eye contact. "I sometimes laugh to keep from crying, but you, my friend, were laughing to keep from—"

"Don't you dare go there," Norman stopped her.

"Facing the truth." Paige went there. "Norman Vanderdale, are you attracted to your wife?" Paige spoke as if she weren't referring to herself. "Come on, you can tell me. After all, I am your wife." She let out a sarcastic chuckle. "You can tell your wife anything. We're best friends."

Norman didn't think this game Paige was playing was cute at all. "Stop it, Paige, you're playing with fire."

"Puhleeze. We've been playing with fire since we both said 'I do.' So come on, Norman, tell your *best friend* what's on your mind." Paige spoke in a teasing manner. The tables were now turned.

"That's just it; we're best friends!" Norman finally snapped. "And best friends aren't supposed to . . ."

"Get married?" Paige questioned.

"No; be attracted to one another." Norman could recall once upon a time when he'd started to develop a slight attraction toward Paige. But she was a married woman, and they were best friends. Besides that, at the time, he was just a fill-in for Blake, the man she'd felt was her soul mate. Even when both Norman and Paige were single, not once had they contemplated dating each other. In fact, the only thing they had in common besides working at the same job was the fact that the two were single.

Paige had sensed Norman's attraction to her at one point. She too realized it was something that was developing simply because they were spending an excessive amount of time together, thanks to Blake practically living at his place of employment. On top of that, Paige had never known Norman to date black girls, not on purpose any-how. He'd been set up on a few blind dates that resulted in a couple of them being women of color, but that was it. As far as Paige knew, Norman's attraction to her had vanished just as quickly as it had developed . . . or had it?

There was brief silence and Norman gathered his thoughts. "I feel so awful. I mean, I've repented a thou-sand times, yet I still feel so guilty," Norman confessed.

"Repented?" Paige was missing something.

"The attraction . . . it was there long before you became my wife. As a matter of fact, it was there when you were another man's wife. It never went away. It's always been there. It's still here. I was just pretty good at sweeping it under the rug and keeping it there while I played the role of your best friend. But, Paige, I wanted more. I wanted you."

Paige just stood there, flabbergasted. Norman's truth had knocked the wind out of her. She and her mother had talked about the fact that Paige and Norman keeping close quarters could lead to them crossing a line that had been drawn when they decided to run off and get married. Paige was adamant that that would never happen. Her mother warned her of the inevitable. So when Paige had just thought that Norman was calling her hot as a compliment, she thought her mother's words were coming to pass. She had no idea that the seed had long been planted in Nor-man, had been watered, nourished, and was now growing like the plant in *Little Shop of Horrors*.

"What's that one scripture? Something about so a man thinketh . . . or lusting after another man's wife? It's ba-sically a sin because it's already transpired in the mind."

"Yeah, I know what you're talking about." It was the same verse the New Day church mother, Mother Doreen, had shared with her when Paige had gone to her for advice about the lusting thoughts she was having about Norman as a married woman.

"My spirit felt so convicted having these feelings about you. My first instinct was to just distance myself from you, but you were going through so much. I couldn't abandon you either. I'd heard the cliché a million times, but for the first time in my life I truly knew what it felt like to be between a rock and a hard place."

Paige just stood and listened as Norman bared his soul to her. No man had ever been so transparent to her before. Unlike women, men weren't emotional creatures who easily revealed their every intimate thought and sentiment like women did. This was like a gift, and Paige would sit there attentive while it unwrapped itself.

"I lied to you . . . by omission," Norman confessed. "This was never just all about the baby. It was about me too. I . . . I . . ."

Paige was on the edge of her seat just waiting to hear what Norman's next words would be. If he just went on and said it first, it would be just that much easier for her to say to him the feelings she too had been suppressing. Maybe for not as long as he had been, but the feelings were there nonetheless, feelings that surpassed those of just a friendship. And it wasn't just an attraction. It wasn't just love. Paige knew what it was like to love someone. But this was different. This felt more like being in love. But no way and absolutely no how was she going to express those words first, only to be humiliated if they weren't reciprocated.

It felt good for her to know that Norman loved her, had been attracted to her, and had imagined being with her. But that didn't mean he was in love with her. She'd have to hear those words from the horse's mouth in order to bare her true feelings. And from the way this conversation was heading, it looked as though Mr. Ed wasn't the only horse that could talk.

"Go ahead, say it. You what?" Paige said, longing to hear those specific words from Norman so that the two of them could stop playing games and start keeping it real.

"Paige, I . . . " Norman walked over to Paige and took her hands into his. He looked so deep into her eyes she felt he could already see the words written on her soul. "Paige Vanderdale, I'm in l—"

"Whaaaa! Whaaa!"

The tiny cry coming from the master bedroom interrupted Paige and Norman's moment of truth. As much as Paige wanted to ignore Adele's crying, she couldn't. Had it been a "my diaper is wet" or an "I'm hungry" cry, she probably would have, just to hear those words she wanted to hear from Norman. But as she raced out of the kitchen heading for the bedroom she knew this wasn't one of those normal cries. Something was wrong with her baby!

Chapter Sixteen

"Oh, my God! Oh, Jesus." Paige stood in the hospital examination room pacing back and forth. "It's been almost an hour. Where is my baby? Where is my baby? What's wrong with her? She couldn't breathe. She couldn't . . ." Paige nearly lost her own breath she was in such a panic.

"Please, honey, calm down." Norman blocked Paige's path and wrapped his arms around her. "Our baby is going to be just fine. The doctors are running tests. God is not going to let—"

"God, God, God!" Paige said sarcastically as she broke away from Norman. "The Almighty who knows all and sees all. Well guess what else God does? He keeps putting me through hell; that's what He does. First He lets me marry this creep, the creep turns out to be an abusive creep, the abusive creep rapes me. Needless to say I get pregnant as a result of the abusive creep raping me. I'm torn, up all night, racking my frickin' brain trying to figure out what to do about it to the point I decide on suicide or abortion. But instead of killing myself or murdering the baby I do the right thing and have it. And now what does God do? He takes the baby away from me anyhow! That's what He does. So I don't want to hear anything about no God right now!" With each sentence Paige's voice had grown louder and louder until she was finally yelling at the top of her lungs in tears.

"Paige, please." Norman struggled to cocoon Paige again. She fought at first but then fell limp into his arms as she wept.

"Is everything all right in—" a nurse started.

"We're fine, ma'am. Thank you." Norman nodded to the nurse that everything was okay and she slowly exited the room, closing the door behind her. The male candy striper who had stood behind her, probably for protection, hadn't gone unnoticed by Norman.

"Why?" Paige cried. "If God was going to take my baby from me anyway, why didn't He just let me do it? Why did He even put her in my womb in the first place?"

"Please don't try to understand God's ways, Paige, "Norman said, rubbing her back. "His ways are not our—"

"Uhhhhggg." Paige pulled away from Norman yet again. "I don't want to hear that church, Bible, and scripture talk. When church ends, real life begins. This is real life."

Norman's eyes tightened. "Did you just quote Jay-Z?"

Paige shrugged. "You know I like to listen to a little secular music every now and then." Paige rolled her eyes. "But it's true. This is real life."

"And God is real, Paige. Come on, you know this."

Paige thought about it for a moment. Her shoulders slumped as if she was lightening up.

"You're just tensed right now. This is a tense situation. And I won't ask you to pray, recite scriptures for encouragement, or to even trust God. I'll do it for the both of us."

Norman's sincerity, hope, faith, and love had just chipped right through the ice that was forming around Paige's heart.

"I'm sorry," Paige apologized. "I didn't mean to get loud with you, embarrass you or whatever. It's just that so much is going through my mind right now. Not knowing is the worst. Your mind begins to make up things. Like what if Adele needs blood or an organ or something? What if I'm not a match? What if Blake is? Then I'll have to tell him about Adele and—"

"Stop it, Paige. Don't allow your mind to go there. Just wait on Go—"

Paige threw her hand up, halting Norman's words. He was a little stunned to have his wife's hand just an inch from his face. "I'm sorry . . . again," Paige said.

"You don't have to apologize, Paige. Not to me anyway." He allowed his eyes to dart upward. "But you might want to, you know, kind of repent to Him."

Paige exhaled. "I think God knows I really didn't mean all those things. Well, I meant them, but He knows my heart. See, I kind of have this love-hate relationship thing with God. He's like the boyfriend, the love of my life, who I can't live with, but sure in the heck can't live without. One minute I love Him and the next minute, well . . . let's just say I don't always get Him. Trying to stay saved is no easy feat for me."

"Well, maybe if you tried listening to J. Moss instead of Jay-Z, it might be just a tad easier." Norman took his index finger and thumb and held them just an inch apart.

"Yeah, well, maybe." The two shared a laugh, but all laughter came to an end when the doctor entered the room . . . without their daughter.

"It's not unusual for this to happen with infants some-times," Dr. Nicholas Wright, the emergency room doctor, told Paige and Norman as Paige sat in the examination room now cuddling Adele in her arms. The nurse had brought her in just a moment after the doctor had entered the room. Paige and Norman had seen Dr. Wright before at New Day. He would visit with another church member named Lorain.

"But, Doctor, she was blue. She couldn't breathe," Paige said, going back into a panic from just the memory of walking into Adele's bedroom just a couple hours ago and finding Adele a deep shade of blue, screaming her lungs out.

"If they're crying, they're breathing, but I'm certain, as a result of the test we gave her, that at some point she had a little trouble catching her breath. Believe it or not, and I know it sounds crazy, but sometimes an infant might have a little trouble catching its breath or remembering how to breathe. I know to adults, who have been doing it for years, it sounds absurd. But breathing can sometimes take a minute to catch on to for newborns. For example, have you ever been snorkeling?" the doctor asked Paige.

Paige tilted her head and poked out her lips, giving the doctor a "really?" look.

"Oh, yeah." The doctor turned his attention to Norman and redirected the question to him.

"Yes, my family and I used to go all the time when we'd go on family vacation," Norman said.

"Well, do you remember what it was like trying to train yourself to just breathe through your mouth through the tube while under water and not utilize your nose?"

"Yes," Norman chuckled, recalling the task. "It took me a minute to get the hang of it. My brain was so used to me breathing out of my nose on the regular, that having to utilize my mouth only was crazy. I have to admit, as a boy, it was scary at first. I felt like I was suffocating at one point. Even though my mouth was available to breathe through that snorkeling tube, I insisted on trying to use my nose and forgetting altogether that I could use my mouth."

Paige just sat there looking crazy and dumbfounded. She couldn't relate under any terms. Noticing the look on her face, Norman said to her, "You have to have experienced it to get it."

"Exactly," the doctor said, pointing his pen at Norman. "You hit the nail on the head."

Both men smiled at understanding the analogy the doctor had used. Paige was done with trying to figure it out. She was just glad her baby was okay. The drive to the hospital had been like her worst nightmare. She'd prayed over and over for God to make it so that her baby was okay.

"Please, God," she had cried while sitting in the back seat of the car next to the baby in her car seat. "Let my baby be okay. I couldn't bear if something is wrong with her. I pray against asthma or any other infirmities that might require lifelong care. I declare that I have a happy, healthy baby girl. In Jesus' name I pray. Amen."

Norman had touched and agreed with her. Of course, that was all before Paige had turned and began to doubt and blame God for even having her in this predicament. And now, as Paige stood up in the examination room with baby Adele sleeping just fine in her arms, she was a believer like never before that prayer worked if you worked it. She might have been wishy-washy when it came to her relationship with God. But God was the same yesterday, today, and would be tomorrow.

"Whatever language that was that the two of you were just speaking," Paige said to the men in the room, "I'm glad you understood one another." She looked at the doctor. "I just need to know that my baby is fine and this isn't something I'm going to have to worry about. That I'm not going to have to sleep on pins and needles with one eye open and both ears sharp making sure my baby doesn't stop breathing during her sleep."

"No, no, Mrs. Vanderdale," the doctor assured her, placing the baby's medical file under his arm. "You have a wonderfully fine and perfect little girl."

"Great." Paige looked to Norman. "Now we can go home and get some sleep." She began gathering her purse and the baby's diaper bag.

"Well, thank you, Doc." Norman stood and shook the doctor's hand.

"Anytime. And with the paperwork the nurse is going to give you with your discharge papers, there is a pamphlet describing what I just discussed. There is also a twenty-four-hour nurse hotline."

"Thank you." Norman thanked Dr. Wright again and shook his hand. He opened the examination room door to let Paige and the baby through.

"Thank you for everything, Doc. Next time I hope to see you at church and not here at your place of employment," Paige said, heading toward the door. She then turned and said, "But can I ask you a question?"

"Certainly," Dr. Wright said. "Shoot."

"How in the world do you know about snorkeling?"

He chuckled and shook his head. "In spite of popular opinion, some Black folk do enjoy snorkeling, water skiing, and swimming with the dolphins on occasion." He then turned to Norman where the two high-fived and then exited the room.

"So how'd she do? What's she doing? Did she cry for me? When's the last time you changed her diaper? How many ounces did she eat? Oh my goodness. Did you remember to burp her after she ate?" Paige hadn't even set her purse and keys down when she entered the house and began bombarding Norman with questions. She still had the mail in her hand she'd gotten out the mailbox.

"She did fine. She's just sitting here in her pumpkin seat, as you can see. She only cried when she needed to be changed, which was just twenty minutes ago, after she ate about four ounces of milk and I successfully burped her." Norman patted himself on the back. "But you know all of this already. I told you when you called me five minutes ago on your way home." Norman put his index finger to his temple as if pondering. "Or maybe it was when you called ten minutes ago. No, it had to be the time you called fifteen minutes ago." Norman snapped his finger. "No, it had to be when you called twenty minutes ago."

Paige put her hands on her hips. "Mister, are you trying to insinuate that I called you every five minutes?"

"I'm not insinuating anything. You did call every five minutes, and I have the call log on my cell phone to prove it," he said.

"Oh, hush." Paige shooed her hand and laughed. "I can't help it that this was my first time away from my little muffin in six whole weeks and I couldn't stand it." Paige made her way over to the baby and began cooing. "Ain't that right, Mommy's little smhoo? Did you miss your mommy? Huh, baby cakes?" Paige tickled the baby's chin.

"So what did the doctor say? Did you get a clean bill of health?"

"Yep. Clean bill of health. I'm good to resume all of my regular activities, which unfortunately means going back to work."

"Ha! You couldn't even go to the doctor's for an hour. How are you going to make it eight hours at work?"

A drab look took over Paige's face. "Ugh. Oh, no. I haven't even thought about that." Paige sat down looking as if she'd just lost her best friend, her eyes watering.

"Well, you have six more weeks of FMLA to think about it. You're twelve-week leave will be up then."

"I'll lose my mind if I resume my work duties."

Norman shrugged. "Then forget about work. Stay home and resume your wifely duties instead."

Both Norman and Paige's eyes darted at one another and locked. Both of their minds traveled to the gutter and then back again.

"I mean your motherly duties," Norman corrected himself.

"Yes, I know exactly what you meant." Paige shot Norman a knowing look as her mind wandered back to that unfinished conversation they'd started in the kitchen three weeks ago. Paige felt, had hoped, Norman was about to confess being in love with her before Adele's hurling cries drew them from the kitchen to the bedroom. Paige had dropped subtle hints over the past few weeks in an attempt to lure Norman back to the conversation. All had failed. Yet here once again it seemed like opportunity was knocking. "You know these awkward little moments can be avoided if you just come out and say whatever it was you were about to say in the kitchen awhile ago."

Norman looked confused.

"You know; the night we had to rush Adele to the hospital," Paige reminded him, although she had a feeling he was playing coy and had known exactly what she was talking about all along.

"Oh, that night," Norman recalled with a nod. He shifted a little on the couch as if trying to get comfortable. "Well, you know how . . ." he started. He was about to go into some long, drawn out pre-speech but felt he was tired of all the awkwardness as well. It was time to give the poor elephant in the room a break and stop making it jump through those stupid circus hoops. "Paige, plain and simply put, I'm in—"

"There you are."

Both Norman and Paige looked up to see Miss Nettie coming out of the kitchen, drying her hands on a paper towel.

"Miss Nettie, I didn't know you were here." Paige looked at Norman and spoke through closed teeth and tight lips. "Norman, why didn't you tell me Miss Nettie was here?"

"Uh, yes, why, Miss Nettie, I forgot myself that you were even here." Norman looked to Paige. "My mother sent Miss Nettie over with some groceries and asked her to prepare a couple days' worth of meals just in case you were busy with the baby."

"Oh, how nice of Mrs. Vanderdale. She sent Miss Nettie to do her grandmotherly duties."

"Don't start," was what Norman wanted to say to Paige. He didn't though. He just shot her a look that said it all. Miss Nettie concurred with a look of her own.

"Anyway, Miss Nettie." Paige stood and went and approached her in-laws' housekeeper. "It's good to see you." She hugged Miss Nettie. "And do send my thanks and regards to my mother-in-law."

Miss Nettie pulled away from Paige and said, "It's good to see you as well." She had a strange look on her face.

"Miss Nettie, what is it? Why are you looking at me so strangely?" Paige asked her.

"Nothing really, or maybe it's just me."

"What?"

"Do you notice that whenever you start talking about the missus that you end up with this accent like you're one of the characters from *Gone with the Wind?*"

Norman couldn't help but burst out laughing. "You notice that too, Miss Nettie? I thought it was just me. That's why I've never said anything."

"I do not," Paige said in disbelief.

"I wouldn't lie to you, child," Miss Nettie assured her. "Sounding like a broke-down Scarlett O'Hara."

Norman roared out in laughter even harder this time.

Paige shot him a glare. "It's not that funny. Besides, I honestly had no idea I was doing that."

"Now that you know better, do better," Miss Nettie said, she then changed the subject as she began gathering her belongings to leave. "I made a spaghetti pie that's cooling on the stove. You can cut it up in squares, freeze it, then thaw and warm whenever you got a taste for it. There's some homemade chicken and noodle soup I done froze up for you already. On the stove I got you some meatloaf, parsley potatoes, and green beans. You can eat those for dinner tonight." Miss Nettie pulled her thin, sheer scarf from her purse and tied it around her hair. "Oh yeah, and I cleaned and sterilized Miss Adele's bottles. Took the liberty of throwing that binky out though. Ain't no need of getting her started on that. Them thangs is just outright nasty. Besides, kids don't need pacifying. That's what's wrong with the spoiled little things now. Then they grow up with a sense of entitlement and . . ." Miss Nettie's words trailed off once she realized Norman and Paige were stone-faced while she went off on her rant. "Oh, well. Never you mind. But you know what I'm talking about."

"Yes, Miss Nettie, we do." Paige smiled as she went and opened the door for Miss Nettie. "Thank you for everything, Miss Nettie. Please send my regards to my mother-in-law." Paige said that last line in a purposeful and jokingly Southern drawl.

"You stop cuttin' up, child." Miss Nettie swatted Paige on the rear as she walked by her and out the door. "Oh yeah, and one last thing," Miss Nettie said before heading down the front porch. "I washed little Miss Adele's blankets. They should be about finished up in the dryer. Take 'em out and fold 'em up while they're warm from the dryer so they don't get all wrinkled and will be nice, flat, and soft for her."

"Is that everything, Miss Nettie?" Norman said, exasperated at all of Miss Nettie's instructions.

Miss Nettie threw her hands on her hips. "Don't worry, that's everything," Miss Nettie said, sensing Norman's irritation. She rolled her eyes and then climbed down the steps, but not before throwing one final task over her shoulder. "Now you can get back to telling the missus that you're in love with her."

Chapter Seventeen

Paige slowly closed the door after watching Miss Nettie walk away. The sense of awkwardness in the room nearly suffocated her. She had to think of something to say, something to do, quick. "The mail!" She hurried over to the end table where she had placed the mail. "Let me see if my million dollar check came today," she joked. Paige flipped through the few pieces of mail. "Here, these are for you." Paige handed Norman a couple pieces of mail that were addressed to either him or current resident. "And these are for . . ." She continued through the pile. "Me." Her tone changed to one of fret.

Detecting the change in Paige's tone Norman asked her, "What is it, honey?"

"Well, it's, uh, something from the jail," Paige informed him.

"With that restraining order, Blake knows darn well he's not to contact you in any shape or form," Norman seethed.

"No, no, it's not from Blake." Paige tore the letter open. "It's from what looks like the prison clinic." She looked up at Norman with fear in her eyes as she pulled the single piece of paper out of the envelope. After reading the first few lines, it was as if the wind had been knocked out of Paige. She nearly fell onto the couch, landing on the baby's pumpkin seat, until Norman caught her fall. It was like the scene when Norman's father had to catch his mother from falling, only this time there was no exaggerating. Paige really had to catch her breath.

"Paige, what is it?" Norman sat Paige down next to the baby. He then picked up the letter Paige had been reading that she'd let fall to the floor. After reading the first few lines, Norman, too, thought he'd need to be resuscitated. "Oh, my God. Is this a joke? Is this a horrible joke Blake is playing on you?" Norman examined the paper and the envelope for authenticity. "Maybe he found out you married me and this is his way of paying you back, some sick form of revenge. Or maybe he found out about Adele. Oh God." Norman threw his hand on his forehead. "This could get ugly." He began to pace.

"Norman, I really don't feel like this is a joke." Paige held out her hand. "Let me see the letter again."

Norman continued reading the letter himself.

"Please," Paige shouted. "Let me see it."

Norman handed Paige the letter and watched as she read. She just started shaking her head as tears filled her eyes.

"This can't be happening to me. It can't," Paige cried.

Norman hated seeing Paige in pain, in such agony. He felt so sorry for her. Just when everything in life seemed to be going okay for her, out popped the devil. Norman couldn't take seeing her like this. He pulled his cell phone out.

"Who are you calling?" Paige stood up to her feet and made an attempt to snatch the phone from Norman's hands. "Don't tell anyone. Don't you dare tell anyone. Do you know how people will treat me?"

"The heck with people, Paige!" Norman snapped. "At some point in your life you can't base every decision you make on what people will think of you. This isn't about people. This is about getting to the bottom of this. I'm calling the number on the paper. Now read it off to me."

Paige stood frozen.

"Read it!" Norman was getting frustrated.

Paige shook her head as tears filled her eyes. "No. No. What if I don't want to know?"

Norman walked over and got in Paige's face. "Are you serious right now? Why would you not want to know?" Norman took Paige's face and turned it toward the baby. "Her, right there; she's all the reason you need to want to know. Now read me the da—" Norman had to catch himself before a cuss word slipped. "Read me the darn number."

Paige took a deep breath and read the phone number she was instructed to call from the paper. Norman dialed. Once he heard the first ring, he held the phone out to Paige. "Here." He nudged the phone toward Paige. "Come on; it's ringing."

Paige exhaled again and then took the phone from Norman. She placed it to her ear until she was greeted on the other end. "Uh, yes," she said, swallowing tears. "My name is Paige Dickenson . . . I mean, Robinson." She slapped herself on the forehead as if knocking some sense into her head. Even though the letter was addressed to Paige Dickenson, that was no longer her last name. "This is Paige Vanderdale. I, uh, received a letter in the mail regarding my husband . . . my ex-husband, Blake Dickenson."

Norman rested his hand on Paige's back to calm her down, comfort her, and let her know that he was there to support her no matter what. Just like all the other trials and tribulations he'd been able to stand by and help Paige get through, he wouldn't forsake her now.

She took another deep breath and gained her composure. "I received a letter in the mail regarding Blake Dickenson. Yes. Umm hmmm." Paige looked at Norman with a deeper fear than ever. "Yes. But I got tested when I found out I was pregnant. Yes." Paige nodded as if the person on the other end could see her. "About six, seven months ago or so. I just gave birth a couple months ago. Yes. Sure. Okay. Thank you. Thank you. Good-bye." Paige ended the call and then slowly handed Norman the phone.

"What did they say?"

"Well, it's not a joke," Paige confirmed. "This letter really is from the clinic prison. And Blake really did test positive for HIV."

Paige and Norman sat in the waiting room of her doctor's office holding hands. She'd just signed in at the reception window and had only been waiting a little over ten minutes, but it had felt like hours. The very next day after she got the letter informing her that Blake had tested positive for HIV, she'd made an appointment with her doctor to get tested for HIV. That was four days ago, but it had felt more like a month.

"Paige Vanderdale," the nurse walked out of the door leading to the examination room and called.

"Yes!" both she and Norman said at the same time, each of them abruptly standing.

"Mrs. Vanderdale, it's good to see you again. How are you?"

"I've been better," Paige sighed.

"Well, come on back."

Paige looked to her husband. "Will you come back with me?"

"Of course." Norman stood and squeezed Paige's hand. She didn't have to ask him twice. There was nowhere he'd have rather been right now than with his wife. He knew she'd need him now more than ever, and was glad when his sister agreed to babysit Adele while he accompanied his wife to the doctor's. He'd been scheduled to be off work anyway and was going to stay home with the baby while Paige went to be tested for HIV per the suggestion of the doctor at the prison clinic. A minute didn't go by after he watched Paige back out of the driveway before he'd gotten on the phone, called Samantha up, and asked her to babysit while he went to be with his wife. She happened to be en route to their parents' house when he'd phoned her. That worked out fine because it was closer to his place than her condo downtown.

Norman packed up the baby and her things, met Samantha at their parents' house, and had just arrived at the doctor's office with Paige about two minutes ago. The wait in the waiting room had felt just as long for him, but finally, it was time for Paige to go back to see the doctor.

The nurse led the couple back to examination room number two. She got some basic information from Paige and then left the room after telling her the doctor would be in shortly to talk with her. Again, the couple found themselves waiting on pins and needles. By the time Paige's doctor knocked on the door and greeted them with a "Hello," they both nearly jumped out of their skin.

"I'm sorry. I didn't mean to startle you," Paige's doctor apologized.

"It's okay, Dr. Benton," Paige breathed out.

"I understand this is a pretty tense situation," Dr. Benton said as she sat down on her stool and opened Paige's file. "But like I said to you on the phone a few days ago when you called to make your appointment, I think you are going to be fine."

When making the appointment, Paige had asked to talk to the doctor personally. It wasn't a matter she felt comfortable speaking with the nurse or receptionist about.

"Yeah, but you also agreed that I should be tested again," Paige said.

"Well, yeah. Whenever you've had sexual contact with someone who has tested positive for HIV, it's a good idea to get tested every six months for a couple years just to be on the safe side."

"But there's a chance he could have, you know, maybe contracted the virus in jail. That means that there is no possible way I can have it."

"True." The doctor nodded. "But did they happen to tell you when he was tested? Perhaps it had been upon some type of entry physical. Maybe he'd been experiencing symptoms for some time and just looked into it while in jail." The doctor shrugged. "I don't know, and because we don't know, we can't take any chances. It's a good sign that the testing you received during your prenatal appointments came back negative, but it would be wise to take a couple more tests at least."

"So, Doctor," Norman interjected. He then looked to Paige for approval. "If I may." Paige nodded her approval for Norman to ask any question he'd like. "Are you saying that even if this test comes back negative, she could take another one and it could come back positive?"

"That is about the reality of it," the doctor said. "But let's have positive thoughts for a negative result. Okay?" Paige nodded and the doctor stood. "Now I'm going to go write you up the order to have the test run. You can go to the lab downstairs and they'll take care of you. And by all means, if you have any questions or concerns, do not hesitate to call my office."

"One more thing, Doctor," Norman said. "Adele; she was given tests when she was born. Would that have included a test for HIV? And if that'd come back positive, wouldn't the hospital have told us?"

"Yes and yes. But it wouldn't hurt to confirm and even counsel with your daughter's pediatrician," the doctor suggested.

Paige made a mental note to do just that. If she needed to be tested again, then perhaps so did Adele.

"Thank you, Dr. Benton," Norman replied.

"No problem. It was good seeing you both. You can pick up the order at the desk on your way out." The doctor nodded and then exited the room.

Paige could not hide the worry on her face, nor did she try to. She just planted her face in Norman's chest and put her arms around him. "I'm so sorry for dragging you into this mess. Your mother is right for being upset that you married me. And not because I'm black, but because I came with a black cloud over my head that produces nothing but storms. What mother wants that for her child?"

"Oh, no, you don't." Norman pulled Paige away from him and held on to her at arm's length. "If you're planning a pity party, you can scratch my name right off the guest list. We are going to get through this and we are going to get through this with our heads held high, looking toward the hills from which cometh our help."

Paige nodded while wiping the tears that had planned on escaping her eyes. "You're right. Let's just do this. Let's get this over with and hope for the best."

"Doesn't sound too convincing, but it's a start." Norman put his hand on Paige's shoulder and the two exited the room.

Paige got the orders for her HIV test and then headed to the downstairs lab where her blood was drawn. After being told it would be about a week before the results were sent to her doctor, Paige headed back to the car hand in hand with Norman to wait out her seven days, which she knew beyond a doubt would feel more like seven years. *God grant me the patience of Job!*

Chapter Eighteen

"Norman, son, it's so good to see you." Mrs. Vanderdale kissed Norman on the cheek as he entered the house with Paige. Even though they'd driven separate cars, they decided to pick up Adele together. Once Mrs. Vanderdale saw Paige entering behind Norman, her smile faded somewhat, but she managed to remain cordial. "Paige, it's uh, good to see you too."

Paige smiled and nodded. "You too, Mrs. Vanderdale." Paige's greeting was genuine. The last thing on her mind was fighting with her mother-in-law. She'd had to deal with the fear of almost losing Adele and now the fear of possibly being HIV-positive. Life was way too short, which was something she was learning day by day . . . the hard way.

"That baby girl of yours is to die for. You should be so proud." Mrs. Vanderdale cleared her throat. "You too, Norman."

"Thank you, Mother," Norman replied, pleased but surprised at his mother's behavior. "Where is the baby?"

"Oh, she's down in the family room with Samantha." Mrs. Vanderdale got close to Norman as if sharing a secret. "She wouldn't even let Miss Nettie help her care for the baby. I think she's got the fever, too." Mrs. Vanderdale pulled back and covered her mouth. "Baby fever that is." She looked at Paige. "I'm sorry. I really wasn't taking a shot at you, I swear."

Paige just nodded and smiled. She was determined not to let her Archie Bunker reincarnated mother-in-law get under her skin. If somehow these were her last days on earth, she wasn't going to give all her energy hating Mrs. Vanderdale when there was so much other stuff to love. But even so, there was still unresolved tension in the room.

"Norman, son, why don't you go get the baby while I have a talk with my, uh, daughter-in-law here."

It looked as though it pained Mrs. Vanderdale to claim Paige as her daughter-in-law. That alone caused Paige to flex a little. But then Norman placed himself in her vision and mouthed the words "baby steps" to her.

As far as Paige was concerned, this woman might have been deliberately planning on taking baby steps forever. Paige would be six feet under before the woman ever made it to a full-out sprint!

Mrs. Vanderdale took a deep breath. "I really would like to speak with you, Paige." She sounded sincere. She appeared sincere as she looked Paige in the eyes.

Norman thought he was going to be the one having breathing problems and end up sprawled out on the couch. He was speechless. Were his mother's baby steps turning in to strides?

"Oh, go on, son. She's safe with me." Mrs. Vanderdale smiled.

Norman hesitated, not sure if this was some trick his mother was playing to get Paige alone and disrespect her behind closed doors. But after the last talk he had with his mother, he was almost certain she knew he absolutely would not tolerate hearing of such a thing. He knew his mother was smarter than to risk seeing her son even less than she had in past years.

"Are you going to be all right, sweetheart?" Norman asked Paige. He knew she was still concerned about the HIV test she'd just taken. He didn't want his mother adding to her worries.

"Yes, go ahead and get our daughter. I'll be fine," Paige told him.

Norman kissed Paige on the forehead, gave her hand a reassuring squeeze, and then left.

Mrs. Vanderdale watched the loving exchange between her son and Paige before clearing her throat and then pointing toward the couch. "Can we sit?"

"Sure." Paige made her way over to the couch.

"Is everything okay? Sam said she was keeping Adele while Norman joined you at the doctor's office. All is well I hope." Mrs. Vanderdale sat down in her favorite chair next to the couch. "Should I have Nettie bring us something to drink? Are you hungry? I'm sure there's something she can whip—"

"No, no, Mrs. Vanderdale. I'm fine. Not much of an appetite these past few days."

"And it shows." Mrs. Vanderdale gave Paige the once-over. "You must share your diet or regime. You look nice."

Paige looked herself over. Between taking care of the baby and the stress of the whole HIV scare, she hadn't been eating well lately, if she even ate at all. On top of that she was due to return to work in a few weeks. She nearly had an anxiety attack every time she thought about that. She hadn't even started to interview babysitters, although between her mother and Miss Nettie offering their services, she really didn't need one. Plus, having family keep Adele would probably give her more peace of mind.

"I think it's what's called a stress diet," Paige admitted to her mother-in-law.

"Oh, one of those. I think I've had my share of those over the years. But then again, you live with Norman now, so you know just what it can be like dealing with him." She rolled her eyes in her head playfully.

Paige simply smiled. Words weren't coming too easy. They seemed to be trapped among all the chaotic what-ifs of her possibly having contracted HIV. If it weren't for that fact, Paige probably would have taken advantage of this one-on-one with her mother-in-law to let her have it for the way she'd disrespected her. Knowing there was a possibility she might have to fight a deadly disease, though, Paige made a conscious decision to save her energy for that battle.

"And then of course there's the stress I put on you as well."

Paige stared at Mrs. Vanderdale. Was she about to do what Paige thought she was about to do?

Mrs. Vanderdale wriggled in her seat. "Look, Paige, you and I both know I owe you the deepest of apologies. I acted a fool and treated you bad the last time you were here. I'm just grateful you even stepped foot in my house again yourself, let alone let your precious cargo spend the afternoon here. Seeing that made me realize that you are the bigger person. And if anybody knows me, they know I like to always be the bigger person . . . or at least appear to be anyhow." She winked. "Because trust me, this old gal knows how to hold a grudge." She looked over to a collection of crystal vases that sat on the mantel. "How do you think I got Mr. Vanderdale to bid on that set of expensive collectibles at an auction last year?"

Paige smiled. She had no problem with women tricking men into doing things for them. It was nice having at least one thing in common with her mother-in-law. But Paige knew she couldn't take credit for being the bigger person.

"Well, I have to admit Adele being here was Norman's doing. And even though Norman and I have never had the conversation, I must admit I did have reservations about whether I wanted Adele around you. It's going to be hard enough with Adele growing up with a black mother and a white father, who one day she is going to have to learn is not her father, that her father is really black, and here all along she's grown up thinking she's biracial. Not all of society is that accepting of families like ours. Heck, in the African American culture alone we're still dealing with the whole light skin versus dark skin thing. And then on top of all that to have her father's mother, whom she will know as her grandmother, act like the, pardon my French, stereotypical bigot, we'll have—"

Mrs. Vanderdale put her hand up. "Please, stop it. You don't have to say anymore. I was awful and I know it. And, Paige, I'm sorry. I'd like to say that I don't know where any of those actions came from, but I think I know exactly where they did. It's part of my family history, kind of like a family curse. I almost want to say it was part of my genetics, something buried deep within my blood that just finally showed itself like a cancer. Whatever excuse I gave Norman for feeling the way I felt about him marrying you is just wrong. Maybe I've felt that way about Black people all my life and just did a great job at hiding it. I don't know, but whatever it is, I'm working on it and I'm going to get fixed."

"I'm glad to hear that you recognize your behavior was not only inappropriate, inaccurate, and offensive, but that you are doing something about it. But what makes you so sure that you can change? That you can be fixed?"

"Honey, because I'm working with the best and he hasn't encountered one person he hasn't been able to fix yet. After all, they don't call my husband the underground Dr. Phil for nothing."

Paige smiled. "Well, praise God, Mrs. Vanderdale. I'm floored."

"You know, my husband thinks God has something to do with all this too. He said that God may have brought you into my Norman's life for such a time as this."

Paige raised an eyebrow. "Come again?"

"Paige, dear, you are the reason why I was able to dig up the roots to this ugly seed that has been growing inside of me all these years, hiding up under the dirt. It made me look back on some past things that I might have said and I might have done, you know, to other Black people. Even my very own staff, who I've humbled myself to also apologize to." She looked off as her eyes watered. "Even Nettie." She shook away her tears. "But now before I meet my Maker I have a chance to change my heart, to change my ways. If it had not been for you coming into my life as my daughter-in-law, why, I might have ended up spending eternal life in hell." Her eyes watered again. "So not only am I sorry, but I'm grateful. Paige, thank you. Thank you."

Paige's heart was warming over like marshmallows atop a cup of hot chocolate. "Mrs. Vanderdale, your apology is accepted."

"I brought you two some hot tea and some of my tea-ade. Wasn't sure if you'd need warming up or cooling off in here." Miss. Nettie entered the room upon Paige accepting her mother-in-law's apology. She was carrying a tray with two teacups, two glasses filled with ice, a tea kettle, a pitcher of her famous concoction, and some small triangular sandwiches.

"Oh, why thank you, Nettie," Mrs. Vanderdale said, quickly wiping away any proof that she was on the verge of crying.

"No problem. No problem at all, Mrs. Vanderdale." After setting the tray down, Miss Nettie looked at Paige and winked. If Paige was accepting an apology when she'd walked in the room, and the only other person in the room was her boss, that meant that Mrs. Vanderdale had to have apologized to Paige. Miss Nettie's spirit was rejoicing inside. She'd go get her praise on in her room later. For right now, a wink acknowledging Paige's win would have to do. "Let me know if you two gals need anything else." Miss Nettie started to leave.

"Nettie, why don't you take a load off and come join Paige and me for a drink?" Mrs. Vanderdale said.

"Oh, no, I still have laundry to get started," Miss Nettie replied.

"Come on, the laundry can wait."

Miss Nettie paused and looked at her boss. "Are you sure, Mrs. Vanderdale?"

"I'm positive. We don't get to spend as much time together since we stopped our little Saturday afternoon . . . well you know."

"Yes, I know," Miss Nettie said. "But you're gonna be mad you've been missing them shows. There's a new one out with doctor's wives and stuff. Them women are a hoot." Miss Nettie shook her head.

"Don't tempt me, Nettie. Now sit down and join us."

"Well, okay, if you're sure, Mrs. Vanderdale."

"I'm positive. Have a seat."

Miss Nettie hesitantly but respectfully accepted her boss's offer to take a break. Nettie went to pour the liquids into the glasses.

Mrs. Vanderdale stood. "Now didn't I tell you to take a load off?" She smacked Nettie's hand away. "What would you two ladies like? I'll fix the drinks."

Both Paige's and Miss Nettie's eyes bucked as they looked at each other in complete shock. They then rattled off their drink preference. Paige just smiled as her mother-in-law handed her a cup of tea. She looked at Miss Nettie who leaned in and lipped, "Told you all you had to do is pray." She looked upward. "He does the rest."

Chapter Nineteen

"Thank you, Jesus. Thank you! Thank you! Thank you!" Paige shouted. She dropped the phone and shouted as her feet had a mind of their own and stomped the ground. "Glory! Glory!"

Within seconds, Norman came rushing out of the baby's room, closing the door behind him. "Paige, I just laid Adele down to sleep. You're going to wake her up. What's going on?"

With a huge smile on her face, all Paige did was take Norman's hands and begin jumping up and down. Her joy became contagious. He smiled and lightweight jumped with her. "What is it? What's going on?"

"It's negative! That was Dr. Benson's office on the phone. The HIV test was negative. They're going to send the actual paperwork showing the results in the mail. But they know how waiting can be, so when they got the results today they called me. It's negative! Yes!" Paige, without thinking, threw her arms around Norman's neck and kissed him on the left cheek. She then kissed him on the right cheek. Finally, her lips landed on his. She pulled back, smiled, and then planted another kiss on him. She was too happy and excited to even think about how he felt about the kiss, whether it was welcomed. Her natural instincts just wanted to lay one on him, and so she did. After the fourth kiss she realized that Norman was just standing there, dumbfounded. That's when it dawned on her that she had possibly driven the bus down a one-way street.

Paige put her hand over her mouth and pulled back. "Oh my. Oh, Norman, I'm sorry. I'm so sorry." She immediately began wiping her mauve-colored lip gloss off of his lips. "I'm sorry. Oh, God, I'm so sorry." Paige was moving ninety miles per hour in an attempt to remove remnants of her kiss from Norman's lips.

Suddenly Norman managed to grab Paige by her wrist. "Paige, stop it!" he ordered.

Paige halted her actions. She looked down, so disappointed in herself. She had vowed that she wasn't going to make any moves emotionally, verbally, or physically unless she knew Norman's feelings for her were mutual. Now she felt as if not only was she going down a one-way street, but that she was headed in the wrong direction. "I'm sorry," she apologized to Norman. "I didn't mean to . . . I just got carried away. I love you, Norman, you know that, and my friendship with you means everything. I never wanted to cross that line and ruin things between us. So I pray you can forget that ever happened."

Norman listened to Paige, and once he was certain she was finished talking he said, "I'll forget that it ever happened. But only if you remember this forever." And on that note, Norman pulled Paige close to him and kissed her like she'd eaten the poisoned apple and he was the Prince Charming who needed to save her life with a kiss.

Paige lay there next to Norman in his bed feeling as if she'd just experienced the downtown Fourth of July parade and fireworks display. She'd never been touched like that before. She'd never been kissed like that before. Held like that before. Made love to like that before. She had to sit back and ask herself if it was all real, if everything had really felt that good. Or was it like the times she'd starved herself all day and by the time she ate, she was so hungry that boo boo would have tasted like a five-star meal? Had she been starving for a man's affection so long that Norman hadn't really been all that and a bag of chips? Maybe in reality, once she came down off her high, she'd come to find that he was just the chips—no salsa, no dip, no nothing extra.

So what? Paige thought. Right now it tasted good and satisfied her appetite and that's all that mattered. A smile spread across her face just thinking how good she felt.

"What's that smile about?" Paige heard Norman ask. She was off in such a daze that she'd almost forgotten he was even lying there next to her . . . and in his bed no less.

"You should know. You put it there." Paige was bold. No need to hold back now. Heck, she'd given the man her body, what more could she hold back from him?

"Ummm," Norman moaned. "You put a lot more than a smile on my face." He grinned.

"Ooooooh, you nasty boy."

"Nasty? You're calling me nasty when you were the one who took your leg and—"

"Stop it!" Paige blushed while covering Norman's mouth with her hand.

He laughed and tried to push her hand off his mouth. "What did you say that thing is called again? The corkscrew?"

"Stop it!" Paige was embarrassed.

"It's true what they say about you Christian girls; y'all some undercover freaks," Norman teased.

"Yeah, but only with our husbands," Paige replied.

"Then you must be speaking for yourself, because I got with this one Christian girl back in the day who . . ." Norman paused. "Oh, shoot, that's right; she was Catholic."

Paige play slapped Norman on his shoulder. "I'm not trying to hear about your past sexual conquests."

"Uhh, hello, need I remind you that you already know about all my sexual conquests? Once upon a time before you got all saved, sanctified, and holy, you used to be my sounding board the next morning after every date."

"Umm, hmm, and your ride to the clinic once or twice as well," Paige reminded him.

"Yep, so you know I've always been clean and I'm still clean."

Paige was suddenly reminded about the great news she'd received a bit ago from her doctor's office. "Yep, and I'm clean too." She pumped her fist. "Yes! God is good."

"Uhh, can you not bring God into the bed with us please? Awkward."

Paige rolled over onto her side and wrapped her leg and arm across Norman's body. "Honey, you, me, and God is the best threesome you could ever ask for."

Norman kissed Paige on the lips. "Yeah, you got that right. Without God, where might we have ended up?"

Paige threw herself back flat on her back. "Uggghh. I don't want to even imagine that. All I know is that I'm glad I can look forward to the rest of my life with Him." Paige looked to Norman. "And you."

They momentarily stared into each other's eyes. Paige was hoping this was the moment she'd hear those words she'd been waiting to hear from Norman.

Norman lifted his hand to Paige's face and rubbed her cheek.

Here it comes. Paige was excited inside.

"The day I had that talk with my mother in the kitchen," Norman started, "the day I first introduced you to her, she asked me something that I didn't answer at the time. She asked me if I loved you."

"Why didn't you answer her?" Paige was confused. Norman loved her; that much she knew. So why wouldn't he share that with his mother? Outside of their four walls, was he ashamed of her? R. Kelly's ex-wife might have been able to take being in the background all the time, but feeling invisible and like her man was ashamed of her, that was more than Paige would be able to bear in a relationship. That's probably why in all her years, she'd never had to travel down that road before. God knew her car would clunk out a mile into that drive.

"I did answer that question. I told her yes without hesitation. But then she asked me if I was in love with you."

"Ohhhh." Now Paige understood his dilemma. That's something he'd never confessed one way or the other to her, let alone his mother. But maybe, just maybe, all of that was about to change.

"I didn't answer because I didn't . . ."

At those words Paige's heart melted like a chocolate bar that had accidentally been left on the dashboard in the summer's sun.

"I didn't think it was her ears that should be the first to hear that answer." Norman placed both hands on each side of Paige's face and said, "Paige Vanderdale, woman, I'm in lo—"

The sound of Norman's alarm clock blasted over his words.

"Oh, shoot," Norman said, turning and reaching to turn the alarm off. "I forgot I set it. I'd planned on taking a nap before heading to work this evening." Norman got up out of the bed and headed to the closet to retrieve his work clothes.

Paige just lay there in disbelief. *Really, God?* "I guess I'm going to go get—" Paige had started to get up out of the bed.

"No, you lay there," Norman told her. "Adele is still asleep. You know the rules. You sleep while she sleeps. Take advantage of the rest. You know you need it with her."

Paige lay back down and watched as Norman headed to his bathroom. Within seconds she heard the shower water turn on. "Oh, well." She flopped back on the bed and realized that at the moment, there really wasn't anything better to do than to sleep. But that was before Norman popped out of the bathroom with a towel wrapped around his waist, dripping wet. That made her want to stay in the bed, but not sleep. She watched as Norman maneuvered around the room to get dressed. Paige didn't know how long her eyes had been glued on him before he even noticed he was being watched.

"What?" he said.

"Oh, nothing. Just admiring my husband. I mean really admiring him for the first time."

"Oh, yeah, and what do you think?" Norman started doing muscle man poses.

Paige looked him up and down and then licked her lips. "I know they say that he who finds a wife finds a good thing. But she who finds a husband finds a great thing. Lord, am I blessed." Paige closed her eyes. "Thank you, Je—"

Before Paige could complete her thanks for Jesus putting Norman in her path, Norman's mouth suffocated hers as they indulged in a deep kiss.

"No, I'm the one who's thankful," Norman said after kissing her. His hands found their way all over Paige's post-pregnancy body. For her own likings and comfort she felt she could stand to lose several more pounds, but for her husband, she was just right. And everything about that moment felt right as Norman led the tango dance their tongues were engaged in.

When Norman finally pulled away, Paige was just mesmerized.

"I gotta go," Norman told her. "But I'll be back." He winked and then exited the room.

Paige fell back on the bed with her arms spread out wide. She eventually heard the front door close shut. "I'm in love," she said out loud. "I'm in love." She smiled. "I'm in love." The smile was gone. She sat up with a serious look on her face. "Girl, you are in love," Paige told herself. "So why are you sitting here telling the walls, the bed sheets, and the pillow instead of the person you're in love with?"

Paige thought about the question she had posed to herself. She didn't have to sit around and wait for Norman to say the words to her first. Many a woman lived a miserable life sitting around waiting for a man to be the first to do something, to say something. Heck, many a woman might have even lost many a man doing that same thing. Well, she was not going to be one of them.

Paige jumped up out of bed, picked her clothes up off the floor, and slid them on. She exited Norman's bedroom in search of her cell phone. Removing her phone from her purse that sat on the living room table, she pulled up Norman's name in her address book and went to hit the send button to call him, but hesitated. Her nerves started to take over. She'd lost her voice. But at the same time, she felt compelled to let Norman know how she felt about him at that moment—at that second. So since she couldn't seem to find her voice, she did the next best thing. Paige began punching in letters into her cell phone.

I'm in love with you, Norman!

She smiled and hit the send button. With a smile on her face, she lay down on the couch to revel in the aftershock of the earthquake she and her husband had engaged in as a consummation of their union. Finally; it was official . . . and in every way it could possibly matter!

Chapter Twenty

"Where is he? Where's my husband?" Paige shouted as soon as she made it through the emergency room doors, struggling to carry baby Adele in her bucket seat. Her words were directed at no one in particular. Heck, if the janitor could direct her to her husband, she'd be fine with that. "Norman Vanderdale. Where is he?" This time she was at the patient registration counter, leaned over practically nose to nose with the receptionist.

The receptionist stood and backed away slightly, not sure of Paige's intentions. In the past, an eager and anxious loved one or two had allowed their fear and emotions to cause them to leap over that desk and demand answers. "Just a moment, ma'am. The patient's name again?" She placed her fingers on the computer keyboard, prepared to punch in whatever name Paige recited to her.

"It's Norman Vanderdale." Paige spelled his last name as the receptionist typed. "I'm his wife. I was called by someone, I don't know, a doctor, nurse. All I can remember them saying is that my husband was in a car accident and was transported here." Paige placed the bucket seat on the ground then put each index finger on her temples and closed her eyes. She was trying to remember any other pertinent information the caller tried to give her before she'd hung up in their ear. Just hearing that her man was in an accident so bad that he wasn't able to call her himself had put her in panic mode.

It seemed like just yesterday when Paige had been in a car accident of her own. She and Blake had gotten into it and she left the house. No one but her and God knew that before her car accident she'd been on her way to Norman's house, possibly to commit adultery. Even though her car had been totaled, she survived the accident. She prayed the same outcome for her husband.

The receptionist punched the keyboard a few more times and then it looked as if all the blood had drained from her face. This did not go unnoticed by Paige.

"What? What is it?" Paige asked. "It's bad, isn't it? It's not just some fender bender, is it?" Paige threw her hands on her forehead. "Oh, God! No. Norman!"

"Look, Mrs. Vanderdale," the receptionist said, "come with me." She came from around the desk and led Paige into a smaller waiting room. "Just wait right here and the doctor will be in shortly to talk with you."

Paige nodded. She didn't want to waste any more words on the receptionist. She needed to save them for the doctor so that she could ask all the questions she could about how she'd need to take care of her husband. When Paige had been in her car accident, she'd had Blake there by her side to help her heal and nurse her back to good health. She'd pay it forward and be there for Norman as long as he needed her. She began to think the worst. Even if he was wheelchair bound for the rest of his life, she'd be his chauffeur, pushing him to and from his desired destinations. She didn't care if he wanted her to push him up a mountain. She'd do it.

Paige set sleeping Adele's bucket seat on the floor. She herself paced the floor for a couple of minutes and then sat down. She sat down for a couple of minutes and then she stood up and paced again. Up, down, up, and down. Finally the door opened. Paige turned with very little patience to begin badgering the doctor with questions.

"Paige!"

Only it wasn't the doctor who had entered the room. It was Norman's parents.

Paige was glad there was now someone else there to comfort her, but the disappointment that it wasn't the doctor with answers broke her down. Tears began to pour from her eyes like the BP oil spill. The running fluid was just unstoppable.

"Paige, darling, where's Norman? Where's my baby?" Mrs. Vanderdale fell into Paige's arms as the two women embraced and hugged like best friends. Paige was grateful she and her mother-in-law had made amends prior to this incident. Right now they needed each other more than ever. At least, Paige needed the comfort of her mother-in-law this moment.

Mr. Vanderdale walked over and began to pat each woman's back. He then went and rubbed Adele's arm and smiled at the sleeping child.

"I don't know," Paige cried to her mother-in-law. "I've been waiting in here forever for the doctor to come tell me something. All I know is that he was in a car accident. That's what the person who called and told me said."

"Yes, the police called us too," Mr. Vanderdale said. "They had Norman's cell phone. We were in his favorites speed dial or something."

"I didn't even get that much information," Paige told them. "I hung up the phone and hightailed it over here."

"This is bad. This is bad." Mrs. Vanderdale turned and buried her face into her husband's chest. "Honey, I know this is bad. I just feel it."

"Please don't put that into the atmosphere, Mrs. Vanderdale," Paige asked. "I've been in here pacing and worrying and just got to the point of praying. I'm praying for the best, so please don't think the worst."

Mrs. Vanderdale stared at Paige for a few seconds before she finally opened her mouth and said, "Paige, I've never done it in my life nor have I asked anyone else to do it for me, but . . . can we pray . . . together?"

Paige simply nodded as tears fell from her eyes. "Yes, Mrs. Vanderdale. We can pray." Paige had held out her hands. Mrs. Vanderdale grabbed both of Paige's hands. "Mr. Vanderdale, would you like to join us?" Paige asked.

Mr. Vanderdale pulled the two women in close and they all formed a prayer circle.

Paige began to pray as if she were praying down the walls of Jericho. As if on cue, upon the closing of the prayer with the three sealing it in Jesus' name and with an Amen, the waiting room door opened.

Paige felt a sense of relief once she saw the doctor enter the room. Now she would find out everything she needed to know on how to take care of her husband. Once she saw a police officer enter behind the doctor, her nerves began to do a jig up her spine. She knew the officer was just probably there to give them a report on the actual accident, but there was this solemn look on his face that gave Paige pause. When the officer removed his hat, a sudden dread filled the room. Both Paige and Mrs. Vanderdale instantaneously held each other. But once they saw the hospital chaplain enter behind the officer, no one was there to catch either woman when they hit the floor.

When Paige came to she found herself lying in a hospital bed. It took her a minute to gather her senses, but then, recalling what had transpired prior to her blacking out, she darted straight up in that bed. "Norman!" she yelled. She looked around the room.

"Sister Paige, calm down." Pastor Margie walked over to Paige and rested her arm on her shoulder.

"Adele?" Paige frantically looked around the room, hoping to see the pumpkin seat containing her child. She didn't see it. Her entire world felt like it was caving in on her. The two people who had become her whole life were nowhere to be found.

"Paige, baby girl."

Paige noticed her father for the first time when he spoke. Her mother's arm was looped through her father's arm as they slowly made the walk from the little couch they'd been sitting on over to Paige's bed.

"Norman's sister has the baby," Mrs. Robinson told Paige. She didn't reply to Paige's first query about Norman. She was thinking that maybe she hadn't been asking for Norman or where Norman was. With the tears that spilled from her daughter's eyes, she knew deep inside she knew the fate of her husband.

"Norman," Paige said again. "Norman, oh my God, Norman." She looked up at her mother. "Mommy," was all she had to say for Mrs. Robinson to release her husband and go throw her arms around her daughter.

Pastor Margie immediately lifted her hands in Paige's direction. "Saints, help me pray," Pastor Margie said to the two church members, women she referred to as prayer warriors, who had come along to the hospital with her.

"It's okay, baby. It's okay," Mrs. Robinson said as she rocked Paige. "You're going to be okay, both you and Adele. Everything is going to be okay."

"No, it's not. I don't have a husband anymore, Mommy. I don't have a friend. My friend. He was my best friend. God keeps taking away my best friends." Paige squeezed her mother so tight she almost squeezed the air out of her. That's when Mr. Robinson intervened.

"Baby girl. It's all right. We're all here for you." Mr. Robinson had nodded to his wife and gave her a look excusing her from comforting Paige so that he could take over. Mrs. Robinson moved away while her husband sat down beside Paige on her bed. "Now, now, sweetie, we're all here for you." He nodded toward Pastor Margie and the two praying women. "You have your church family. You have your family: your mother and me . . . your beautiful daughter. And you have Norman's family, who are out there." He nodded to the door.

Paige shut off the waterworks as if she had a knob to do so. She looked her father dead in the eyes and said, "But where is God?"

Chapter Twenty-one

"Paige!" Mrs. Vanderdale ran and threw her arms around Paige as soon as Paige reentered the waiting room where she'd received the news about Norman's death. "You okay, sweetheart? You passed out. You scared us." She used her hand to brush Paige's hair back. "You okay?"

"Yes, I'm okay," Paige lied. She was a wreck, but she had to keep it together for the sake of . . . She heard a small cooing noise and saw Adele in Samantha's arms. "Adele!" Paige went over and took her daughter from Samantha's arms, pressed her against her chest, and held her tight. She twisted her upper body from left to right while kissing the baby's forehead. Paige knew she had to stay strong for Adele. Babies could sense things. "What do I tell her about all this? What do I tell her about the man who signed her birth certificate? What do I tell her about the man whose last name she carries? Huh? How do I fix this mess now? I was in a hole and yet I kept digging dirt. Now look at me," Paige cried.

"No, Paige. Please. Do not beat yourself up," Samantha stood from the couch she'd been sitting on with the baby and said. "You and my brother did what you thought you needed to do for this baby. My brother signed that birth certificate because as far as he was concerned, Adele was his baby. He was her father. That was not a lie. He married a woman he was in love with. That woman, you"—Samantha pointed at Paige—"had a beautiful baby girl while she was his wife. That's my brother's baby.

That's my niece," Samantha declared, "and nothing is going to change that."

Paige stared at Samantha, the bleached blonde who was a little rough around the edges but had a flair about her. She was a cross between Paris Hilton and Jodie Foster. "What did you say?" Paige was fixated on Samantha's mouth as she awaited her response. It was like she wanted to be able to see the words come out.

"I said my brother is that little girl's—"

"No, not that. You said something about Norman being in love with me. How do you know? How do you know that? Did he tell you? Did he say those exact same words? That he was in love with me?" The more Paige spoke, the more intense she became. And with every line she spoke, she got closer and closer to Samantha. "When? When did he say that to you? Tell me! Tell me!" By now Paige had let one hand loose from the baby and was shaking Samantha's shoulder. Paige knew for certain she'd been in love with Norman, but—and as selfish as it might sound—she needed to know that Norman had been in love with her too. She needed just that one thing to be able to help her get through her loss. "Tell me. How do you know, Samantha? How do you know he was in love with me? Is that what he said?"

"Paige, stop it!" her parents ordered her in unison. Mr. and Mrs. Robinson had followed Paige back into the waiting room after they bid Pastor Margie and the church members farewell.

"How do you know your brother was in love with me?" Paige continued, even as her mother slid the baby from her arms.

"Samantha, tell her," Mrs. Vanderdale shouted, hoping that by doing so, it would calm Paige down.

"The officer! The police officer!" Samantha yelled as she tried to peel now both Paige's hands from her shoulder.

As if Samantha had summoned him, the police officer that had followed the doctor into the room earlier reappeared. "Is everything okay in here? The nurse told me I could now speak to the deceased's wife."

Just hearing the officer's last words, Paige yelled out like a wounded animal and squatted down to the floor. "Noooooooooooo!" That word, deceased. It sealed everything. It made it real. Paige was a widow and the honeymoon had just begun. "Noooooo!"

"Oh, God, help us," Mrs. Robinson lifted her hands in the air and said, then threw herself into her husband's chest.

Mr. Robinson, with the help of the officer, got Paige over to the couch while Mrs. Robinson tried to calm down Adele, whose mother's scream had scared her into a crying fit.

"Paige, just calm down, please," Mr. Robinson pleaded with his daughter. "Let the officer talk to you, honey, please."

Paige eventually managed to calm herself down and look at the officer, giving him the hint it was okay to proceed with his questioning.

"Mrs. Paige Vanderdale," the officer started, "like I told everyone else, I'm so sorry about your loss. Your husband's car veered off the road into a pole. It was a one-car accident. Passerbys phoned in the accident. When medics arrived at the scene, your husband was pronounced dead. From what the doctors said, it was more than likely an instant death upon impact. He was driving about fifty miles . . ."

Paige was trying her best to stay focused. The officer's words were going in and out. The feeling was just so surreal. She couldn't believe it was happening. She couldn't believe she was sitting there listening to the details of her thirty-year-old husband's death. Too young to die.

"We checked his alcohol level," the officer said, "and—"

"Norman doesn't drink," Paige interrupted.

"Yes, I know. Your in-laws shared that with me," the officer told Paige. "Medically it doesn't seem like anything might have triggered him to lose consciousness or anything. If a full autopsy is performed, the doctors can learn more, but . . ." The officer's voice seemed to lower a notch. This caught Paige's undivided attention.

"But what?" Paige said.

"We did find this." He pulled out a plastic Ziploc baggie that had a cell phone in it.

"That's Norman's phone." Paige got excited. It wasn't Norman, but it was a possession of Norman's. That's all Paige would have left of him anymore: possessions and memories.

"Yes, it is," the officer confirmed. "When we found it there was a recently typed text. He hadn't had a chance to send it yet, but more than likely he was responding to a text that had just been sent to him. And according to the time the text was sent and the time the nine-one-one calls started coming in, we believe that texting while driving was the cause of the accident."

"No! Can't be possible," Paige said. "Norman never texted and drove. In all my times of riding with him, I never once saw him text and drive."

The police officer wasn't going to argue with Paige in her emotional state. She'd just suffered a major loss. Instead, he held out the bag to her. He hit a button and the screen lit up. Paige looked down to see the text Norman had typed but had not yet sent. Her name appeared in the "to" box.

I'm in love with you t

Paige couldn't believe she was sitting in the front pew of New Day Temple of Faith staring at her husband lying dead in a casket. Little Adele lay asleep in her arms. Every now and then her tiny mouth would form into a smile, then a frown, and then a smile again. Paige imagined she was seeing an angel, perhaps Norman. And just maybe every time Norman tried to go away Adele would get upset, and, to appease her, he'd return. Would that be how Paige's own dreams would play out from now on?

Weeping sounds began to flow from Paige's throat as her body began to heave.

"Let me take the baby," Samantha insisted as she wiped tears of her own and then took Adele from Paige's arms. She kissed her niece right beside her lips, causing the little infant's smile to spread wide. Samantha, too, took it as a sign that her brother had made it to heaven and was now an angel watching over his baby girl. He was now an angel in heaven looking out for the little girl he'd vowed to sacrifice his life for, in not just words, but in action and deed.

Paige sat there numb as people viewed Norman's body in the casket and then came over to her and Norman's family to give their condolences. All Paige could do was nod and accept their hugs and kisses to the cheek. She couldn't even speak. God only knows what would have come out had she been able to speak. She was so angry that every time things looked as though they were falling into place, the devil would come over and flip the puzzle over, destroying the almost perfectly put together picture. She was tired of it. She was sick and tired. She was sick and tired and outright mad!

Where was God during all this craziness? Come to think of it, perhaps it was because of God she was even dealing with all this craziness. Her life seemed less traumatic before she got saved. The devil wasn't messing with her at all because he already had her. There was no threat. It's kind of like that deranged ex: they deal with the breakup until they find out there is somebody else in your life and then they absolutely lose it, trying to do any-and everything to win you back. Paige was seriously contemplating getting back with the ex if it meant he'd lay off.

"I'm so sorry about your loss. May God bless you."

"Norman was such a good man."

"God is going to pull you through. He's a comforter."

After about a couple dozen more sentiments somewhere along those lines, the funeral service started. Paige's body was present, but not her mind. Afterward, she couldn't even remember what song the choir sang, or what the five people who wanted to speak final words about Norman said. Had the obituary been read out loud or had the guests been asked to read it silently on their own? Did Pastor Margie get many Amens when she gave the eulogy? Paige was oblivious to all of this. She'd just sat there as if she was watching somebody else's life and not living her own.

"Come on, Paige honey."

When Paige looked up and saw her father extending his hand to her in order to help her up off the pew, she figured the service must be over. That was confirmed when Paige looked up and saw that the casket was long gone. When had they closed it? When had they wheeled it out? Paige watched as several people volunteered to remove the flower arrangements from the sanctuary and carry them outside to be transported to the burial site.

Mr. Robinson helped his daughter up and escorted her out to one of two limos, the one that was assigned to take them to the cemetery for the burial. This was too much for Paige. She thought she was going to pass out like she'd done back at the hospital. If she could, she would have ordered the driver to just take her home so she could crawl into the bed and bury her head under the pillow. The rest of the world could go on and do whatever they wanted if they so chose, but that wasn't her choice. But then she'd remember there was Adele. She had a daughter she had to be strong for, who she had to live for. So throwing in the towel wasn't an option. She'd have to bear with the remainder of the day's events at least.

Once they arrived at the cemetery, everyone gathered around the casket that appeared to be levitating over a hole six feet deep. Pastor Margie spoke a few more words before the service was concluded and people were invited back to the Vanderdale home for the repast.

"How you holding up?" Mrs. Robinson asked as they rode silently in the limo. Mr. and Mrs. Vanderdale rode cuddled up with one another. Samantha sat next to Adele, who was in her car seat, while Paige sat sandwiched in between her parents.

Paige couldn't even respond to her mother. All she could do was just shake her head. She was weak and in a daze. She could barely hold her head up the same way she could barely hold her daughter earlier during the funeral. She could barely walk without the support of others. She was in total disbelief that this was her life. She was in total disbelief that she'd waited what seemed like forever for her and Norman to finally be headed down the same road together, sharing the same sentiments toward one another, which was absolutely true love that had been a long time coming. It was right there up under her nose like a steak to a hungry bum on the street who hadn't eaten in days. The bum had the decency to close his eyes and say a prayer, blessing and thanking God for the steak, then when he opened his eyes, the steak was gone. That was the thanks the bum got for blessing and thanking God? That described to a tee how Paige was feeling.

Every time she decided that God might be this okay dude after all, He'd show His true self or He'd not show up at all. She was tired of the relationship and just as soon as she was able to get some clarity, she would have to re-evaluate whether she wanted to continue the relationship at all. The on-again/off-again thing was about to send her to the looney bin.

"I know it must be hard," Mrs. Robinson said when Paige didn't reply to her initial inquiry. She could tell how her daughter was doing just by looking at her: not well at all. She tried to find some comforting words. "Even though you and Norman hadn't even been married for a year, you two had been friends for years. Good friends. Everybody knows that. Everybody knows how hard this must be for you. But you will make it. You have a whole team of supporters here for you."

Once again, all Paige could ask herself was where was the captain of this so-called team? Where was God? Everybody else always seemed to be around, but where was God? Especially when all this bad stuff happened in her life. *Why can't He be there to stop it all? To just stop it? All the pain? All the hurt? Yet He just keeps sitting idly by watching it pile on and on like a pyramid. A pyramid that is about to crumble any day.*

Paige rode in silence all the way to her in-laws' house, where tons of cars were already parked upon the limo's arrival. The limo driver parked at the front door and then walked around to let them out of the car. Miss Nettie stood at the door, holding it wide open for all to enter. She'd attended the funeral but passed on the burial in order to get home and make sure everything was in order and to greet the guests.

"Thank you, Nettie," Mr. Vanderdale said, the first one to enter the house.

Miss Nettie nodded at everyone but spoke to Paige. "How you holding up, dear?"

Paige just looked into Miss Nettie's eyes and shook her head. It showed; she wasn't holding up too well at all.

"Looks like you might need to lie down and rest for a spell. It ain't about entertaining folks. They here to pay their respects and that's fine, but if you don't take care of yourself, keep your body and mind right, then what good are you going to be for that little girl?" Miss Nettie nodded toward Adele, who was being removed from her little car seat bucket-style carrier by Samantha.

Mrs. Robinson looked to her daughter. "Is that what you want to do, Paige? Do you want to go get some rest? You do need to eat though, but I'm sure we can bring a plate of food to you."

"Yes, I'd like to lie down, but I'm not hungry though." Paige's throat was scratchy and dry.

"Nettie, can you lead Paige to the yellow guest room, please?" Mrs. Vanderdale asked. "Samantha and the rest of us will tend to Adele. She's probably about ready to go down for a nap as well."

"Sure, Mrs. Vanderdale." Miss Nettie took Paige by the arm. "Come on, baby." She led her up the stairwell.

Once Paige reached the top step, she was in awe of the long hallway. Straight ahead she could see a circular veranda through a set of double French doors. She'd never been given a tour of the home, but even from the outside she could tell it was a magnificent dwelling. Right now wasn't the time to take an official tour though. She just wanted to dive into the nearest bed.

Well, Miss Nettie didn't take her to the nearest bed. They passed at least four bedrooms before Nettie finally opened the door to a room that had yellow walls and a gold-painted ceiling. A white canopy bed sat to the left with the head rails against the wall, while about fifteen to twenty feet straight across was a private veranda that could only be entered by way of that room. There was a white dresser and a white chest that matched the two white nightstands that rested on each side of the bed.

"That right there is the bathroom." Miss Nettie pointed to one of two other doors.

"What's that room?" Paige pointed to the other door.

"Oh, that's just the closet. If you want to put on something more comfy than that dress and heels you're wearing, I'm sure there is a guest robe and slippers or something in there that will suit you." Miss Nettie walked over to the queen-sized bed and pulled back the yellow coverlet trimmed in lace.

"Thank you, Miss Nettie," Paige said as she kicked off her heels and sat on the bed.

"There's the remote if you feel like watching a little television." She pointed to the nightstand where a remote control for the television rested.

"No, I just want to lie here and rest my eyes for a minute. Please let everyone know I'll be down within an hour. I just need a moment."

"Well, you take all the time you need. I'm sure everyone understands." Miss Nettie headed over to the door.

"Thank you, Miss Nettie."

Miss Nettie just smiled and nodded, and went to close the door behind her.

Paige closed her eyes. When she opened them again, Miss Nettie was standing next to her with a tray of food.

"Figure I'd bring you up a bite to eat since you never came down."

Paige sat up, rubbing the sleep out of her eyes. "What do you mean? I just got up here."

Miss Nettie chuckled. "Child, you been sleep for three hours. The house is clear. Your parents said they'd call you in the morning."

"Where's—"

"She's sleeping sound in her nursery." Miss Nettie responded to Paige's inquiry about baby Adele's where-abouts before Paige could even finish it.

"Her nursery?" Paige had a confused look on her face. The only nursery she knew of Adele having was at their apartment. "She's home?" Paige sat up in worry. "Who's with her?"

"Now just calm yourself down." Miss Nettie set the tray down on the bed. "She's right in the room across the hall."

Paige still gave Nettie a concerned look.

"Come on and take a peek. Settle your nerves so you can get some food in you."

Paige stood up and followed Miss Nettie straight across the hall. Miss Nettie opened the door to a room half the size of the one Paige had slept in, but elegant and beautifully decorated nonetheless.

"Wow," Paige couldn't help but exclaim once she walked into the room with a white ceiling and soft pink walls. A beautiful canopy crib draped in pink and white sheers sat in the middle of the room. There was a wooden rocking horse, and an oversized rocking chair with padding and pillows. There was a pink chest and matching toy chest. The carpet was a thick, plushy white. Paige felt as if she were walking on marshmallows. On the rear wall was a painted portrait of Norman, Adele's newborn picture, and a portrait of Paige. "How? When?" She was at a true loss for words.

"Mrs. Vanderdale had it done," Miss Nettie told her.

"That's my Facebook profile picture," Paige said, fascinated as she pointed to her painted portrait. "I don't understand." She continued to look around. "They did all this knowing that Adele really isn't even their . . ."

"Isn't really their what?" Miss Nettie pressed while walking over to Paige. "Go ahead; Adele isn't even their what?"

Paige swallowed and practically choked on her words.

"Umm hmmm, 'cause you better not think of fixing your mouth to say what I think you were going to say."

Paige felt convicted enough, but that didn't stop Miss Nettie from making her feel even worse.

"You and Norman done came up with this bright idea involving that baby. The man signed the birth certificate and everything. Wasn't your goal for Adele to be his? For Adele to be theirs? Isn't that what you wanted the family to accept? Well, missy, that's exactly what happened. So now that Norman is gone, don't you dare . . ." Miss Nettie couldn't even get her last words out, her lip was trembling so much, as well as the finger she was pointing in Paige's face.

"Miss Nettie. I'm sorry, I didn't mean to—"

"Never you mind." Miss Nettie shooed her hand. "I know you probably just talking out of emotion right now, but the next time you need to take a minute to think before you speak. As a matter of fact, do yourself one better; think before you think. Think about the bed you made and have to now lie in. Good thing about it though, you've managed to make quite a comfortable bed for yourself. You got a whole family behind you who took you in, and has accepted you and your daughter as their own. Yes, Mrs. Vanderdale has her ways, and I must admit, the day Norman brought you home I was ecstatic."

Miss Nettie clapped her hands together and smiled. "Everyone else might not have seen or even turned a blind eye to Mrs. Vanderdale's ways when it came to other folks—Black folks namely, but I knew she was a good woman. I knew she was just a product of her family curse but that God would change her heart, change her mind. God would hold up a mirror to her face and finally show her who she was."

Paige recalled a similar statement Samantha had said when they first met. Apparently Samantha and Miss Nettie had conversed about this matter before.

"Well, when you walked through the door, I knew my prayer had been answered. Whoooo weeeeee," Miss Nettie recollected. "Norman knew his mother was special, which was why he didn't come around much," Nettie continued to share. "But I could see all that was about to change. A lot changed. The change is good, and you are the cause of that change. And what I won't allow to happen is for this family to take ten steps back." She looked at Norman's portrait on the wall. "You couldn't tell that boy that baby wasn't his daughter." She pointed to Adele sleeping in the crib. "And now you can't tell the Vanderdales that she's not theirs. So if you plan on breaking their hearts, I suggest you do it now so I can get to praying for their healing."

"No, Miss Nettie." Paige shook her head. "It's not like that." And it wasn't. The thought had never come to mind that just because Norman was no longer with them that she'd go on about her life forgetting she ever married him and the reason why she'd married him. "I would never do that. It's just that . . ." She looked around the room. "I had no idea they really accepted Adele like this. I'm just . . ."

"See, that's what I don't get about some Christian folk. You pray to God and ask Him to do something for you, then when He does it you're shocked that He did it?" Miss Nettie shook her head. "Had you not truly prayed in faith?"

"I don't even want to talk about God right now and what He does. All I know is what He didn't do." Paige headed back over to her room. She took the tray off the bed and placed it on the floor.

"You're not going to eat?" Miss Nettie, who had followed her, asked.

"I just lost my appetite," Paige said as she got back in bed and pulled the covers over her.

Miss Nettie stared at her for a minute. "Fine, then I'll just take it back downstairs and wrap it up. It'll be in the fridge when you get ready for it." Miss Nettie picked up the tray. "It's late and looks like the baby is down for the night. No need dragging her out and I'm sure you don't want to be apart from her. I'll just let Mrs. Vanderdale know you and li'l Miss Adele will be staying the night." She turned to exit the room.

"Miss Nettie?" Paige said.

Miss Nettie turned and looked at Paige.

"Tell Mrs. Vanderdale I said thank you . . . for everything."

"I'll let you tell her yourself when you get ready," Miss Nettie said, leaving the room.

Little did Paige know, her chance to talk with Mrs. Vanderdale would come sooner than she thought.

Chapter Twenty-two

"Oh God!" Paige grabbed her heart that felt like it was beating out of her chest. "Mrs. Vanderdale. You scared me."

"I'm sorry, dear. It's just that I really didn't get a chance to eat earlier I was so busy talking to everyone." Mrs. Vanderdale was leaned over a foiled pan with a fork. "When my stomach started growling louder than Norm's snoring, I knew I needed to come down and get me a bite to eat." She chuckled, but Paige saw right through it. It was fake, a mask; she was trying to be strong.

"I can't imagine how you as a mother must feel right now," Paige said. "I hope to never know what it feels like to lose a child. The pain I'm feeling I'm sure is tenfold for you. He lived in your womb for nine months. He was connected to you in ways he could never be connected to any other human being on this earth. And even though, as his wife, the Bible says we became one, he was born one with you." Paige walked over to Mrs. Vanderdale. "I know all about masks, Mrs. Vanderdale. And you don't have to wear one with me. You don't have to laugh when you really want to cry. You don't have to smile when you're really pissed off. And you don't have to stand up straight and keep a straight face when you really just want to hunch over in pain."

Mrs. Vanderdale threw her hand over her mouth to stifle the growing sob trying to roar from her throat. She began to sniffle. Her sniffle turned into a deep gasp as she placed her other hand on her stomach and knelt over in pain, a pain she was suffering due to the loss of her child. "Oh, God!" she exhaled. "My baby!" She dropped the fork and Paige raced over to her side and embraced her.

"It's okay," Paige told her as she held the weeping mother in her arms.

"A mother is not supposed to bury her child," Mrs. Vanderdale cried. "It's unnatural. It's inhumane even. Why would God . . ."

"I know, I know," Paige comforted her. After a few moments, Mrs. Vanderdale collected herself and Paige looked at her in her eyes. "Now you ready?"

Mrs. Vanderdale had inquiring eyes. She had no idea what Paige was talking about.

"Are you ready to go ahead and say what you need to say to me? Go ahead. Just get it over with."

"I . . . I don't know what you are talking about." She turned away as if she didn't want Paige to be able to seek out the truth in her eyes.

"Mrs. Vanderdale, you know exactly what I'm talking about. Just go ahead. I'm ready for it. There is nothing you can say to me that I haven't already said to myself. So just say it so we can move on. Our relationship started out rocky to say the least. We've come this far. No need to hinder it by holding back words that need to be said."

Mrs. Vanderdale's chest began to rise up and down. She became warm, and it had nothing to do with the random hot flashes she sometimes suffered. Although it looked as if every ounce of her being wanted to blow a fuse, she just stood there contemplating; contemplating on whether to speak now or forever hold her peace. But like Paige said, if she didn't speak now, would it really be peace she'd be holding within?

Taking a deep breath, Mrs. Vanderdale decided that speaking her piece would be the wisest decision. She thought that taking that deep breath would have allowed her words to flow free and calmly, but it didn't as she exploded. "Why did you have to text him?" she cried out. "You knew he was driving. You knew he was on his way to work. Why did you have to send that text?" she screamed. "If you hadn't sent that text, he would have never . . . he wouldn't be . . ." Mrs. Vanderdale couldn't even finish her sentence before she just burst out in tears.

Once again, Paige embraced Mrs. Vanderdale. "I'm sorry. I'm so sorry," Paige cried. "I'm beating myself up over the what-ifs. There is no other way to say it. If it hadn't been for me sending him that text, Norman would be alive. He'd be alive. There would have never been a text for him to reply to. He would have just driven to work safe and sound. But I was a coward. I should have just told him a long time ago face to face that I was in love with him. No, I had to send him that text . . . while I knew he was driving."

Now both Paige and Mrs. Vanderdale were crying and comforting one another.

"I know everybody is thinking that," Paige said. "I'm thinking it, so I knew you were thinking it and I owe it to you to allow you to say it. It's a valid question. And it's a question that deserves an answer." Paige pulled herself together, went and grabbed a paper towel and wiped her face. "I sent the text because I meant it. I am in love with your son. I needed him to know, for some reason, at that very moment, at that very second. I didn't even think about the fact he was driving or that he would try to text me back. Like always, I was only thinking about myself. And now my husband is . . ." Paige couldn't even say the words. She just burst out crying again.

This time Mrs. Vanderdale rushed over to comfort her. "I'm sorry. I didn't mean to make you feel this way. It's just that—"

"No need to explain yourself. Like I said, what you've been thinking the past week, I've been feeling. I've been asking myself those same questions and I've been blaming myself. I have to live with this, Mrs. Vanderdale. I have to live with the fact that I'm responsible for my husband's—"

"No, I won't let you live with that burden. That's too much for any person to bear. I don't feel that way and I won't allow you to feel that way." When Mrs. Vanderdale saw that Paige wasn't really paying her any attention, that she was heaped over crying, she stood Paige straight up and looked into her eyes. "I don't blame you for Norman's death. Yes, the question of the whole texting was on my mind, and that if you hadn't texted him he might still be alive. But we have to face it; Norman made a decision to text and drive. Norman made a decision to read a text and drive. Honey, you can't be blamed for that. And, dear, I don't blame you. Do you hear me, Paige Vanderdale? I don't blame you for my son's death. I blame you for his happiness."

Mrs. Vanderdale's last comment made Paige's tears dry up. She looked up at her mother-in-law.

"It's true. Norman had never been as happy and content in his life as he was these last few months, and that we owe to you. Norman had never thought a woman worthy enough to bring to the Vanderdale doorstep. Norman had never shared being in like with a woman, let alone being in love." Mrs. Vanderdale turned her back in shame. "I hate to say it, but until he called me up and told me about you, I thought the poor boy was gay." She chuckled.

"Yeah, he told me that," Paige confirmed.

"What?" Mrs. Vanderdale turned around in horror. "He knew that I thought that?"

Paige nodded. "Uhh, yeah. He kind of got a kick out of letting you think that."

Mrs. Vanderdale shook her head and let another chuckle escape. "That Norman. I swear."

"He was something else indeed," Paige said. "God, I'm going to miss him. He's been a part of my life for so many years. Norman and I, we're the epitome of being friends before lovers. We knew almost everything about one another. We shared some of the most intimate details of our lives with one another. We would have lasted forever. I just know we would have. The circumstances under which we became husband and wife were a little unorthodox, but we were real. It was real. Our marriage was real. Our love for one another was real." Paige shook her head as she stared off. "But now it's gone. True love was right at my fingertips and now it's gone. What am I going to do?"

"For now, you're going to stay right here . . . with us," Mrs. Vanderdale said. "We're all going to get through this together."

Paige was stunned by Mrs. Vanderdale's offer.

"I won't take no for an answer. I won't be able to think straight with you and Adele over at that apartment all alone. You need family right now, and that's not to take away from your own family who I know is there to love and support you. But perhaps it's time for me to be selfish right now." Mrs. Vanderdale put her nose up in the air. "I want you here." She grabbed Paige's hands. "I want to know everything there was to know about my son, all the things he'd told me if he and I would have had a closer relationship. I want to hear his good deeds and his mistakes. I want to know how you got him into church. And maybe I just might want you to take me to that church of yours myself. I kind of liked that Pastor Margie, although I must admit I was surprised that your pastor was white. I thought you went to a Black church."

Paige smiled. "Church has no color. And even Jesus doesn't if you ask me. Folks can argue about what color He is until they are blue in the face. I was never one to care about what Jesus looked like; I just cared about being like Jesus, even if He was green. I wanted to be able to relate to Jesus for His deeds, not His skin tone and wooly hair. I was always more concerned with what about Jesus and His teachings was going to make me a good person versus whether He was black, white, Chinese, et cetera.

"When I was in school I had some awesome teachers, some black and some white. I could relate to what they were teaching me and how they were teaching it. Whether my geometry instructor was black or white, I got the message. I received what I needed in order to pass geometry and was able to apply it to future mathematical courses and parts of my life. But back to your original statement; yes, the majority of the congregation is African American, but the church is the body." She pointed to Mrs. Vanderdale's heart. "That's where the real church is. That is the real temple Jesus wants to dwell in . . . not just some building." Paige was oblivious that even in her pain and anger toward God, she was giving Mrs. Vanderdale a word.

"I get it. And I guess I'm starting to get a lot of things. From what I've been able to see through you, Norman, and even Miss Nettie over the years, this Jesus fella really can change people for the better. He really can change situations." She looked to Paige. "You think what He does for everybody else He can do for me? You think He can give me the strength to get through the loss of my son? Because it hurts." Mrs. Vanderdale started to cry again. "Words can't even describe. I still feel as if the true realization that my son is gone hasn't hit and that one day I'm just going to lose my mind."

"Well I know one thing for certain and two things for sure. Jesus is a mind keeper, and all is possible through the strength of Christ Jesus. You can lean on Him."

"Then does that mean you'll stay? And you'll take me to your church? And we'll get through this together?" Mrs. Vanderdale grabbed hold of Paige's hands and was almost begging her. "I don't want to go through this alone. I know I have my husband, but men don't always understand a woman's emotions and how we deal with things. Even with him by my side tonight in that bed, I still felt alone. And I just don't want to go through this alone."

"And you don't have to," Paige told her. "You have me. And more importantly, you have Jesus." Guess this meant Paige would have to get back into God's good graces just long enough to introduce Him to someone else.

"So does that mean you'll stay? Just for a while?"

Paige thought for a minute. "I kind of don't like being in that apartment without Norman. I haven't even been in his room since having to pick out something for him to wear at his . . ." Paige nodded. "Yes, I'll stay, at least until I can find another place. I just don't think I can go back to the apartment and live."

"Well just know you and Adele can stay here as long as you like."

"Thank you. I appreciate that. And thank you for loving and taking in my daughter as if she were your blood. That nursery . . . I had no idea."

"I'd do it for any of my grandchildren." She smiled.

"Well, thank you for doing it for Adele. It meant a lot and really touched my heart. Thank you, Mrs. Vanderdale." Paige took Mrs. Vanderdale's hand into hers to let her know with her touch that she genuinely was thankful.

"Oh for Pete's sake. Cut it out with all that Mrs. Vanderdale stuff. All my friends call me by my first name. We are friends now, right?"

Paige smiled. "Right . . . Naomi. We're friends."

***

"This is the last of all the boxes," the worker said to Paige as he removed a stack of three boxes from the dolly.

"Thank you so much," Paige said as she unpacked her things into the yellow guestroom that was now officially her bedroom in the Vanderdale home. In what was now her home. After all, she was a Vanderdale. She bore the last name.

"All the furniture and items marked for storage are all at the storage unit per your request."

"Oh, thank you. I'll probably be needing your services in a couple weeks. A girl from church is moving and I'm donating a lot of the things to her, so I'll be in touch."

"We appreciate the business, ma'am. Have a good one." The gentleman exited the room.

Paige had packed up her and Adele's personal items, but all the furniture had been placed into storage. A lot of the items Paige was donating to her church SWATC Ministry, which was a ministry one of the sisters at the church who was a survivor of domestic abuse had founded. It stood for Sheltered Women and Their Children. It assisted victims of domestic abuse any way that it could. One way was to help with the transition from the shelter to the woman and her children living on their own, away from the abuser. A woman from their church had managed to get out of an abusive relationship a couple months ago and had been in a shelter ever since. She was finally moving out on her own with the help of the SWATC Ministry and the resources they'd tapped into on the woman's behalf. Paige had furniture in storage from not only her and Norman's apartment, but from the place she'd had before she even moved in with Blake, all the way down to some of her and Blake's furniture. She couldn't think of better use than to help out a woman who was basically starting over in life. And maybe getting rid of a lot of things from her past she'd managed to keep a hold of would give her an easier new start as well.

Heck, she was basically starting over in life too. She'd started life over before, but now it was with a baby. She looked over at Adele, who was stuffed down inside a little infant swing, staring at the toys that hung above her head.

"I can do this," Paige told herself. "I have to do this . . . for us." She continued to unpack when she heard a knock on the door. "Come in."

"How's it going?" Miss Nettie asked, poking her head in the room. "You need any help?"

Paige shook her head. "Oh, no. This is all just personal stuff. Clothes and whatnot. I got it. So much of this stuff was Adele's newborn stuff that I'm just going to keep it packed and donate it."

"You've been at it all day. Why don't you finish up tomorrow?"

"Ahh, I just want to get it all finished up tonight, rest, and be ready for church tomorrow." Paige got excited. "You do know Naomi is going to church with me tomorrow, don't you?" Paige had to admit that if it wasn't for the fact Naomi wanted to go to church so badly, seeing she was still upset with God, she probably wouldn't have gone herself. Truth be told, she was all churched out right about now.

Miss Nettie looked over her shoulder and down the hall to make sure nobody else was around. She then entered Paige's room completely and closed the door behind her. "Do I know the missus is going to church with you tomorrow?" Miss Nettie whispered. "Child, that's all she's been talking about. The woman has had me teaching her church etiquette all week." The two women laughed softly. "We done went over there to that Christian store on 256 in Pickerington and bought her a Bible and a Bible case. She even got a prayer cloth." The women chuckled again.

"She is dead serious, huh?"

"Serious ain't the word." Miss Nettie sat down on the bed. "I just feel like for so many years God used me to plant the seed in Mrs. Vanderdale's life. Here you come along and watered it. And now God's about to make it grow." She clapped her hands, stomped her foot and shouted, "Hallelujah!"

"Glory to His name," Paige added out of habit. She then sat down on the other side of the bed. "Won't God do it? I mean look where Naomi and I started. And now look where He brought us." Paige supposed God perhaps still was somewhat in the midst of things.

"Yeah, I mean, you're on a first name basis with the old woman like y'all the best of friends."

Paige smiled. "And strangely enough, she kind of feels like a friend. When I'm talking to her it's like talking to . . . Norman. It's just crazy."

"No, ma'am," Miss Nettie assured her. "It's God . . . and He ain't crazy. Everything is happening in divine order." Miss Nettie stood up. "Want me to take the li'l miss?" Miss Nettie nodded over toward Adele.

"No, God no. All you folks do is spoil her rotten. When I go back to work here in a couple of weeks, I'm sure all everybody is going to do is carry her around. The child probably won't even learn how to crawl and walk until she's two."

"You're probably right. That Sam has got that baby rotten. Now that that baby is here, we see more of Sam than we've seen of her since she moved out of this place. I think she's got the bug: the baby bug. Maybe she'll settle down and find a nice fellow to give her one."

"It's a lot easier than that these days," Paige assured her. She stared off while lifting a pair of pants out of a box. "There are so many single mothers it ain't funny. Working, trying to raise kids." She looked over to Adele. "Kind of like how I'm going to be when I go back to work."

Miss Nettie shook her head and stood. "I still don't see why you're going back to that job. I mean, you really don't need to. Mrs. Vanderdale said you can stay here as long as you like, rent free. Besides that, you got money."

Paige did have money. She hadn't really touched any of the settlement she'd received from her divorce, not even to purchase that Louis Vuitton luggage set she'd been eyeing for years. No, she'd get that with her own hard-earned money.

"And that baby of yours has plenty of money," Miss Nettie continued. "Norman had made her beneficiary of his life insurance policy. She's even the heir of his trust." Miss Nettie put her hands on her hips. "And do you know that boy has never taken a dime out of his trust? He's worked for everything he's ever gotten. And you know what? I don't think he did it to prove a point to his parents. He did it to prove a point to himself, that he could do it." Miss Nettie shook her head. "That boy was some kind of special."

"I know," Paige said. "More special than he'll ever know."

Miss Nettie looked up to see tears flowing down Paige's face. "Oh, now, now. I didn't mean to get you all started up." She walked over and patted Paige's back. "Take a break. I insist." Miss Nettie removed the same pair of pants from Paige's hands she'd been messing around with the past few minutes. "Bring yourself on downstairs and eat something." She whispered in Paige's ear, "I made me up my own personal batch of pig's feet. Got some neck bones and sauerkraut, too. Even got some deviled eggs with beets in the fridge and . . ."

Before Miss Nettie could finish reciting her menu, Paige was gagging. She grabbed her stomach and raced into her bathroom. She barely made it to the commode before she started throwing up in the toilet. Hearing all the hurling going on in there, Miss Nettie entered the bathroom and quickly retrieved a rag from the linen closet. She wet it and made it available to Paige to wipe her mouth.

Paige stood up, flushed the toilet, and went to the sink to brush her teeth. It wasn't until she rinsed her mouth and started to dry it that she realized Miss Nettie had been standing there eyeing her knowingly the entire time. "What?" Paige said to Miss Nettie.

"Oh, nothing, 'cept for the fact you might not want to go getting rid of li'l Miss Adele's newborn things just yet."

Chapter Twenty-three

Paige sat in church the next day just admiring Naomi praise and worship God. No one would ever know that was her first time ever being in church, outside of weddings and funerals. Obviously, all Miss Nettie's lessons had paid off. But Paige knew genuine praise and worship when she saw it. Like so many others, she'd faked it enough times herself to know when it was the real thing and when it wasn't. With Naomi, it was the real thing.

As excited as she was that Naomi was so into the service, she just couldn't seem to get into the service herself. Her mind kept drifting a million miles away. *Could I really have let this happen again?* she kept asking herself.

Ever since having Adele, her period hadn't really gone back to normal, so heck, she didn't know if she had missed her period, if it was late, or what. What she did know was that she hadn't gotten on birth control and when she and Norman made love for the first and only time, they hadn't used a condom.

"Jesus!" Paige shouted out.

"That's right, sister, you praise Him," Naomi said, slapping Paige on the shoulder.

Pastor Margie was preaching so tough that most of the congregation was on their feet. Paige hadn't been, until just now, when Naomi pulled her to her feet.

"I swear she's preaching to me," Naomi said.

"Because trust me, saints, you do not have to be the old you anymore," Pastor Margie preached. "You have

a choice to move beyond the past. You have a choice to
move beyond the pain from the past. The pain you caused
and the pain inflicted upon you."

"Amen!" Naomi shouted, then elbowed Paige. "Did you
hear that? It's the truth, 'cause I ain't me no more."

Paige watched with a wide smile on her face as Naomi
lifted her hands and jumped up and down. "Go on,
Naomi. Get your praise on." Before Paige knew it, she was
smiling, jumping up and down, and praising right along
with Naomi. Here Paige thought she was bringing Naomi
to church to show her how it was done, and Naomi had
been the one to show Paige a thing or two. She reminded
Paige of just who God was and how in all times He should
be honored, worshipped, and praised. No matter what
circumstances life held for Paige, she was still standing.
God had brought her through, and for that, she shouted,
danced and praised side by side with her mother-in-law.

"Pastor Margie, this is my third Sunday in a row and
I must say the spirit has been higher and higher each
time," Naomi said to Pastor Margie after service. "It's
really helping me get through the loss of Norman. I'm
going to have to invite my husband next Sunday."

"Please do. We'd love to have him," Pastor Margie said.
"And tell Paige we hope to see her next Sunday as well.
We missed her this week."

"Yes, she hasn't been feeling well. I know what it's like.
Some days I can't believe Norman is gone. I get physically
ill and can't get out of bed. But this right here"—Naomi
pointed to the church ground—"this helps get me through.
I grab that Bible and get to reading. It seems like whatever
page I land on is just the Word I need." A sour look came
across Naomi's face. "Is that bad? That I just flip to any ol'
page in the Bible? My housekeeper, Nettie, said as long as

I'm reading the Word is all that matters. That there ain't no punishment in skipping around, or even jumping right to the end." Naomi laughed.

Pastor Margie joined her in the brief moment of laughter. "Well, Nettie is right, but eventually you might want to commit to just sitting down and reading the Bible from start to finish. If you like, I can help you. Maybe the two of us can meet up for coffee or something and do some reading together. That way if you have any questions, I can address them for you."

Naomi's eyes grew the size of saucers. "Are you serious? You'd really do that for me?"

"I'll do it and have done it for anybody who needs it. A babe in Christ, a seasoned saint, what have you. You'll find that you can read the Bible, even the same verse, over and over again, but God always has a new revelation for you in due season."

Naomi looked a little confused.

"Never mind." Pastor Margie smiled, patting Naomi's shoulder. "Let's just take it one verse at a time. You'll see what I mean."

"Okay. Well I'll be calling you sometime this week," Naomi told her. "I'm really excited about this. Thank you, Pastor." Naomi gave Pastor Margie a huge hug then headed off to her car, giving everyone she walked by an excited, "Praise the Lord," "God is good," and "Hallelujah." She was so full of joy, so full of peace, and so full of thanks. She didn't know how she would have gotten through this time of loss if Paige hadn't invited her to church and introduced her to Jesus Himself. And she made it up in her mind that she was going to drive straight home and thank Paige.

After a little over a twenty-minute drive, Naomi pulled up to her house, got out of the car, ran into the house, and dashed right toward the steps.

"Honey, is everything okay?" Mr. Vanderdale asked, who was in the sitting room in his chair reading the Sunday paper.

"Oh, sweetheart, I didn't even see you sitting there." Naomi turned back around and walked toward her husband.

"That's because you dashed through here so quickly." He laughed, kissing his wife on the cheek as she bent over to hug him.

"I'm sorry, it's just that I have to hurry and thank Paige. That church, honey, it's the best thing that could have ever happened to me." She looked up. "I take that back. Jesus is the best thing that could have ever happened to me."

"Well, that's good to hear, but Nettie's been talking about Jesus for years."

"Yes, I know. I know. And I'm so glad she told me all about Him, because I finally met Him, and thanks to Nettie, He wasn't a stranger." She snapped her finger. "Guess I owe Nettie a thank you too."

Mr. Vanderdale was glad to see his wife doing well. The first week of Norman's death she'd seemed to have cried almost twenty-four hours a day. The only time he could recall her not having a constant flow of tears was the day of the funeral. She was putting on a front and being strong for everyone. He honestly thought that was how she'd spend her remaining days. But the joy and the peace she was displaying now was not a front. It was genuine. And to be honest, he couldn't think of a time ever since meeting her where such pure joy and peace rested upon her.

"You just do that, honey," Mr. Vanderdale told his wife. "And thank them both for me. It does me so well to see you this way."

Naomi kissed her husband on the forehead. "I love you, dear. We'll get through this. This past month having to deal with Norman's death has been hard, but now with God on our side, I think we'll get through this. I know we will."

"I know we will too," Mr. Vanderdale agreed, taking his wife's hand and planting a kiss in her palm.

"I'm going to go check on Paige. How is she? Has she been down any today?"

"I haven't seen her. Samantha peeked in on her when she came over to go riding. Of course she brought the baby down and we played and cooed with her for a while. Miss Nettie's home from church. She checked on Paige as soon as she got here."

"Well, okay. Let me go lay eyes on her myself. Besides, I need to relay a message to her from her pastor."

"Okay. Tell her I hope she's feeling better and that perhaps she'll feel up to joining us at dinner later."

"Will do," Naomi said as she ran off to see about Paige. "Knock knock," she said while simultaneously knocking on Paige's door once making it up the stairs and to Paige's room.

"Come in," she heard Paige call out from the other side.

Naomi entered the room and saw Paige sitting up in bed reading a book. "How are you?"

"I'm good," Paige answered.

"Pastor Margie sends her well wishes. She missed you at church today."

"How was church today?" Paige asked.

Naomi's face lit up. She raced over and sat next to Paige on the bed. "It was awesome. You should have been there, but I took notes. Pastor preached on healing, and not just physical ailments, but healing in your heart, mind, spirit, soul. It was just so amazing." Naomi went on for about twenty minutes straight reiterating the service to Paige.

Paige had placed her book down and was fully engaged in Naomi's words. She even found herself closing her eyes and swimming in the words of the hymn Naomi sang that she said a dancer had ministered to.

"Naomi, my God, you have a lovely voice. Norman never told me you could sing."

"Well, now, I can carry a note or two," she said modestly, blushing all the while.

"What I just heard you do was more than carry a note. Your voice is amazing. I got lost in it."

"Thank you. You are too kind."

"Don't let Pastor Margie hear you singing like that. She'll insist you join the choir."

"I have to join the church first." Naomi had a knowing look on her face.

"Really?" Paige sat up straight in the bed, whereas before she'd been leaned up against the pillow propped behind her. "Are you truly thinking about joining New Day?"

"I really am, Paige. It just feels right. It feels like . . ." Naomi searched for words.

"Home?"

"Yes, home."

"I know what you mean. That's how I felt from the minute I walked into New Day. Jesus didn't even have to court me. I fell in love instantly. Dedicated myself to Him and joined the church all on the same day."

"Thank you, Paige."

"For what?" Paige asked, confused.

"For inviting me to your church."

"Oh it was nothing. Besides, Miss Nettie said she'd invited you to her church a million times."

"Yeah, she had. I just never felt led to go to church. My family wasn't into church. There was no grandmother or auntie to drag us to church. It's not that my family didn't believe in God, it's just that, I don't know, church wasn't something we did." Naomi shook her head as her eyes filled with tears. "I just wish instead of making sure Samantha and Norman had designer clothes, went to private schools, and had the best family vacations, that I could have given them what really mattered: Jesus."

Paige let Naomi get out her tears.

Once Naomi gathered herself she looked up at Paige. "Thank you! Thank you! Thank you so much." She grabbed Paige's hands and squeezed them tight.

"Naomi, please. You don't have to thank me for inviting you to church. That's my job as a saint, to bring in—"

"No, no. I'm not talking about that." Naomi shook her head. "Thank you for giving my son what I didn't. Paige, you took him to the water and he drank it, like the woman at the well Pastor preached about at Bible Study last week. He's gone, but before he left us, he got saved. He allowed Jesus into his life-his heart. My son is in a much better place. I know that now. Knowing that allows me to sleep at night now. It doesn't mean that I don't still miss Norman. It doesn't mean that it doesn't hurt, but knowing that he is at the right hand of the throne . . ." Naomi exhaled and tears ran down her face. They were tears of complete joy.

Before Paige knew it, her lips were spread into a huge smile and tears of joy were streaming down her face too. Naomi's joy and peace was simply contagious. When Naomi stood and announced she was going to get out of her church clothes and take a nap before supper, Paige didn't want her to leave. Like a small child, Paige wanted to follow Naomi to the bathroom and wait outside the door until she was finished. Naomi reminded Paige what it was like when she first fell in love with Jesus. For Paige, it was like something was ignited in her. Naomi had just unknowingly helped rekindle that fire that Paige never wanted to go out. And since it was Naomi's spirit that seemed to keep that fire burning, Paige was going to make it a point to be a moth to Naomi's flame.

Chapter Twenty-four

"Is she Mommy's little angel? Is she?" Paige cooed and played with three-month-old Adele. She'd just fed and burped her. Now they sat in the rocking chair in the nursery while Paige got some play time in before laying her daughter down for the night.

"She's everybody's angel," Miss Nettie said, entering the nursery with a laundry basket in her arms. "Just coming to put little missy's clothes away."

"Oh, Miss Nettie, you can just sit that down. I'll put them away," Paige told her.

"I got it. That's my job."

"Actually, it's my job. That's what mommies do." Paige stood with Adele in her arms and walked over to Miss Nettie. "Here, let's switch. You take this one, and I'll take that."

Miss Nettie set the basket down on the floor and took Adele from Paige's arms. She then walked over to the rocking chair, sat down, put Adele over her shoulder, and began patting her back while she rocked and hummed.

Paige picked up the basket, walked over to Adele's dresser, and set the basket on top of it. She then began pulling out drawers and putting the clothes from the basket in their proper place.

"So, do the Vanderdales know they are about to be grandparents . . . again?"

"Miss Nettie, I am not having a baby." Paige let out a nervous chuckle. "I told you that the other day."

"Oh, you mean when you were bent over the commode having pregnancy sickness?" Miss Nettie laughed. "You might not be having a baby, and that's your choice, but, child, you as pregnant as a banana is yellow." Miss Nettie laughed again at her own joke. "I take it you ain't been to the doctor to confirm it yet, huh?"

"Miss Nettie, there is nothing to confirm."

"Sure it is, and not marching your tail down to the doctor's office to pee on a stick ain't gon' change the fact that you's with child. Not hearing the doctor say you pregnant ain't gon' take away that fact that, child, you's pregnant." Miss Nettie laughed again.

This time, Miss Nettie's laughter got under Paige's skin. "You think this is funny, Miss Nettie? You think all this going on in my life is a joke? Well it's not." Paige's voice was rising with each word.

"Shhhhhh." Miss Nettie put her index finger on her lips and looked down at Adele whose heavy eyes kept closing and then opening. She was fighting sleep.

"I'll just put these away later." Paige stormed out of the room, leaving the basket half filled with Adele's clothes on the dresser.

It was five minutes later when Miss Nettie laid a sleeping Adele in her crib. She couldn't make it to Paige's room fast enough. Paige's door was cracked open. Miss Nettie didn't even bother to knock. She just waltzed right in and found Paige pulling her nightclothes out of her drawer.

Paige quickly turned around upon realizing that someone had entered her room unannounced and uninvited. "I'm about to take a shower and get ready for bed. So if you'll excuse me, Miss Nettie . . ."

"Oh, no, you don't!" Miss Nettie closed the door behind her and marched over to Paige, wagging a finger at her. "You are not going to brush this off. You are a grown woman. So stomping off like a big baby and running away from your problems is not becoming."

"Key words, Miss Nettie: my problems. This has nothing to do with you."

"I'm not trying to get in your business. I'm just here to help."

"You want to help? Then ask God why He keeps throwing all these monkey wrenches in my life. Ask Him that and then come back and give me the answer." Every time the going got tough or Paige was called on her actions, she always managed to blame God somehow. Jesus was supposed to be her sheep, not her scapegoat. Looks like she needed to catch whatever it was Naomi had so that the peace and joy could resurface again.

Paige rolled her eyes and then slammed her dresser drawer closed after pulling out a nightgown. Paige headed to her bathroom where she'd planned on shutting the door, leaving Miss Nettie on the other side so that she'd get the hint and leave her room. Well, she managed to close the door and leave Miss Nettie on the other side, but no hint was received on Miss Nettie's part as she decided to say what she had to say through the bathroom door.

"You can run from me too, but you can't hide. My words still gonna reach ya. I'll talk to God all right, but I'm not about to question Him. And what you are not going to do is try to flip the script and be mad at God either, especially not after all He's done for you."

Paige flung the door back open. "Look, Miss Nettie. I love God. I have my moments where I get mad at Him, where I question Him. I'll admit that. But then here comes Naomi shining His light. And you too. But give me my moments. And right now I'm having a moment. Right now all I can think about is what God didn't do for me. He didn't save my husband. My husband is gone, Miss Nettie. And now here I am a single mother with one over there and one on the . . ." Paige cut her words off. No, she hadn't been to the doctor and, no, she hadn't taken a pregnancy test, but she knew. She felt it—that and the fact that she hadn't had a period. She was pregnant . . . again. And now, again, just like the last time, she had no husband.

"But God did give you what you wanted didn't He?" Miss Nettie asked.

Paige had a puzzled look on her face. "What? I don't understand." Paige threw her hands up. She was too frustrated and had too much on her mind to subject herself to Miss Nettie's riddled words.

"Then let me pull it apart for you so that you will understand." Miss Nettie stared Paige in her eyes. "You didn't want to be a divorced woman and pregnant," Miss Nettie said. "Guess now you's widowed and pregnant."

Miss Nettie's words punched Paige in the gut. Her head fell downward. Miss Nettie lifted Paige's face by the chin and looked dead into her eyes. "Next time, be careful what you pray for." And on that note, Miss Nettie exited the bathroom, closing the door behind her.

Paige stood in the bathroom alone for a minute taking in Miss Nettie's words. That old woman sure knew how to get up under her skin by speaking the truth. And God knows the truth could pull the skin back and reveal all the nastiness that lay beneath. But Paige knew that Miss Nettie was right in every word she'd spoken. God did seem to be giving Paige everything she asked for . . . and then some. It was the "then some" that Paige didn't know if she was prepared to deal with.

After finishing up her shower, Paige walked across to the nursery to go peek in on Adele. She wanted to make sure she was still sound asleep and to give her a kiss good night.

"Naomi, what are you doing in here?" Paige whispered, entering the nursery to find Naomi standing over Adele's crib.

"Oh nothing." Naomi smiled. "Just staring at the little angel who is responsible for all this." She raised her arms and then let them fall to the side. "This little girl is what's going to keep us all connected. She brought us all together. And even though her blood doesn't pump the same as Norman's, she was his. He couldn't have been more proud the day you gave birth than had you given birth to his own flesh and blood."

"Well, Naomi," Paige started. Naomi had just cracked open a door; Paige decided she'd push it open just a little more and walk all the way through it. "I think there is someone else who's going to keep us connected."

Naomi thought for a moment. "Oh, what we talked about before; Jesus."

"Well, yeah, Jesus too," Paige said, slowly walking over to the crib. "I mean, someone who will be flesh and blood." Paige made it over to the crib and looked down at her sleeping daughter.

"Who?"

"Adele's little brother or sister, who will probably be born in about eight months, give or take a week or so." Paige said it so nonchalantly, as if she were sharing details of the weather.

An excited yelp tried to escape from Naomi's mouth, but she managed to cover her mouth and hold it in as not to wake up her sleeping grandchild. Huge, excited, tear-filled eyes stared over her hand in surprise at Paige.

Paige took Naomi by the elbow and escorted her out of the room so that they wouldn't wake up Adele. Once out in the hall, Naomi clasped her hands together and jumped up and down.

"A baby? Are you saying what I think you are? That you're going to have another baby? Norman's baby?"

Paige nodded. "I think so."

Naomi hugged Paige, still jumping up and down.

"Perhaps I'm jumping the gun," Paige told her after she managed to calm down. "I haven't been to the doctor's yet."

"Well have you taken a pregnancy test at home?"

"No, but I haven't had a period either. And I've been throwing up. And sleeping all the time."

"Go throw on some sweats and some shoes or something," Naomi ordered. "I'll grab my purse and keys." She turned to walk away.

"Wait," Paige said, reaching out to grab Naomi, stopping her in her tracks. "Where are we going?"

"A Walgreens, CVS. I don't know; someplace we can get one of those sticks for you to pee on," Naomi said before heading toward her bedroom to change out of her pajamas.

"But I plan on calling my doctor in the morning and making an appointment." Paige had come to that decision in the shower after her talk with Miss Nettie, or, rather, her talking-to from Miss Nettie.

"Do you think I'm going to get any sleep tonight knowing this? Or not knowing this? You could be carrying Norman's . . ." Naomi couldn't even get her words out before she got all choked up.

"Okay, okay. We can head out. Give me five minutes. I'll meet you downstairs."

Paige kept her word. Five minutes later she and Naomi were in her car and pulling up at the first drug store they drove to.

"I can't believe I'm out at night buying a pregnancy test with my mother-in-law. This is insane," Paige fussed as they stood in line, waiting to check out. "I'm too grown for this. I feel like a teenager who has been doing something she has no business doing and now she thinks she's in trouble."

"Well, this won't be trouble. It will be a blessing," Naomi assured her.

Finally it was their turn to check out. The clerk picked up the pregnancy test and before scanning it gave a questioning look to both Paige and Naomi.

"We might be having a baby," Naomi said excitedly to the clerk, grabbing Paige's hand.

"Is that so?" the clerk said with raised eyebrows.

"Yes. Well I mean, she might be having a baby." Naomi pointed to Paige. "But it's mine too."

The clerk's eyebrows rose even higher.

"Oh, no. I don't mean it that way. It's mine and my husband's."

The clerk put her hand up. "Please, ma'am, no need to explain. I get it. I have cable."

Paige just shook her head and stayed out of the conversation that Naomi was doing a fine job of creating the wrong impression with. Paige paid for the pregnancy test and the two headed back out to the car. They were back home and in the house in five minutes.

"Where are you going?" Naomi asked Paige as she headed up the steps.

"To my room to go take this test." Paige held up the box.

"Oh, no, you don't. I want to be right there when you find out whether I'm going to be a grandmother again. Use the bathroom down here."

"Really, Naomi?" Paige tried to whisper, but her voice carried . . . all the way to Miss Nettie's room.

"What in the world is going on out here?" Miss Nettie said, coming out of her bedroom, tying her robe around her waist and donning a satin cap.

"Is everything okay down here?" Now here came Mr. Vanderdale down the steps. He stopped when he reached Paige, who was on the second step from the bottom. "You okay?" he said to Paige. "Naomi told me you guys had to make a run to the store to get something because you hadn't been feeling well." He looked down and saw the test in Paige's hand. "What's that you're about to take?"

Paige glared at Naomi as if to say, "Now see what you've done?"

"Oh, go on and tell 'em. We're all family anyhow," Naomi insisted.

Paige took a deep breath and opened her mouth to tell Mr. Vanderdale and Miss Nettie what was going on: that she was about to take a pregnancy test. But before she could even get a word out, Naomi spouted it off.

"Paige thinks she's pregnant. She's about to take a pregnancy test."

"Well, well," Miss Nettie said. "Deciding to face the truth after all, huh?" Miss Nettie gave Paige a proud smile.

"Oh, my," Mr. Vanderdale said, coming down the steps and taking a seat in his favorite chair in the parlor. "A baby?" He looked up quickly at Paige. "Norman's baby?"

All three women sucked their teeth and snapped their necks sideways.

"Well, I had to ask," he said, wishing he could tuck his head back into a shell like a turtle.

"Anyway, get going." Naomi shooed Paige. "We'll all be waiting down here for you."

"This is so embarrassing," Paige said under her breath as she made her way to the bathroom.

Mr. Vanderdale sat in his chair tapping his fingers on the arm of the chair. Naomi paced the floor while Miss Nettie sat on the couch rocking back and forth. Finally Paige entered the room.

"What did it say? Where is it? Let me see," Naomi said as anxious as could be.

Mr. Vanderdale stood. "Hold on, dear. Give the girl a moment to speak."

Miss Nettie stood from the couch and walked toward where the other three were standing.

Paige looked from one to the next and then finally said, "We're having a baby . . . again."

Chapter Twenty-five

Paige sat out on the back patio reading while ten-month-old Adele played in her playpen. It was Sunday afternoon and Mr. Vanderdale and Samantha were off riding horses. Mrs. Vanderdale was just returning home after having gone out to lunch with Pastor Margie after church.

"So here you two are," Naomi said, walking out on the patio. "Where's everybody else at? Riding?"

"You know it," Paige answered. "Everybody's doing their same ol' thing. Including me." Paige lifted her book, which had been resting on her seven-months-pregnant belly, and then dropped it to her knees. "I think I made a mistake in deciding not to go back to work. I don't know what to do with myself these days. I mean, I've read more books in the last few months than I did in college." She looked over at Adele. "I mean, Adele keeps me busy and I love being a stay-at-home mom. It's just that during down time, I can't help but think about . . ." Her eyes saddened.

"I know, I know." Naomi walked over and sat next to Paige on the swinging bench. She patted Paige's knee. "I miss him too. But look at what God has done for us." She touched Paige's stomach. "We have an extension of Norman growing inside of you. Pretty soon we'll be looking into Norman's eyes. Do you know what a gift that is? Do you know how much God must love us to do something like that for us? No, this baby is not Norman and could never replace Norman, but that huge void we have in our lives due to his absence, something tells me it's going to be filled to some degree."

"I never really thought about it like that," Paige said.

"That's what you have me here for," Naomi said. "To remind you how good He is. Even when everything looks bad, there is something good within it." Naomi paused before continuing. "I thought I wasn't going to make it when I lost Norman. I felt like death myself. I honestly didn't know how I would make it after that funeral, but with you staying here that night . . ." She shook her head. "Then you decided you and Adele would move in. Then I go to church with you and now . . ." She looked at Paige's growing belly. "He's just so faithful. All I can do is lift my hands in praise."

As Paige sat there and watched Naomi lift her hands, close her eyes, and let tears fall down her cheeks, she was reminded, yet again, of the goodness of the Lord. That darn God just would not let her break up with Him. Paige found herself doing the exact same thing as the older woman who sat next to her. Before Paige knew it, Naomi began praying aloud.

"Father God, I thank you for who you are in my life. I thank you for my life and for all those you have brought into my life, and yes, Lord for all those you have taken. For, Lord, you are the author of my life and I trust the story in which you have penned for me. When the load was getting heavy in life, thank you for always being there to someway, somehow, make the load seem lighter. Father God, I thank you for my grandbaby who's here and my grandbaby that's on the way. But Lord, I thank you most for putting Paige into my life. Whatever circumstances you had to stir up in order for the story to read as planned, I thank you."

It was then when Paige's mind wandered from Naomi's continued prayer to the words she'd just spoken. *"Lord, I thank you most for putting Paige into my life. Whatever circumstances you had to stir up in order for the story to read as planned . . ."* That's when it hit Paige. Everything that had happened in her life was all part of God's plan. It was exactly how the story was supposed to be written. What Paige saw as a setback had really been a setup by God. Adele was what had connected her and Norman as husband and wife. Adele was a product of rape. So was Paige to think that she had to endure and suffer all that she had in order for destiny to be fulfilled? As faith filled as she tried to be, that was just a little difficult for her to accept. But if she was to believe that Jesus endured all He had in order for destiny to be fulfilled, how could she not believe that about herself? And she hadn't gone through a quarter of what Jesus had.

"In Jesus' name, amen and amen," Naomi said upon completing her prayer. She then looked over at Paige, who she found just staring at her. Paige wasn't saying a word, just staring at her with a smile on her face. "What is it, dear?"

"God just never ceases to amaze me is all," Paige said. "Or should I say the God in you?"

"He is amazing, and if you can see Him in me, then that must mean I'm doing something right."

"Well then you must be, 'cause I see His light shining all over you." Paige waved her hands as if tracing Naomi's silhouette.

"Stop it." Naomi shooed her hand and stood. "You acting like I'm the one who led you to Christ. I would have never walked down to that altar a few months ago and got saved and joined New Day if it weren't for you."

"Yeah, well getting saved is one thing. Trying to stay saved is a whole other ballgame. I guess you could say you help keep me saved. And you know what, Naomi?"

"What is it, Paige?" Naomi said, walking over to Adele's playpen and smiling down at the child playing.

"I would do everything all over again, mistakes and all, if it meant having the opportunity to have you in my life."

"Paige, dear, how sweet," Naomi said, looking back at Paige heartfelt. "That means a lot, knowing what all you have been through. I'm just glad you were able to give your life to Christ so that He could get you through it."

"Amen. To God be the glory, Naomi."

"To God be the glory."

"Her heartbeat is fine. She seems to be growing well," the doctor told Paige. "Looks to me like you have a nice healthy baby girl who in less than a couple of months will be welcomed into this world."

"I could have told you she was growing," Paige said as she sat up on the examination table. "I've gained five pounds since my last visit."

"Well, I don't know if that's the baby growing or you." The doctor shot Paige the eye. "I'm going to need you to slow down on the sweets. If you feel like a snack, try popcorn or fruit or something."

"Blah blah blah, Doc," Paige said jokingly. "It's easier said than done. Besides, I'm only seven and a half months pregnant. Let me enjoy these last few weeks. This is the only time when indulging in ice cream and Little Debbie snack cakes don't make me feel guilty. Let me enjoy the moment."

"Yeah, well you won't be saying that when the baby is no longer the cause for the numbers on the scale."

"Oh, you sure do know how to take the fun out of this whole pregnancy thing," Paige teased again. "But I know I have to make healthier choices. I'll try. I'm not promising you anything, but I'll try."

"Good. Do you have any more questions?" Paige's doctor asked her as she prepared to leave the room.

"Not really concerning the pregnancy." Paige hesitated.

"Oh, then concerning what?" the doctor asked with concern.

"I've taken a couple HIV tests now: the one when I first found out I'd been in contact with someone who tested positive, and when I went through the series of testing with this pregnancy. They both came back negative. I had my other daughter tested as well and her test came back good. Am I in the clear?"

"I'd say you were in the clear as far as testing for contact with your . . . ex-husband was it?"

Paige nodded.

"Then I'd definitely say you haven't been infected by him."

Paige exhaled. "Thank you, Doc. But I'm still thinking about taking just one more for good measure in the future."

"No problem." Her doctor smiled before opening the examining room door. "Just let me know and I can set something up for you."

"Oh, Doc, one last thing."

"Yes?"

Paige rubbed her belly. "She'll be tested too, at birth, right?"

The doctor smiled and nodded. "We can definitely do that."

"Thanks, Doc."

"Anytime. You can schedule your next appointment on the way out. And lay off the sweets," she threw over her shoulder before leaving the room.

"I hear ya, Doc," Paige called out as she gathered her things.

She was as happy as could be. She learned she was having a baby girl during her fifth-month ultrasound. She was glad she'd taken Miss Nettie's advice and not donated Adele's baby items. Naomi wanted to give Paige a baby shower. Paige discerned that she only wanted to do so in order to make up for missing her last showers. But Paige told her it wasn't proper etiquette to have a baby shower for every single child a woman has unless there was a huge gap in time of pregnancies. That wasn't the case for Paige. Not only did it seem like she'd just had a baby shower yesterday, but she was having the same sex, so she could pretty much reuse everything she'd received for Adele, which was all in great condition. She didn't need anything new . . . except for one thing.

"I've got to find me a place for me and my girls," Paige said to Miss Nettie as they stood in the kitchen after Paige had returned from her doctor's appointment. "I can't stay here forever. I mean, Norman's gone. I know they are the girls' grandparents, but are they technically still my in-laws?"

"Technically, legally, and all that other stuff don't matter," Miss Nettie said as she prepared lunch. "It's what's in your heart."

Paige nodded in agreement.

"So what's your heart say?"

"Honestly, Naomi is more than like a mother-in-law. She's even more than just a mother. And don't get me wrong. I love my mother more than anything in the world, my father too, because God knows I'm a daddy's girl, but Naomi is like all of that rolled into one and the icing on top is the fact that she's my friend. She's my children's grandmother. She's genuine. I just never imagined in a million years, let alone one, I'd ever be saying this about the woman I met in this here house last year. I love her . . . maybe too much, so much so that I'm depending on her for my own happiness. I can be having the worst day ever where I feel like life is too much, but then here she comes along with that amazing spirit of hers and the Jesus in her makes me feel like going on."

"Then maybe it is time for you to go," Miss Nettie said.

Her comment caught Paige off-guard. She was expecting for Miss Nettie to at least try to talk her out of it if just until after the baby was born, not dang near be ready to help her pack. "Well, geesh, I know who won't miss me when I'm gone." Paige rolled her eyes.

"I'm just sitting here listening to you talk and sounds to me like you're giving Mrs. Vanderdale more credit than you're giving the Lord."

Paige was offended. "I'm absolutely not! I know better than to put anybody before God."

"We all know better, but that doesn't mean sometimes we don't do it without realizing it."

Paige looked as if there was never a time in which she'd voiced more glory to man than God. Had she?

"Why does it take your mother-in-law entering the room to remind you of how good God is, what He's done for you, and what He's brought you through? Now I know sometimes we need encouragement and God will use man to encourage us, but my God, child, sometimes you've got to encourage yourself!" Miss Nettie declared. "Like my pastor says, it shouldn't always take a song or someone exalting to get you to realize how blessed you are and to just thank Him. To Honor Him. To acknowledge Him. To remember Him."

"That wasn't what I was saying," Paige said.

"It's exactly what you said. My body might be in its sixties, but my hearing is twenty-five. My eyes, too, for that matter. I see how you are whenever you're with Mrs. Vanderdale; you like a bee and she's honey. It's like you're more dependent on what she has to say about God than God Himself."

"That is not true and I will not stand here and listen to this craziness of yours any longer."

"Good," Miss Nettie said, walking over to Paige and pushing her down in a chair. "You can sit there and listen then since ya don't feel like standing." Miss Nettie rolled her eyes, and went back to preparing lunch and fussing at Paige at the same time. "You like some young girl in love; heck, from what I see on television, some of the older ones, too. Y'all always expect somebody else to come along and give you the fairytale or dream that you've pictured or created in your mind. Always looking for someone else to create, give, or be the source of your happiness. Build it yourself. Create it yourself. With God all things are possible. You don't have to sit and wait around for someone else to make you happy, to believe in yourself, to think you're beautiful. Make the choice on your own. Bunch of lazy folks is what I say. When you get to the point where you can't even create your own happiness, that is lazy to the tenth power."

If Paige wasn't mistaken, it sounded like Miss Nettie had slammed a plate down on the counter.

"God is a jealous God and you know it. You keep giving Mrs. Vanderdale all that credit and see what happens. You walking a fine line in admiring the God in Mrs. Vanderdale. She's not your crutch. Yes, I do believe God placed her in your life and you in hers for a reason, but when you get to the point to where you can barely walk your walk without someone pushing you along, then you need to separate yourself. Perhaps your spirit needs to be rehabilitated, learn how to walk again on its own."

"Naomi is the grandmother of my children. I'm not going to separate myself from her. That would not be fair."

"Stop being all literal. Child, you know what I mean. Put away childish things. You's a grown woman now.

Time to leave the nest and trust God. I mean, what do you expect anyway? To never find a man again? To never find a daddy for those children? You plan on doing that sitting up under your deceased husband's mama?"

"Well . . . I . . ." Paige had not taken a moment's time to think about her future as far as finding another mate. Her outcome with men hadn't been favorable for her. Maybe she could do better all by herself. Life with the Vanderdales was good. She had not a single complaint, but what if God had a Boaz for her? How would he feel about spending holidays with her former in-laws versus his family? Because she couldn't imagine experiencing those times without Naomi and Norman Senior.

Paige grabbed her head, as if that would stop all the thoughts from spinning within.

"You okay?" Miss Nettie sounded concerned. "I didn't mean to upset you, it's just that in less than a month you will have not one, but two little girls depending on you. All y'all gon' pile up on Mrs. Vanderdale's strength? You got to be strong on your own. You need to find your strength in the Lord, not man." Miss Nettie stared at Paige for a moment. "When's the last time you opened up your Bible? And I'm not talking about when scripture is being read at church and the preacher asks you to open your Bible and turn to chapter and verse whatever. I'm talking about when do you take time out of your day to get into God's Word?"

"Well, I used to do it all the time before . . ."

"Before Naomi started reciting scriptures and praying." Miss Nettie let out a tsk. "See, you can't possibly think somebody else's obedience, prayers, studying the Bible, fasting, and walk with Christ is gonna get you in heaven. It might keep you alive and get you out of bad situations, but heaven ain't gon' admit two for the price of one. Child, the price was paid by one for all, but you gotta walk that walk. Child, Jesus is what's gon' get you into heaven and not nobody else. And that's all I'm trying to get you to see."

Paige took in all of Miss Nettie's words and then nodded her understanding. Without saying a word she exhaled and then stood to walk away.

"And where you going? Lunch is ready," Miss Nettie said.

Without turning around Paige shot over her shoulder, "Going to call a lady from church who does real estate. It's about time I find me a new place to live so that I can start living again . . . on my own . . . literally."

Chapter Twenty-six

"Norm, do something," Naomi said in a panic, pulling on her husband's arm. "Talk some sense into her. Maybe she'll listen to you. She can't leave. It doesn't make sense for her to leave." She looked over at Paige, who stood next to Adele in her car seat, a diaper bag in one hand and a suitcase in the other. "Look at her. She's nine months pregnant and about to have that baby any day. Who will be there to take care of her?" She looked down at Adele. "And my granddaughter. She can't do this alone."

Paige had to admit that Naomi had a point. It would appear to others like this was an odd time to be moving. Sure she'd relocated from one place to another at the end of her pregnancy with Adele as well. But she'd had Norman then. This time around she was a single mother with another child on the way. This could be looked at as a time in her life when she needed the most help, so why not just stay with the Vanderdales and get that help? Because Paige knew that the longer she stayed, the harder it would be for her to leave. She wanted to start a new life with Adele and her new baby in her own new place. She knew the pitfalls of getting comfortable with something and not wanting to leave. She'd learned that with Blake. Had she left that man when he first showed her his true self, her story might have been reading a little differently right now. And although she couldn't change her decisions of the past, she could make better decisions for her future.

"Ye of little faith," Paige said, almost offended by Naomi's lack of confidence in her.

"Oh, I'm sorry. I didn't mean it the way it sounded. It's just that being a single parent is hard."

"And you would know that how?" Mr. Vanderdale said to his wife.

Naomi stuttered for a moment. "Well, uhh, Peggy Sue; her daughter's husband ran off with some gal from work and left her to parent alone their two children. Peggy said she's been having the hardest time. Her daughter can hardly get dinner prepared at a decent hour or get house chores done. Peggy Sue said she got so tired of going over to visit to find her grandchildren living in such conditions that she ended up having to hire her daughter a housekeeper."

"Well, if things start getting too bad for Paige," Miss Nettie interjected, entering the room with Adele's play-pen all folded up, "I won't mind going over and helping her out on my time off. But truth be told, I think she'll be able to handle everything just fine." Miss Nettie gave Paige a supporting wink.

Although Paige appreciated Miss Nettie's support, she didn't feel she needed it. She was 100 percent certain she'd be okay. She was a grown woman. She needed to be on her own. A grown woman with one child and another on the way. When Paige informed her mother that she felt it was time to move away from Norman's parents, her mother had even suggested she come stay with her and Mr. Robinson.

"What sense does it make to jump from one lily pad to the next?" Paige had told her. "I need my own pond, Ma. I have to move on and figure out what I'm going to do with myself, because I sure don't have the slightest clue right now."

Paige might not have had a clue in the world of where she was going in life, but she knew where she wasn't staying: with her parents or Norman's.

"I just don't understand why you'd want to move out when you're due any day." A fretful look rose upon Naomi's face. "Was it me? Was it something I said or did? I know what it is. You haven't forgiven me for the way I treated you when Norman first brought you home. I'm sorry. Please forgive me. I'm so sorry. Just don't go."

"Please, Naomi, you know that was like ages ago," Paige reminded her.

"But you know how you can hold a grudge," Naomi said. "That Tamarra girl you told me about. She was your best friend and now you won't even speak to her."

"She does have a point there," Miss Nettie reminded Paige. She too had been privy to the Tamarra betrayal during one of her and Paige's talks. Paige had definitely found confidants in the two older women. But she had no idea they'd use her stories against her.

"Well I'll be," Paige huffed. "See if I share anything else with the two of you. And for all practical purposes of forgiving, I did forgive Tamarra. I am not holding a grudge. I just choose to no longer entertain her. Forgiving someone does not mean you have to keep company with them."

"Yeah, she's got a point too," Miss Nettie said to Naomi, not realizing she was playing both sides of the field.

Naomi put her hands on her hips. "Why, Nettie, whose side are you on anyway?"

"Now, now, ladies." Mr. Vanderdale put his hands up to referee. "Let Paige's farewell be a peaceful one. Besides, she's only moving about twenty minutes away to Malvonia." He turned to his wife. "You act like she's leaving the state of Ohio."

"You just don't understand. I need her," yelled Naomi to her husband. "Having her and Adele here was like . . ." Naomi's words were buried under her weeps. She just stood there with her face buried in her hands.

Mr. Vanderdale was about to go over and comfort his wife, but Miss Nettie put her hand up to stop him. She nodded to him that he could go and she would tend to the situation. Miss Nettie had been much more than a live-in housekeeper over the years. She'd been a friend to his wife, a confidant and a comforter. She always managed to handle his wife so he knew this time wouldn't be any different. He parted a small smile at Miss Nettie and then exited the room.

"Mrs. Vanderdale, I understand how you feel," Miss Nettie started. "You lost a child, and at the time of his death, this right here was his life." She pointed to Paige and Adele. "They were a big part of his life, so you feel like having them here is like having him here in a sense." Miss Nettie gave Naomi a few seconds to allow her words to sink in and then asked, "Am I right about it?"

Naomi lifted her face from her hands, looked at Miss Nettie, and then nodded.

"And you," Miss Nettie said to Paige, "well, you and I have already talked about this before, which is why we decided you needed to go. You can't keep using Mrs. Vanderdale as a—"

"Wait a minute," Naomi interrupted. "Nettie, did you just say that you talked to Paige about leaving?"

"Well, yes, ma'am, I told her—"

"So this is all your idea? I knew it! I knew my Paige would have never decided to leave on her own. You're the one who got it in her head that she should move out?" Naomi didn't even give Miss Nettie a chance to answer. "How could you do that? What is it, jealousy or something? Are you upset that I don't have time to watch those stupid reality shows with you anymore because I'm spending time with Paige and my grandbaby?" Naomi took a step closer toward Miss Nettie. "Or let me guess; you're mad that after years of you inviting me to your church that I went with Paige. That's it isn't it? You're jealous, and I'm surprised because you know jealousy is not of the Lord." Naomi kept walking toward Miss Nettie.

Miss Nettie held her hands out. "Now look, Mrs. Vanderdale, you might want to back up. Keep in mind I served five years before coming to work here. You can't handle some of this whoop I can pull out of a can if need be." It was true; Miss Nettie had been a former patient of Mr. Vanderdale's during his days as a therapist in the prison system. Miss Nettie felt it necessary to remind her boss of such.

Naomi gasped in shock. "Are you threatening me?"

"Whoa, whoa, whoa," Paige said, holding up her hands and walking in between the women. "Emotions are high right now." She turned and placed her hands on Naomi's shoulders. "I know you want to blame somebody for something . . . anything . . . everything. Trust me. I've been there. But don't blame Miss Nettie for my leaving. I've only known this woman for a little over a year. You've known her a lifetime so you know as well as I do that Miss Nettie don't blow smoke up nobody's behind. She speaks the truth and dang on it, as much as we both probably hate to admit it, the woman is always right."

Paige's comment caused both Naomi and Miss Nettie to chuckle. Paige was glad she was able to cut up the tension before it got bad and words got to flying, words the women might regret having said but weren't able to take back by any means.

Naomi looked at Paige, squinted her eyes, and shook her head while saying, "And isn't it just scary that some-one can be that connected to God where they just know things . . . just know everything? I mean, have you ever met anyone like that in your life?"

"Well, actually I have." Paige laughed, thinking of New Day's church mother, Mother Doreen. That woman has a spirit of discernment that made Paige not want to come to church on Sunday after a night of partying when she first got into church. It wasn't until now when Paige realized how much Miss Nettie reminded her of Mother Doreen.

"I'm sorry, Mrs. Vanderdale," Miss Nettie apologized, "if I disrespected you in any way, or if you think I'm interfering in family affairs."

"Oh, Nettie, for God's sake how many times do I have to tell you that you are family? We're practically like sisters. As a matter of fact, I confide in you way more than I do either of my two blood sisters. Sometimes sisters have disagreements. And misunderstandings. And in this case, I misunderstood the whole issue about you and Paige having a talk. I jumped the gun without even listening to all the details. I know you would never steer Paige wrong. Like Paige said, I just needed someone to blame. I'm sorry, Nettie."

"Me too," Miss Nettie said in return. The two women smiled and embraced.

Naomi pulled away and gave Miss Nettie a serious look. "Were you really going to kick my butt?"

Miss Nettie smacked her lips. "I'm a saved and changed woman . . . which means only if I'd had to." Miss Nettie broke out in laughter. "I'm just kidding. I'm all about turning the other cheek, but you know while I was locked up I had to talk a good game in order from getting my own tail beat. 'Spite popular belief, not all black girls can fight."

Both Naomi and Miss Nettie laughed and embraced again.

"Hey, what do you say I sneak and watch a couple of those reality shows with you?" Naomi said to Miss Nettie.

Miss Nettie raised an eyebrow and gave Naomi a serious look. "You're not gonna tell that husband of yours are you? He thinks I'm a bad influence for getting you hooked on those shows."

"There's some things sisters have to keep between themselves, sista," Naomi said, then bumped Miss Nettie with her hip. The two women cracked up laughing.

"Well, now that my work is done here, can me and my daughter go?" Paige said, a little disappointed that her mother-in-law had so quickly recuperated from the fact that she was moving out. "Besides, the movers expected me about fifteen minutes ago."

"Oh, Paige, I forgot you were still here," Naomi said. "Drive safely with that precious cargo. I'll call you tonight before I turn in." She turned to Miss Nettie. "Come on, I've been dying to find out if that pregnant rapper chick stays with her husband who had turned it up."

Paige laughed as she watched Naomi hustle off with Miss Nettie to go indulge in her guilty pleasure of reality shows. For Paige, on the other hand, it was time for her to go face her own reality; and her reality was that she was a pregnant, twice-married, once-divorced, widowed single mother . . . without a plan.

Chapter Twenty-seven

"Hold it right there. Say cheese."

"Cheese," Paige said and one-and-a-half-year-old Adele mocked as the photographer with H2J Photography snapped the family portrait. The flashing light caused baby Norma, who was just about eleven months younger than her older sister, to flinch and blink multiple times back to back.

"Okay, Vanderdale family. I think that's it," the photographer said as he began to pack up his things.

"Thank you so much. I really appreciate you coming and setting up at the house," Paige told him. "This is our first family portrait. It made it just that much easier not having to drag the girls out to some other location. I think they did well seeing they were right at home."

"Well I'm honored that you allowed H2J Photography the honor for your first family portrait. And what a beautiful family you are."

"Thank you." Paige looked from Adele to Norma. "I do have some beautiful daughters."

"You do, and no offense, but I was more so referring to the mommy."

Paige was stunned by the photographer's blunt comment. She was even more stunned that it made her feel all funny inside. The last compliment she'd received from a man was from Norman. Unless her doctor complimenting her on how well she was pushing Norma out counted.

The photographer noticed how flushed Paige was. "I'm sorry. I didn't mean to make you uncomfortable."

"Oh, no, you're fine," Paige said, trying to play it off. The last thing she wanted him to do was to think she didn't know how to take a compliment. But as she played back her words, she reconsidered them, hoping that he didn't take them literally, since he was in fact, fine. "I mean you're not fine, fine as in looks. I mean you're fine as in okay. You didn't make me uncomfortable."

"Uh, okay. I think." He kind of frowned. "I mean, I know I'm no Denzel fine, but I'd like to think I'm a nice-looking brotha."

Paige threw her forehead in her hand. "Oh, geesh. That didn't come out right. I'm sorry . . . Ryan, right?"

"Well, at least you remembered my name," the photographer said. "That takes away some of the sting of you calling me ugly."

Paige laughed. "Now you know I didn't call you ugly. Stop putting words in my mouth."

Ryan laughed as well. "I know. I'm just messing with you." Ryan finished packing up his backdrop, props, and camera equipment. "Give me a few days to get together some proof pictures for you to look at. I'm going to add borders, maybe get some red eye out, editing, you know, make them look the best they can."

"Dang; all that to make me look good?" Paige huffed. "And here I thought all this time I had a natural beauty. Now who's calling who ugly?"

"See, there you go." Ryan pointed and smiled.

"Ummm, hmmm. Got you back." Paige laughed.

"That's good. I ain't mad at ya. As a matter of fact, I like a woman with a sense of humor. It's just a bonus that she looks good, too." Ryan winked and then headed to the door.

This man was blatantly flirting with Paige. Had he been flirting the entire time? She wouldn't have noticed. She'd been too busy trying to get Adele and Norma to smile for the camera. But now Mr. Ryan had her full attention indeed!

"Let me leave you alone before you call my boss and tell him I was harassing you."

"I wouldn't call it harassment," Paige said, walking him to the door. "You're just doing what you've gotta do to get a girl to order up lots of pictures. I know how y'all do it. But you can stop trying to butter me up. I'm probably going to buy every take anyhow."

"Ahhh, you're on to me. Dang it." He snapped his finger.

"It's all good. I ain't mad at ya, Ryan." There was a brief silence. Paige wasn't sure if she'd purposely said Ryan's name all sexy, or if his sexy name matched his sexy self. Medium brown skin. The kind where team light skin and team dark skin, as unfortunate as it is that those teams even exist, would have to fight for him. His dark brown eyes and smooth bald head with a goatee had enough gray hairs to make it attractive. He looked young though. Around his early thirties. Too young to have all those gray hairs. So Paige assumed he'd endured some stress in his life. "Do you have kids?" It was too late for Paige to take her query back. She'd assumed his stress may have come from kids. She'd wondered and that thought had escaped her mouth.

"Yes. I have two kids. Boys. Five and six. Two baby mamas, but don't judge me. I got caught up. Made stupid decisions." He stood at the door. "You ever made stupid decisions? Did things you wish you could take back?"

Paige thought about that question. Those thoughts occupied her mind momentarily, stopping her from judging Ryan, which was exactly what she was about to do before he posed that question. "I've done more stupid things than I care to admit," Paige confessed. "So trust me"—Paige raised her hands in surrender—"no judging here."

"Yeah, that's what they all say," Ryan said, sounding a little down, "until they meet my babies mamas." He laughed. "No, really, I'm just kidding. I actually only have one baby mama. We had our sons back to back. I hadn't married her yet, but I was going to. I just . . . I don't know, in all honesty I just wanted to play the field, see if the grass was greener. I wasn't that good to her." Regret filled his eyes. "She deserved better." He stared off momentarily and then brought his thoughts back to the present. "I'm sorry. I didn't mean to go there as if you're Oprah or something." He chuckled. "It's just that's the one thing that bothers me is the way I treated my sons' mother."

"Well, I'm sure she'd like to hear that. 'I'm sorry' goes a long way for a woman. Sometimes we just want a brother to acknowledge his wrong, without making excuses for it."

"Yeah, I hear you, but it's too late for all that now." He turned the doorknob and opened the door.

"It's never too late to say that you are sorry."

"It is when the person isn't here anymore."

When Ryan looked up at Paige, she saw a familiar look in his eyes. It was one she'd seen a million times before when she herself had looked into the mirror after Norman's death. She had so many regrets, like how she played around and didn't just tell him sooner how in love with him she was. They could have lived a little bit longer as husband and wife—real husband and wife.

"I'm . . . I'm sorry to hear that," Paige said as she stood holding on to the open door.

"It's okay. But hey, I'm here to make a milestone—your first family portrait ever. Not to have an Iyanla and Oprah moment."

Paige chuckled. "It's okay. Sometimes we just need to let things out. To let things go."

"Yeah, and let God."

"Oh, you're a Christian."

"Catholic."

Paige did a poor job of hiding the slight frown on her face.

"What?"

"Nothing. I just have never met a black person who was Catholic."

"If Sammy Davis Jr. can be Jewish, can a brotha be Catholic?"

Both Ryan and Paige shared another laugh.

"You're funny, Ryan," Paige said.

"You too, Paige." Awkward silence. "Well, I better go. I have another appointment I need to get to. Watch your e-mail. In a few days you should have something from me. And if you have any questions in the meantime, you know how to reach me. I did give you my card didn't I?"

Paige looked over on her coffee table. She spotted the business card Ryan had given her. She walked over and picked it up. "Got it."

"Great. You have a good day." Ryan nodded and was on his way to the next appointment.

Adele sat on the couch shaking her baby sister's rattle in her face while Paige closed the door and then stood up against it. She felt good. Perhaps laughter was the best medicine. She couldn't remember the last time she'd laughed so much. She liked that. God must have known exactly what she needed. Although she didn't realize it, she hadn't given Ryan the glory, not one little bit. It all went to God. She'd grown a great deal since moving back on her own. A work in progress indeed!

***

"Paige, these pictures are simply beautiful," Mrs. Robinson said as she looked at the photos Paige had spread out on the dining room table. She'd brought the girls over to visit her parents as well as show off the portrait package she'd purchased from H2J Photography.

"Aren't they?" Paige had to agree. "Ryan did a phenomenal job. I'm going to make sure I recommend him to the church the next time we need photography services, like at an anniversary banquet or something."

"Oh, I just love this one of just Adele and Norma," Mrs. Robinson said, holding up a picture of Norma lying on a fluffy brown rug and Adele sitting next to her with her hand on her belly.

Paige leaned over and looked at the picture. "Oh, yes. That is one of my favorites. Ryan came up with that pose. Even though he's only been doing photography for a few months, he's like a pro. This is really his calling. He said he was definitely walking out on faith when he quit his job with benefits to just try something he's always been interested in."

"And how'd you learn all that about this . . . Ryan?"

"Oh, he shared it with me while he set up in the living room." Paige stared off as if recollecting the conversation with Ryan. "It takes a God-fearing man to be led by faith."

Mrs. Robinson gave her daughter somewhat of a glare. "Nothing like stepping out on faith. At least you know you're always headed in the right direction."

"Ain't that the truth?" Paige said.

"You must give me a big one of this photo." Mrs. Robinson held up a picture of Paige up close making a funny face. It was just so natural and she looked genuinely happy. Her dimples were in full effect.

"Oh that silly picture." Paige shooed her hand. "Ryan just threw that in there to be funny. I was actually just trying to make the girls laugh. I had no idea he was pointing the camera at me." Paige shook her head and went on to look at another picture. "That Ryan."

"Yeah, that Ryan is right." Mrs. Robinson tsked.

Paige looked up at her mother. "What was all that about?"

Mrs. Robinson looked across the dining room and into the sitting area, where Mr. Robinson was down on the rug with Adele, while Norma was lying in the playpen. "Y'all all right in there, honey?" she called to her husband.

"We're just fine," Mr. Robinson replied.

"Come on." Mrs. Robinson grabbed Paige's hand and led her into the kitchen.

"Mom, what's wrong?" Paige asked with a worried look on her face.

"Hopefully nothing, but I swear things are starting to feel like déjà vu."

"Mom, what on earth are you talking about? You're starting to remind me of Miss Nettie, speaking in riddles and whatnot."

"Paige, honey, sit down," Mrs. Robinson said. She and Paige went and sat down at the table. Mrs. Robinson clasped her hands and then thought for a moment before she spoke. "Paige, you are all right. You are a good person. It's okay to be alone with you."

Paige was none the wiser as to where her mother was going with this conversation. "Mom, please. Just say whatever it is you are trying to say."

"Baby, I'm just trying to choose my words carefully because I don't want it to come off the wrong way, but, please, before you go bringing a man into your life and those girls' life, spend some time with yourself. Date yourself. Court yourself. Get to know yourself. Who you are. Who you are not. What you like about yourself. What you don't like about yourself. Spend some time making sure you are a person you can spend the rest of your life with so that you are sure somebody else can spend the rest of their life with you as well."

Paige was silent for a moment, her face laced with confusion. "Mom, where is this coming from?"

"From my heart." She grabbed her daughter's hands. "Look, love. I don't know if you've noticed it, but you've said Ryan's name a million times, and every time you do, your face lights up like a big ol' Christmas tree."

Paige smiled. "I didn't realize I was doing that."

"See, even now you're glowing at just the thought of him. I want to see you light up like that at just the thought of who you are and who God says you are. No man can define you, Paige. Dang it we've had this talk before." Mrs. Robinson threw Paige's hands away and turned her head in frustration.

"Mom, I hear you loud and clear. And yes, maybe I am a little smitten by Ryan, but trust me, it's not that serious. He hasn't suggested anything but business between us."

"But the minute the check clears for those pictures, trust me, he's going to come sniffing around and you gon' go lifting your skirt so he can get a good whiff."

"Mother!" Paige was offended.

"I don't mean literally lifting your skirt and letting the boy between your legs. I mean you are going to play into his attraction toward you. Because trust me, if he's got you acting all giddy and stuff right now and he hasn't even made a move, you can rest assured that once he really starts to pursue you, the smallest of things is going to have you all stirred up over him."

"Mom—"

"Don't 'Mom' me. You know I'm right and this is one time when I don't want to be. Paige, it's just like when you brought Norman over here to tell me you were married to him. That fear I had about you not giving yourself time with you is the same fear I have now."

"But that was different and you know it. Norman and I got together under some very unusual circumstances. It just so happens we were friends. Then we were lovers. I absolutely was not trying to use Norman to fill a void in my life."

"And I realized that then, but can you say the same now?"

Paige opened her mouth but then paused. She didn't want to tell her mother a lie, but how sure could she be that the words that came out of her mouth would be the truth? She honestly hadn't even thought about it. Sure, she'd thought about Ryan. She couldn't help it. He'd boosted her ego. His spirit and words were like a ray of sunshine after a never-ending storm. She hadn't analyzed those feelings though, and perhaps just maybe that was her mother's point. Had she ever just sat down and analyzed herself, let alone the choices and the decisions for herself? But now it wasn't just about her anymore, which was another point her mother was about to make. She had two children that would be affected by every decision she made.

"Paige, you have two girls," Mrs. Robinson said. "Do you want your daughters to be you?" She put her hand up quickly and spoke. "Before you get offended, let me explain. I don't say that to hurt you or to even slightly suggest that you are not a good person. But as a mother, don't you want your children to be better than you are? I wasn't no saint, but I wasn't an outright heathen either. But, Paige, honey, I made some decisions and choices in my life that I can't take back or change. Do I regret them? No. Because I believe that it's okay to make a costly mistake in life as long as you learned a priceless lesson. And I've learned indeed.

"Parents would like to believe that their children don't understand or notice some of the bad choices we make in

life, but unfortunately, it's our children who often times
have to live with the consequences of our bad choices or
wrong decisions. I watched my own parents make poor
judgment calls. I learned from half of them and repeated
the other half myself. And that's how life is sometimes.
We either learn from our and other people's mistakes, or
we imitate them and learn the hard way. As a parent, heck
as a person, you are going to make mistakes in life, but if
you can consciously make a choice for your children to
witness as few of them as possible, wouldn't you choose
that for them?"

Mrs. Robinson had finished her talk and was now
allowing Paige the time to let her words sink in and
respond.

"Mom, I hear you. I hear you and I'm listening," Paige
told her. "And, Mom?"

"Yes, dear?"

Paige smiled, got up, and walked over to her mother.
"Thank you." She placed her lips on her mother's forehead and held them there for a warming kiss. "Thank you
for loving me enough to tell me the truth."

Chapter Twenty-eight

"Besides, he's Catholic. That would never work," Paige said to herself as she paced her bedroom floor with her cell phone in hand. She'd just finished listening to a message Ryan had left her. The words of his message replayed in her head.

"Hi, Paige. This is Ryan. I was just following up to make sure you received your delivery of the photos and that they were to your satisfaction. I um, was also wondering, if uh, you might want to have dinner with me or something. I know I'd like it. I'd like it a lot. Give me a call back. You have my number. Take care."

"It's just dinner. Doesn't mean I'm trying to fill a void," Paige reasoned with herself. "Heck, it just means I'm hungry." She pictured Ryan's beautiful self. "Starved!"

Next Paige recalled the conversation she'd had with her mother. It convicted her spirit, which meant there was a part of Paige that didn't want to be alone with Paige—even at the dinner table. Just like Sheree Graham said in her book; maybe she first needed to figure out what she was bringing to the table.

"But I'm okay. I'm a good person. I can be with myself. Heck, I sleep with myself every night." Paige was bound and determined to convince herself that calling Ryan wouldn't be a selfish act. Perhaps all he wanted was someone to break bread with. Nothing more and nothing less. So on that note, Paige went over to her corner desk where her home computer sat and fumbled around. "Where did I put that business card?"

With every intent of accepting Ryan's dinner invitation, try as she might, Paige could not find that business card. She and Ryan had e-mailed each other a couple times after he'd sent her the proofs in order for her to pick out the pictures she wanted in her package. She could easily log on to her computer and e-mail him her answer, but the same way she wouldn't want to be asked out via e-mail or text, she wouldn't reply either way.

"Dang it! Where is that card?" Paige sat for a moment trying to recall the last time she'd had it. Coming up blank, she figured it was a sign from God. It was His way of keeping her from doing the wrong thing. Well, she wouldn't necessarily call it the wrong thing. Then again, she couldn't call it the right thing either. But none of that really mattered because since she couldn't find his number, she wouldn't be doing anything . . . she wouldn't be calling Ryan at all.

She sighed and then stood. "All right, I hear you, Lord. Maybe I need to chase after you the way I was chasing after that phone number." Paige had to laugh at herself on that one. *As a matter of fact, that's exactly what I'll do,* Paige said to herself before exiting her bedroom.

She went into Adele's room and peeked in on the sleeping princess. She smiled, then closed the door, leaving it slightly cracked. She then went and checked on Norma. She walked over to the crib and waited until she saw Norma's little chest rise. There was something about a mother needing the reassurance of proof that her small infant was breathing, especially after that scare she'd had with Adele when she was a baby.

After checking on the girls, Paige went and retrieved her Bible from her Bible bag she kept in the laundry room. She kept it there because the laundry room led to the garage. On the Sundays when she headed out to church, or the occasional Wednesday Bible Study she could make it to, it would be right there in sight. She hated the times she'd get so sidetracked with getting the girls together that she'd leave her Word.

With Bible in hand, she headed to her room. Wearing a pair of sweats and a T-shirt, she lay back on her bed. She'd change into her pajamas after reading the Word. She opened the Bible to a random page and began to read. She'd read about three verses before realizing she hadn't absorbed a single word she'd read.

"I got it!" Paige said, setting the Bible down next to her and then going to get her cell phone. She immediately went to her call log and searched for all incoming calls that she'd missed. "Now let's see," she said as she scrolled down the numbers. There were two numbers in her log that weren't assigned to someone's name and that she didn't recognize. She'd have to listen to Ryan's message again and hit the prompt afterward that would tell her what time the call came in. She'd then match the time of the message with the time of the number received on her call log. So that's exactly what she did.

Once she was certain of what number belonged to Ryan, she took a deep breath and prepared to dial his number. Before doing so, she checked the current time. It was 8:30 p.m. Nine o'clock was the unofficial "too late to call somebody" time. That meant she still had a half-hour window. Paige dialed all seven numbers and just before hitting the send button she paused. "Why am I acting so desperate?" she asked herself. "I couldn't even focus on God's Word for thinking about this man."

Paige sighed and threw her phone onto her bed, which landed right next to her Bible. "Now that's a sign." Paige laughed. "If I need to be calling on anybody, it needs to be you, Lord." She laughed as she went back over and picked up her Bible. "I hear you, Lord." She lay back, placed the Bible in her lap, and found the scriptures she'd attempted to read earlier. Before beginning to read she looked up and said, "Thank you for saving me, Lord . . . from myself."

"'Happy birthday, dear Adele . . .'" all in attendance at the three-year-old's birthday celebration sang.

"Happy birthday, angel," Paige said as she stood behind her daughter. "Now make a wish and blow out the candles."

The little girl thought for a moment, took in a deep breath, and then blew the fire out of all three candles, with the help of her mother.

"Yay!" Everyone clapped.

"What did you wish for, sweetheart?" Mr. Vanderdale asked as they all sat around the dining room table at the Robinsons'. Norman's parents, Paige's parents, Samantha, and Miss Nettie were in attendance. Paige decided she'd wait until each girl turned five to throw them a real birthday party with kids and goodie bags. For now, family and friends would suffice.

"She can't tell you what she wished for or else it might not come true," Naomi said.

Bypassing what her grandmother had just said, Adele couldn't wait to let the secret loose. "I wished for my daddy to come see about me."

One could have heard a pin drop the room grew so silent. Paige and the Vanderdales had made it a point to show Adele pictures and videos of Norman, the man who'd signed her birth certificate. He was the man she'd only spent the first couple months of her life with. The man who was the son of her Grandma Naomi and Grandpa Norm. The man who she knew as Daddy. It looked as though now pictures and videos were no longer enough. Adele wanted her daddy in the flesh.

"Who wants cake?" Paige said, quickly saving anyone from having to verbally respond to Adele's words. This wasn't the time or the place. They'd just sung "Happy Birthday," and it was a happy birthday. Paige wanted to keep it that way.

"I do!" Adele shouted. "But can I have my cake and my daddy too?"

Paige's derailment from Adele's wish wasn't long-lived. Adele had quickly put the train right back on the track. Paige looked to Naomi, her eyes begging for her to come up with a save this time.

"You do have him," Naomi said. "And where did Grandma Naomi tell you Daddy is?"

"Right here!" the bubbly three-year-old, who came across as if she'd been here before in a previous life, exclaimed, pointing at her chest. "He's my heart!"

"He's in your heart," Naomi corrected her and then kissed her on the cheek. "I'll take some of that cake too."

"Yippeee. I share my cake. I share my cake."

The mood that had almost come down a notch was quickly lifted as Paige served cake to everyone. They all ate and chitchatted for the next hour or so until the Vanderdales and Miss Nettie headed out.

"Dinner next Sunday after church? Our house?" Naomi said to Paige as they walked out the door.

"We're there," Paige told her before giving the three departing guests a hug good-bye. Paige waved once they got in the car and drove off. She then closed the door.

"Those are some really good people right there," Mr. Robinson said, putting his arm around Paige. "You did good marrying into that family. I can't think of a better father you could have picked to be your children's daddy." He kissed Paige on the forehead.

"Thanks, Dad." She smiled. "Well, I'm going to get the girls packed up and we're going to head home. I have choir rehearsal in the morning."

"You joined the praise and worship team again?" Mrs. Robinson said, excited.

"Yes, I thought I told you. I've been back singing in the New Day choir for about six months now."

"Well, praise God!" Mrs. Robinson said, not one to overuse out of habit so-called church-folk sayings, but it blessed her soul, for lack of better words or description, to see her daughter getting back on track.

The last year and a half she'd watched Paige grow as a woman, as a person, tremendously. Paige still stayed closely connected with the Vanderdales, the girls going over there at least once or twice a week, but Paige didn't use them, namely Naomi, as a crutch or as a means not to be alone. She didn't go back to work at the theatre, but Nettie still came over a couple times a month to help her keep the house in order. And, not surprisingly, Samantha had been the best auntie in the world, babysitting the girls a time or two while Paige attended church functions such as the New Day Singles Ministry meetings.

What blessed Mrs. Robinson the most was seeing her daughter getting back into the Word, the Lord, where Mrs. Robinson knew her daughter was safe. If she was going to place her daughter in any man's hands, it would be God's. Although she wasn't in church every Sunday, she knew one thing for certain: her daughter's heart was safe with Jesus.

Chapter Twenty-nine

"'Take me to the king,'" Paige sang as tears fell from her eyes during her church solo. The words to the song truly struck a chord with her. She had once been all cried out, churched out, too, for that matter. There were times she'd felt so abandoned by God that she nearly detested anyone bringing up His name. Her life had been a roller coaster, going down hill after hill. There had never seemed to be many up moments, a time where she could catch her breath, think straight long enough to comprehend, and make sense of everything that was going on around her. But this last year, once she'd learned to trust God once again with all her heart, things had changed . . . for the better.

She was back to taking care of herself, living healthy and eating healthy. She'd lost all her baby weight, from both children, and was comfortably in a size fourteen, sometimes twelve. She walked on the treadmill for an hour a day and got playtime in with her girls. She read them Bible stories, and after putting them down every night, she'd spend quality time reading the Bible herself. She sought out God and prayed over any situation that stomped her, even if it was just a conflict over what to make for dinner. Now of course not everything called for fasting and praying. Some things simply called for the use of good old-fashioned wisdom. But at least Paige was in a place where, if she needed to call on God, without a doubt she knew He'd be there. And He was with her now as her song moved the congregation to tears.

"'Take me to the king,'" Paige finished off, holding that last note for so long she knew for sure God was the air she breathed.

"Hallelujah!" the congregation shouted.

"Glory!" some cried out with hands lifted.

The spirit was so high in the sanctuary that the organist continued playing the melody of the song while praise and worship went forth.

"He's worthy," Paige cried out. "So worthy." She just shook her head back and forth, in awe of all that God had brought her through.

After ten minutes of basking in the spirit of the Lord, Pastor Margie was able to begin to preach. Paige went and took her place next to Naomi. Mr. Vanderdale sat on the other side of his wife. He didn't come to church regularly, but he came every so often.

After service, Naomi helped Paige retrieve the girls from children's church. They followed the Vanderdales back to their house. Paige tried to have dinner with the girls' grandparents at least one Sunday a month. Today was that Sunday.

"Auntie Sammie," Adele said once she entered her grandparents' house and saw Samantha sitting on the couch watching television while flipping through a magazine.

"T-Sammie," little Norma cried out as well, on the heels of her big sister.

Samantha slid off the couch, down onto her knees in order to be eye level with her nieces. Thank goodness the couch was behind her because she needed it to balance her and catch her fall when the girls slammed into her. They each threw their arms around her neck and smothered her with kisses.

"Now that's what I call a greeting." Samantha laughed as her nieces tackled her. She then planted a kiss on each of their cheeks. "Hey, Paige, Mom," she said, getting up off the floor and dusting herself off. "Dad, I've been here an hour. We were supposed to ride and do pictures of Sunrise and Champagne." Samantha held out her hands and made a duh look.

"Oh shoot." Mr. Vanderdale popped himself upside the head. "I completely forgot all about the photo shoot with the horses."

"Obviously," Samantha said, rolling her eyes. "I even called your cell phone and left a message."

Mr. Vanderdale pulled his phone out of his suit jacket pocket and looked at it. "I switched it on to airplane mode before I went into church. I forgot to turn it off after church." He proceeded to do so.

"Well, can you go hurry up and slip into some riding clothes? Surely the photographer is set up by now. He's been here forty-five minutes. Thank goodness once Stuart gets to talking there's no stopping him. He's kept him company outside, but who knows how much longer he'll be willing to stay? You go get dressed and I'll let him know you're here and that we're ready."

"All right, sweetheart," Mr. Vanderdale said, removing his tie as he walked up the steps.

"Sorry, Sam," Naomi apologized. "I invited him to church today forgetting all about the fact today was picture day for the horses."

"It's okay, Mom. We're good," Samantha said. "Let me head out before the photographer packs up and leaves." She looked down at her nieces. "You girls want to come see Sunrise and Champagne? Wanna see the horses?"

"Yay. Yes." The girls screamed out and jumped up and down, clapping their hands.

"Then let's go," Samantha said as she took them by the hands and led them outside.

Paige and Naomi were the only two remaining in the room.

"I feel so bad. Norm and Sam are entering the horses in some contest. They have to turn in photos of them with the horses. Sam's had this appointment scheduled for a month." Naomi shook her head. "Them and their horses. I can't stand the smell of them personally."

Paige laughed and shook her head.

"Come on. Let's go to the kitchen and see if Nettie has any of her concoction whipped up. If there isn't, she can whip us some up as soon as she gets in from church. She should be arriving any minute now."

Paige followed Naomi into the kitchen and sat down at the nook while Naomi went and opened the fridge.

"Voilà!" Naomi said, pulling out a pitcher of Miss Nettie's favorite beverage. She then retrieved two glasses and filled them each with the refreshing liquid. About a half hour later Miss Nettie entered the kitchen dressed in a plum dress with white buttons down the front. It had a white collar and she wore white shoes over her nude-colored stockings. "So sorry I'm late. Church went over a bit and then Sister McKenzie 'bout talked my ears off," Miss Nettie said, rushing through the kitchen with her Bible in its Bible cover. "Let me get changed and I'll be right out to get you all a snack together and get dinner started."

"Take your time," Naomi called out to Miss Nettie. "Norm and Sam are out there with the girls doing pictures with the horses anyway."

"Is Stuart tending to them and helping? I sent him a text reminding him about the shoot," Naomi stopped and asked.

"Yes, Nettie, Stuart is on it. Now just calm down and catch your breath."

Miss Nettie hurried off to her living quarters down the hall and disappeared behind her bedroom door.

Naomi whispered to Paige. "She thinks this house can't run without her."

Both let out a chuckle and took a drink from their glasses.

"Paige, Mom," Samantha stuck her head in the back door and said. "You guys have got to come see the girls taking pics with the horses. It's wayyyyy cute." Just as quickly as her head had appeared in the door, it disappeared.

"Well, come on," Naomi said, rising up from off the stool. "Let's go see America's next top models."

Paige chuckled, and with her drink in hand, followed Naomi out to the back deck.

When they walked outside, they could see Mr. Vanderdale up on his horse with both Adele and Norma sitting in front of him just a-smiling with their ruffled and lace Sunday dresses on. The photographer, whose back was toward the two women just entering the scene, was just a-snapping away. With the camera glued to his face, he was walking around getting his models from several angles.

"Adorable," Naomi clasped her hands and said to Paige. "You know what? I just realized we all don't have a picture together. What do you say we go crash this photo shoot? I mean, the photographer is here. I'm sure he won't mind. What do you say?"

Paige shrugged. "Why not? But let me go inside and get my purse so I can touch up my face."

"That's fine. I'll go on out there with them and make sure it's all right with everybody."

Naomi headed off the deck and Paige headed back in the house. She retrieved her purse and then went into the bathroom to touch up her makeup and fix her hair. A couple minutes later she was back outside heading off the deck down toward where the family awaited.

"Paige, come on," Naomi waved to her as she stood with the girls and her husband, already taking some pictures.

"I'm coming, I'm coming," Paige said, removing her heels so that she could get down to the photo shoot quicker. Walking on her tiptoes to avoid the feeling of her feet sinking into the ground was painful on her calves and her toes, in addition to slowing her down. Once she was about a foot away from the photographer, who was snapping away, Paige stopped, bent over, and slipped her shoes back on her feet.

"Paige?"

"Umm hmmm . . ." Paige started and then her words trailed off as she looked up. "Ryan! Oh my God." Paige hugged him and he returned the hug as if they were old high school sweethearts who had just reunited again after years of being apart.

"Paige Vanderdale. I didn't even put two and two together with the last name."

She was certain Ryan wasn't trying to kid her. He wouldn't have thought he was doing a photo shoot of Paige's extended family, considering she was black and they were white. "Uh, yes, I inherited this wonderful family through my husband."

Ryan raised an eyebrow.

"God rest his soul," Paige was quick to say, letting Ryan know she was as available as a hooker at a truck stop.

"I thought these two beauties looked familiar though," Ryan said, referring to Adele and Norma. "They are getting so big. But still as beautiful as ever . . . like their mother."

Paige subconsciously immediately looked down at Ryan's hand in search of a wedding band. All his fingers remained bare. Of course that didn't mean a whole lot. Paige had witnessed several married couples at church not wearing rings. Some had never even owned wedding rings but had been married for years.

"So what have you been up to?" Paige fished. *Please don't say married.*

"Nothing too much. I've just been taking care of my kids, focusing on school, and serving God," he admitted. He held his camera up. "And taking pictures."

"Speaking of taking pictures," Samantha said, who was standing off to the side allowing her parents to take pics with their grandchildren. "Can we get the family portraits out of the way and get back to the horses?"

"Oh, yes, I'm sorry," Ryan apologized to Samantha. He turned to Paige. "You getting in the pics?"

"Oh, yes, of course." Paige walked over to get into the picture. "Come on, Sam."

"You guys first," Samantha said. "Then I'll get in."

Ryan proceeded to take pictures, and pose and position the family. He put people in and out of the pictures until there was a nice selection they could ultimately choose from. "Last one. Everybody say cheese," Ryan ordered, snapping a family portrait of all six Vanderdales.

"Cheese!" they all said for the final family portrait. A couple of them even clapped, knowing in advance they'd taken a spectacular photo shoot.

"Now back to the horses," Samantha said.

"Come on, kids," Naomi said to her granddaughters. "Let's head in the house and see what Miss Nettie has prepared good to eat."

The girls followed their grandmother into the house. Paige watched them head off and then stood there for a moment realizing all eyes were on her.

"Oh, I guess I better go and let you all get back to your business of taking pics of the horses." Paige let out a chuckle. The chuckle dragged on as if she was stalling for some reason. It was almost as if she didn't want to leave. There was silence as everyone waited for her exit. "Okay, well, I'll see you all inside. Well, except for you that is," she said to Ryan. "I guess, I uh, won't see you again. But it was good seeing you again this time. Today. How, uh, did you end up getting this gig anyway?" A fine job Paige was doing of prolonging her presence in front of Ryan.

"You gave me his card a long time ago? Remember?" Samantha chimed in, trying to hide her agitation.

Paige raised an eyebrow trying to recall when. So Samantha decided to help her recollect, hoping it would hurry her along. She was more than ready to finish up.

"Back when you gave us photos of you and the girls," Samantha said. "I mentioned how good of a job the photographer did. I was considering back then doing a photo shoot of the horses. You ended up having his card in your wallet and gave it to me."

"Oh, yeah. I remember now," Paige said. She did, in fact, remember. And that helped to explain why that day she was looking for the card to accept Ryan's dinner invitation she couldn't find it. She'd passed it on to Samantha. She had to admit, back then would not have been the time to try to build a relationship with any man. She had to rebuild her relationship with God, and, per her mother's advice, with herself as well. She had a wonderful relationship with her daughters also. Life was good. And the same way Ryan had made her feel all some kind of way when she'd first met him was how he was still making her feel.

As far as Paige was concerned, there was no time like now to get to know Ryan. The thing was, did he still want to get to know her? There was only one way to find out.

"So, are you still hungry?" Paige asked Ryan. She only noticed the confused look on his face, not the crazy looks Samantha and Mr. Vanderdale were giving each other behind her back.

"Pardon me?" Ryan asked, expressing his confusion with his contorted face.

"Uhh, well you know, the last time we were in contact, you'd left me a message, inviting me to dinner. I'd lost your business card though. Well, I guess I actually hadn't lost it. I'd given it to my dear sister-in-law and didn't remember that. I was going to e-mail you, but that just didn't feel personable. I guess now thinking back I could have e-mailed you, asked you for your phone number, and then called you."

Paige let out a nervous chuckle. Ryan just stood there lost in her words.

Paige's words were all over the place as she continued talking ninety miles per hour. "But of course I didn't think of that at the time, so I didn't call you. Not only that, but it probably wasn't a good idea at the time. I don't think I was being honest with myself in thinking that I wanted you to do more than just fill a void in my life. That would not have been fair to you at all. You seemed like such a really nice guy and all. I mean, you still do, it's just that . . ." Paige went on and on and on. Five minutes later she ended with, "You know what I'm saying?"

"No," Ryan said, trying hard not to laugh in Paige's face, but letting one slip out. Shaking his head he said, "I have absolutely no idea what you are saying."

Samantha, clearing her throat, walked up next to Paige and Ryan. "What she's saying, Ryan, is that if you're still down for it, she'd loved to go to dinner with you."

Ryan put his head down as if he didn't want anyone to see him blushing. Paige tightened her lips and elbowed Samantha.

She shot her a look and mouthed, "What did you do that for? I didn't need your help."

"Like heck you didn't," Samantha said out loud.

"Excuse me?" Ryan said.

Samantha put her hands on her hips and sighed. "Look, Ryan, in a minute here I'm going to charge you money for my time, so either you want to take my sister-in-law here, the mother of my two beautiful nieces, out to dinner or you don't. Either way, I'd like to finish this photo shoot. I hate to break out my Paris Hilton spoiled brat alter ego, but dude, I frickin' have a date after this, so could we please wrap this thing up?" Samantha threw her arms up in the air, and let them drop as she rolled her eyes and stomped away, mumbling "Geesh," under her breath.

So now stood Paige and Ryan face to face.

"Well, what she said," Paige spoke.

"Well, to answer your initial question then"—Ryan gave Paige the once-over with wanting eyes—"I'm starved."

Paige exhaled. She could breathe again. That awkward moment of asking Ryan out on a date . . . or not necessarily asking him out on a date but accepting his proposal to go out on a date a year ago . . . or whatever it was, was over. Ryan agreed he wanted to have dinner with her and that's all that mattered.

"Great." Paige clasped her hands together. "I'll, uh, give you my number and everything before you head out."

"Oh, no need to," Ryan told her. "I still got your number." He winked and then finished his business at hand.

Chapter Thirty

"Well look at you," Mrs. Robinson said when she opened the door to find Paige dressed to the nines with Adele and Norma in tow. "You clean up fabulous! And did you lose more weight? Girl, what did I tell you about all that insanity workout business? It's just that; insane. I don't want you killing yourself trying to lose weight for no man or—"

"Mom, stop. You're doing it again," Paige said, putting her hand up, then leading the girls inside her parents' house. "We've been there, prayed that. It's about me now, what I like and what makes me happy. It's not about what other people think, will think, or might think. It's especially not about a man," Paige assured her mother as she walked into the living room. "I have not been doing no insane workouts. I follow this personal trainer named Andre LaVelle on Facebook. He teaches that being healthy and staying healthy is a lifestyle that goes beyond sixty days of madness." Paige cleared her throat. "Now thank you very much for the compliment, and thank you for agreeing to keep the girls while I go out with Ryan."

Following her daughter in complete "I told you so" mode, Mrs. Robinson said, "See, now ain't you glad you waited until the time was right before you decided to give Ryan the time of day? You're in such a better place now. You're so happy with yourself and your life that now you can be happy with someone being in your life. Timing is everything."

"Yes, it is, and yes, you were right, Mother. You are always right," Paige said, laying down the girls' overnight bags next to the couch. Even though Paige's dinner date with Ryan was at seven, she hadn't planned on being at the restaurant with him more than a couple hours. It was Friday night and the girls didn't have preschool the next day or anything, but Mrs. Robinson still thought it would be a better idea if they just spent the night instead of Paige dragging them out at midnight—her words—tired and half asleep. Holding on to the mantra that her mother was always right, Paige simply agreed. Besides that, what single mother didn't want to take advantage of sleeping in on a Saturday morning?

"Are you being sarcastic with me?" Mrs. Robinson, with a look of uncertainty, raised an eyebrow.

"No, Mom, you always are right, and boy oh boy do I learn the hard way."

"Awwww, sweetie." Mrs. Robinson wrapped her arms around her daughter and just hugged her.

Paige's eyes got bugged. She was not used to this type of physical connection with her mother. Growing up, her mother was not the "hug on and let's say I love you" type of mother. That was something Paige had resented her mother for for so long. Fortunately, once Paige got into church, got saved, and learned about deliverance, she was able to let go of that foolishness. Slowly, and almost awkwardly, Paige put her arms around her mother.

"There's my two favorite girls," Mr. Robinson said, entering the room and greeting his granddaughters. The girls immediately ran over to him.

"Well, what are we? Chopped liver?" Mrs. Robinson joked.

"I know, right," Paige agreed. "I remember the days when I was his favorite girl." Paige playfully poked out her bottom lip and pouted.

"Oh, now, you know you're still my favorite girl too."
Mr. Robinson went and planted a kiss on his daughter's
cheek.

"Thanks, Dad." Paige bent down and held her arms
out. "Come here, girls. Give Mommy a kiss bye-bye."

The girls ran into their mother's arms. They planted
kisses on both her cheeks.

"I love you, girls," Paige said, returning their kisses.
"Tomorrow when I come pick you up, I'll have a lunch
packed and we'll go to the park. Okay?"

"Ooooh, yes, Mommy." Adele clapped. "I love it when
we go to the park. Can you push me on the swings first
this time, and not Norma in that dumb baby swing?"

"I'm not a dumb baby," Norma said, poking out her lip.

"I didn't say you were a dumb baby. I said the swing
was dumb, but you're too scaredy to ride the big girl
swings like me."

"I'm not a scaredy."

"Then prove it. Ride the big girl swing with me tomorrow."

"I will."

"Bet you won't, 'cause you're a scaredy."

The girls argued.

Figuring it was time to break them up, Paige interjected. "Don't worry. Mommy has plenty of time to push
you both on the swings, whether it's the big girl swing or
the baby girl swing. As long as we're together and having
fun is all that really matters, right?"

"Right, Mommy," the girls agreed, now back on good
terms.

"All right, Mom." Paige stood up straight. "I'll be by to
pick them up around two o'clock tomorrow afternoon."

"Okay, sounds good. Depending on how much they
wear me out, I might go to the park and picnic with y'all."

"That would be nice." Paige turned to the girls. "Girls, wouldn't y'all like Grammy to come to the park with us tomorrow?" She looked at her father and winked. "And perhaps Grandpa, too."

"Yay!" the girls cheered.

"Hey, how'd I get caught up in this?" Mr. Robinson asked.

"Oh, come on, Dad. Remember how you used to take me to the park and push me on the swings?" Paige leaned in and said softly, "The big one and the stupid baby one?" Paige and her father shared a laugh, and at the same time a memory.

"Those were the days," Mr. Robinson said, staring off with a sentimental look in his eyes.

"And God is so good, you get to relive them with your grandchildren. Now how many people get blessed enough to experience that?" Paige added.

"All right, you've talked me into it. Picnic tomorrow at two," Mr. Robinson agreed.

"Yay!" the girls cheered again.

"Now, girl, go on and get out of here before you be having the neighbors join us tomorrow and it turns into an all-out block party," Mrs. Robinson said. "And don't worry about packing a picnic. I'll take care of that."

"Sounds good to me," Paige said. "All right everybody. I'm out of here." Paige gave her girls one last hug and then was out the door.

It took her about twenty minutes to get to the restaurant where she was meeting Ryan. She was ten minutes early, but to her surprise, he was already there waiting when she walked inside the restaurant.

"Man, where is my camera when I need it?" Ryan said when he saw Paige enter with her nice-fitting red trousers that flared at the bottom, black patent pumps, and royal blue puffy sleeved blouse. Her gold handmade earrings she'd gotten from a lady at church who had her own jewelry business went perfectly with the bracelet her wrist don that she'd picked up from Burlington Coat Factory. She'd watched on television that it was no longer the style to match her purse with her shoes, so she opted to carry a neutral-colored patent Versace bag. It was just one of the few items she had kept that Blake had purchased for her.

"Well, hello to you too." Paige smiled and kissed Ryan on the cheek. This was their third date since reconnecting at the photo shoot a couple of months ago. They'd talked on the phone several times in getting to know one another. So far Paige liked everything she knew about Ryan. The fact that he had children from a prior relationship didn't bother her any more than it bothered him that she had two children from a prior relationship as well. Paige hadn't told him, though, her entire baby daddy issue. She just always referred to Norman as both the girls' father. She'd mentioned the fact that Norman was her second marriage, but again, she didn't go into full details. Although they were getting close, they just weren't quite there in their relationship where she felt comfortable sharing everything.

Not Ryan though. He was an open book. What Paige saw would be exactly what she got. Nothing more and nothing less. "I know how women are," Ryan had told her on their first date. "You might as well tell them everything or don't tell them anything at all. Either way they'll swear up and down you're hiding something from them. So I just choose to keep it one hunid out the gate."

"That's all good," Paige had replied. "But I hope you don't mind if I spoon-feed you. Sometimes less is more. Besides, if I told you absolutely everything about me so soon, that would take all the fun out of the getting to know each other stage."

"No, it won't. It will just mean that the past will be laid out on the table and we can get on to making a future . . . together."

Paige loved how Ryan never even had to think about what he wanted to say to her. It was like the words were just right there on the tip of his tongue waiting to spill out. And every word Ryan spoke to Paige felt like Bible to her. *He couldn't make up a lie that fast if he wanted to,* she had told herself. And even if he could, Paige could sit and listen to his lies all night, and that included tonight.

"Shall we?" Ryan said, extending his bent arm for Paige to loop her arm through. She did just that and he escorted her over to the hostess booth. "My party has arrived," he told the two chatting hostesses who stood behind the podium.

Paige smiled a huge smile. The way he strutted her over there, one would have thought he was escorting Miss America down the runway. She felt so wanted and desired.

"Party of two," one of the hostesses said while grabbing two menus. "Right this way."

Ryan released Paige's arm and instead guided her with his hand on the small of her back. She hoped to God the tingling electric sensation going through her body did not transfer to his hand. Or perhaps it was actually an electric current running from his hand to her back. She had no idea. All she knew was that their energy flowing together felt right.

The hostess sat the couple at a table and their waitress did a follow-up by taking their drink orders. Ryan ordered a glass of wine while Paige, who didn't drink alcohol, ordered a Coke product. Ten minutes later they were sipping their drinks, had given their food orders, and were partaking in an engaging conversation as always.

"You know, we've been getting to know one another for a couple months now. I know that's not a long time, but it's been long enough and I'm just surprised that there's something you haven't yet offered."

All of a sudden the pit of Paige's stomach felt like someone had hidden an Easter egg that nobody ever found and now years later here it sat rotting in Paige's belly. So Mr. Playa Playa was just trying to be smooth all along. All the while Paige thought he had really been trying to get to know her, and what he'd really been trying to do is get in her—

"And here are your entrees," the waitress said, setting their requested meals in front of them. "Is there anything else I can get you right now?"

"No, I'm fine," Ryan said.

"No. Maybe a doggie bag here in a minute because I think I'm about to lose my appetite." Paige folded her arms.

"Okay," the waitress said in a sing-song voice with a look on her face like she needed to get out of the line of fire and fast. She had obviously walked into the middle of something and now she wanted to disappear as quickly as she had appeared. "I'll be back to check on you guys in a bit. Enjoy your meals." She shot them a quick fake smile and then hurried off.

"What was that about?" Ryan asked. "That little comment you made to the waitress about losing your appetite. Did I do something wrong? Say something wrong?"

"No," Paige said, shaking her head. *Not yet.*

"Okay. Just checking," Ryan said before blessing their food and then taking a bite of his steak. "Anyway, like I was saying before the waitress brought our food . . ." He paused and chewed.

"Yeah, what were you saying?" Paige said, anxious for him to finish sticking his foot in his mouth. He'd already had a taste of his toes.

"Well, we've been hanging out for a bit and I'm just surprised that there's something you haven't yet offered." He took in a forkful of his potato and chewed while staring at Paige. She 'bout hoped he choked on it before he could get out the words she knew he was about to say. What she didn't know was exactly just how Mr. Smooth Operator was going to word it. "You haven't offered me an invitation to your church."

Paige's mouth dropped. "Is that it? Is that what you've been expecting from me? An invitation to my church?" She burst out laughing.

"Am I missing something?" Ryan asked, cutting into his steak. "Was there something else I should have been expecting after two months?" Before two seconds could even pass Ryan caught on. "Ohhhhhhh. I get it. You thought . . ." Within seconds both Paige and Ryan were laughing hysterically at Paige's assumption.

Paige's subconscious drifted back to the time she thought Norman was telling her she was hot-as in looks. She'd felt more like he was laughing at her than with her. But with Ryan, she knew he was laughing with her. There were no doubts in her mind that he was for her and not against her; not that she ever felt Norman was against her. Then again she'd never felt Blake was against her and yet he'd been her greatest enemy. But life was good. Life was fresh. Life was new and no remnants of her past would be permitted—the good parts or the bad. And she certainly wouldn't compare Ryan to any other man in her life—the good or the bad.

Paige wanted something different with Ryan, something she'd never had before. Something she never even prayed for, asked for, or wanted. She wanted God to surprise her. She liked surprises. And as she melted in Ryan's laughter, eyes, and conversation, she just hoped the surprise was all good. She'd had enough bad ones to last a lifetime.

Chapter Thirty-one

"Paige, honey, I've been calling you all morning. Maybe you just had a later night than you anticipated and are still sleeping. But it's almost two o'clock in the afternoon and I haven't heard from you. I just wanted to make sure we were still on to take the girls to the park. They woke up first thing this morning talking about it." Mrs. Robinson chuckled as she left a message on Paige's voicemail. "Please call me just as soon as you get this message." Mrs. Robinson ended the call, but stared at the phone.

"Is everything okay?"

"Oh God!" Mrs. Robinson almost jumped out of her skin when her husband approached her from behind.

"You okay? I didn't mean to scare you. What's going on? Why are you so jumpy?"

Mrs. Robinson turned around and looked into her husband's concerned eyes. Hers, filled with worry, stared back at him.

"Sweetheart. What's going on? What's that look for?"

"Nothing, I hope." Mrs. Robinson walked away just a few feet. She cupped her chin with her index finger and thumb as she thought.

"What do you mean you hope?"

She turned back around to face her husband. "Well, it's almost two o'clock and I haven't heard from Paige. That's not like her. She would have at least checked on the girls by now."

Mr. Robinson thought for a moment. "Yeah, she usually would have." That was true. Anytime Paige had left the girls with her parents, even if it was just for a couple of hours, she would call to check on them. "When's the last time you talked to her?" Now Mr. Robinson was somewhat concerned.

"She called me last night during dinner with Ryan. She sounded all giggly and giddy." Mrs. Robinson paused. "Do you think . . ." Her words trailed off. "No." She shook the thought out of her head.

"No, honey, go ahead and say it. Do I think what?"

"Do you think that maybe he gave her something?"

"Something like what?"

"That stuff. That stuff people put in people's drinks so that they can take advantage of them? That could explain why she was all giggly and stuff like a schoolgirl."

"Umm." Mr. Robinson shook his head. "Although we've never met this Ryan fella yet, the Vanderdales have. I'm sure they would have noticed something fishy about him. The fact that he's met some of her family alone would scare him off from doing any nonsense like that. We know who he is and where to find him."

"Do we really? What's his last name? Where does he live? What's his phone number? Oh God!" Mrs. Robinson began pacing and biting her nails.

"Come on now, Susie. Calm down. You're thinking the worse. It's all that ID channel business that's got you stirred up."

"Yeah, maybe you're right," Mrs. Robinson agreed, knowing she was a true ID channel addict, intrigued by the evil that existed in this world. "I'm sure the Vanderdales could get a hold of him if we needed to. But we don't need to, right? Because Paige is safe and sound, sleeping in like a baby. And can you blame her? Those two girls are a handful." Mrs. Robinson tried to talk herself down from her worry high.

"Speaking of which, why don't you head back into the kitchen and finish getting the stuff packed for the picnic. I'll wait out here to let Paige in, because I'm sure she'll be pulling up any minute." Mr. Robinson went and kissed his wife on the forehead for reassurance.

"Okay. I better get back in that kitchen. Those two are probably covered in peanut butter and jelly by now." She laughed and then reluctantly headed back into the kitchen, even though everything in her wanted to pick up the phone and call her daughter again, but she remained strong and didn't.

After going back into the kitchen and packing up the picnic, Mrs. Robinson sat the girls in front of the television, where her husband was sitting in his chair reading the newspaper and watching CNN.

"Do you mind if I put on a cartoon channel for the girls?" she asked her husband, who was more focused on the newspaper.

"Oh, no, I don't mind at all," Mr. Robinson replied.

"But we don't wanna watch TV. We want to go to the park," Adele said, looking like a brown mini Paige.

"Yeah, 'cause I'm riding the big girl swing today," Norma said, looking like a fair-skinned version of her big sister.

"I know, and we are," Mrs. Robinson assured them. "But we have to wait on Mommy. Remember I told you that in the kitchen? Now let's watch some cartoons. That Mickey Mouse sure is something isn't he? And Tweety Bird, she is just darling."

"Tweety Bird is a he," Adele said.

"Nuh, un. It's a girl bird," Norma begged to differ.

Adele laughed at her sister. "Tweety Bird is a boy bird, isn't that right, Grandpa?"

Mr. Robinson lowered the paper and looked to his wife for an answer. She shrugged.

"Tweety Bird is whatever you want it to be," was Mr. Robinson's reply.

"Yeah, just like God. God can be black or God can be white," Adele said.

"Yeah, just like God," Mr. Robinson said, then quickly turned his attention back to his newspaper before his granddaughters could drag him into another one of their debates.

The girls sat and watched two cartoons before Adele finally spoke up again. "I'm done watching cartoons. Time for the park." She stood up as if what she'd said was final.

"Yep, time for the park," Norma concurred.

Both Mr. and Mrs. Robinson stared at each other.

"Okay, let me call your mom again." Mrs. Robinson stood up and walked over to the phone and dialed Paige's number. It rang and rang and rang until it dumped her into voicemail. This was the case for both her cell and land line. Once again, Mrs. Robinson left a message. "Paige, this is not like you at all." This time around Mrs. Robinson sounded more perturbed than worried. Maybe she was just so worried it was making her mad. Nonetheless, she left her message. "These girls have been waiting patiently to go to the park. It's going on three o'clock. I don't think your father and I can hold them off any longer. Besides, the sandwiches are going to get soggy. Just meet us at Blacklick Park. I'm sure you'll find us on the big girl swings." Mrs. Robinson let out a small laugh that didn't do too good of a job at hiding the worry that was seeping back into her voice. "See you soon. Love you."

Mrs. Robinson hung up the phone, and before turning around to face her husband and grandchildren, she wiped away the lone tear that slid down her face. Something was wrong. Something was very wrong. Mother's intuition.

***

"Do you want to drop by Paige's house before we head back home?" Mr. Robinson had asked his wife as they packed up the car after spending two hours at the park with the girls.

Mrs. Robinson thought for a moment. "No, no. Let's just go home." Of course she wanted to go to her daughter's house to see what was going on. But once scene after scene of episodes from the ID channel popped into her head where family had found their loved ones dead, the last thing she wanted to do was have her grandchildren there to witness something bad.

"Grammy, did you see me on the big girl swing?" Norma asked excitedly, but got no response. "Grandma, did you?"

"Huh, what?" Mrs. Robinson said, snapping out of her thoughts about her daughter.

"Did you see me on the big girl swing? I went wayyyyyyy high."

Mrs. Robinson didn't want to lie to her granddaughter, but she did anyhow. "Yes, Grandma saw her big girl." She hadn't though. She'd been too busy looking around, hoping, and praying she'd see Paige walk up to them at the park. That never happened. The same way she had spent the last two hours thinking about Paige's whereabouts, she spent the twenty-minute ride home doing the same thing.

When Mr. Robinson pulled up into the driveway, Mrs. Robinson barely let him put the car in park before she went barreling out of the car and into their house. The first thing Mrs. Robinson did was go over to the phone and check her messages.

"You have twenty unheard messages," the automated system said. Mrs. Robinson sucked her teeth. She'd wished she'd listened to her husband a long time ago about checking and clearing out the messages on the voicemail. Mrs. Robinson wasn't a big talker and didn't really have people she spoke to on a regular basis, so she hardly was ever on the phone. But when Mr. Robinson missed a doctor's appointment they both had forgotten about and would have been reminded of had they checked the messages and heard the reminder call from the doctor, they could have avoided the fifty dollar no-show fee they'd been charged by the doctor's office.

Mrs. Robinson had promised to do better with checking messages, but that was months ago. So now here she had to go through about fifteen minutes' worth of messages to see if Paige had tried to call. And after going through about sixteen messages, Mrs. Robinson came to one that nearly made her heart skip a beat. She listened intensely. Just to make sure she'd heard the message correctly, she listened again. "Oh, God. Oh my God! Samuel!" she called out to her husband. "Samuel!"

When Mr. Robinson, who had been in the kitchen with the girls unpacking the picnic items, made his way to his wife, he found her standing there trembling with the phone in her hand. She was shaking so badly he thought the phone would shake right out of her hand. "What is it, honey?" He walked over to her and took the phone.

"Listen. Listen to the message," Mrs. Robinson pleaded.

Mr. Robinson placed the phone to his ear and replayed the message. He was speechless as he removed the phone slowly from his ear. "Oh, my God. When did we get this message?"

Mrs. Robinson hated to say. "Two weeks ago." Tears poured from her eyes as she kicked herself for not keeping her word and checking the voice messages regularly. Now because of it, Paige could be in trouble.

"If this message is two weeks old, then that means he's already out," Mr. Robinson said in horror. "He's already been released."

"That means he's been out of jail a week already."
Horror covered both Mr. and Mrs. Robinson's faces.
"He's got my baby," Mrs. Robinson said. "They done let
that man out of jail and he went and finished what he
started. Oh, God. He's done something to our daughter;
I just know it!"

Chapter Thirty-two

"I hate you! I hate you! I hate you!" With a piece of paper crushed inside each one of Paige's fists, she looked up to the heavens and cried out. Tears streamed down her face like a flowing river that had no ending place. If her eyes could shoot darts, she'd aim them at God's heart . . . if He even had one. As far as Paige was concerned, if God had a heart for her and He loved her as much as the Bible had professed, then why would He do something like this to her heart? Why would God tear it up into a million little pieces and serve it up to Satan on a silver platter . . . time and time again?

Paige sat on her bed and uncrumpled each document she held in her hands. She flattened one out and then the other. Her eyes went back and forth from one to the other. "God, you are supposed to be my joy. I know that no man can steal my joy, but I never once thought you'd take back something you gave me . . . and to take it back so quickly." Paige snickered. "Then again, I guess your Word does say that the Lord giveth, the Lord taketh away." She shook her head. "Guess some of these folks are right complaining about how the Bible contradicts itself." Paige balled her fist tight, closed her eyes tight, and screamed at the top of her lungs like she was about to explode. "My entire life is a contradiction. I don't trust joy anymore." She opened her eyes looking upward. "I don't trust you." Tears spilled endlessly from Paige's eyes. Time and time again Paige had given her trust to God, but it

seemed as though time and time again, He let her down.
Well this was it. No more of that on-again and off-again
crap with the Almighty. It was over between them. Trust
was the most important thing in a relationship. No trust,
no relationship. God had shown Paige exactly who He
was. Well she believed Him. He was a man . . . woman . . .
being . . . whatever that couldn't be trusted—ever!

"Why?" Paige cried out.

Had her daughters been home, Paige's wails would
have probably scared them to death. At the moment Paige
would have thanked God the girls were safe and sound at
her parents' house, but she wasn't about to thank God for
a darn thing! All she could fix her mouth to do right now
was curse Him.

Paige looked down at the HIV test results. They were
the last of the last HIV tests results she and her girls
would be having done. She'd made that decision a couple
weeks ago when she'd had her blood drawn. Although she
felt as though she was safe from not having contracted
the disease from Blake, considering the first two tests
were negative, she wanted to take another one for general
purpose. Third time was a charm . . . and final confirmation. That and the fact that she was getting closer than
ever with Ryan. She had no plans whatsoever to give her
body to him anytime soon, but they'd kissed and whatnot.
And after their date last night, she knew beyond a doubt
that one day she'd give him her heart.

If she didn't know any better, she'd say that last night on
their date she'd given him her soul, and he had given her
his. Before last night there had been so many details of her
life she felt compelled yet scared to share with him, and so
she'd kept the details locked and tucked securely within
her soul. There'd been so many intricate details she hadn't
laid out, one being the fact that her husband from her first
marriage had tested HIV-positive. She didn't want the ulti-

mate whammy, and the thing that forced her to reveal this detail, to be having to tell him that she was HIV-positive. So, she decided to go ahead and get one last test. Those test results were one of the wrinkled-up documents that now lay on Paige's bed. When Paige received the negative test results in this morning's mail, she was ecstatic. She'd done a Holy Ghost dance right there in her living room.

She'd cried tears of joy and then gathered enough composure to go on and read the rest of the mail. Now here she sat still crying, but now, after being greeted in the mailbox by the other document that lay on Paige's bed, she was no longer crying tears of joy. Just like always, she hadn't had a tight enough grip on joy and the devil had skipped along and snatched it out of her hand . . . and God had let him.

"No, no, no! He can't have my daughter. He can't!" Paige punched the letter she'd received in her mailbox today from Blake's attorney. They were kindly informing Paige that they'd learned of Adele's existence. In short, the letter said that they did the math and realized that unless Paige was, in fact, having an affair with Norman during their marriage, then Adele was Blake's child, in spite of Norman's name being on the birth certificate. A copy of the birth certificate was attached to the letter.

Paige read the attorney's letter again for the umpteenth time. Whenever she read the line about them filing an order for a paternity test, she cringed. "I could go away," Paige spoke. "I could pack up my babies and just go." She looked over at the family portrait of her and the girls that Ryan had taken that rested on her nightstand. "Isn't that right, little ones? Mommy can go away and it can be just the three of us. We'll live happily ever after. Just us. No man." Paige smiled, visualizing her fantasy. "Maybe a Caribbean island somewhere. We'll spend days on the beaches building sandcastles." She talked to the picture as if her daughters might respond. "How's that sound to you?"

Paige was taking her own thoughts seriously even though she knew one could run but they couldn't hide. The letter in hand had proven that. She'd tried to run from her problems, yet everything had caught up with her and seemed to be crumbling down. As much as she'd wanted to celebrate her negative HIV test and the positive life she wanted to start with Ryan, she couldn't because the black cloud of Blake trying to take her daughter away from her had consumed her.

"How did he even know? How did he even find out about Adele?" Paige asked herself. She tried to think of who could have told him, but they didn't have any mutual friends who could have passed on that information to Blake.

Fear tore through Paige's heart. "Maybe he hired someone to watch me. Maybe all this time someone has been watching every move I've made." With that thought, chills ran through Paige's body. She jumped up and ran over to her bedroom window and closed the open curtains after double-checking that the window was locked. Next she ran into her bathroom. Behind the shower curtain was a window that she usually kept open. The sound of running water mixed with the sounds of nature while showering always gave Paige a wave of peace. Now to know that someone might have been right outside her window each time she showered made her skin crawl.

As she approached the shower curtain, it moved and Paige's heart just about beat right out of her chest. *It's probably just the wind,* that voice in her head told her. Had she been watching herself on a theatre screen she would have been fussing and calling herself all kinds of idiots for not turning around and running. But this was reality and the naïve voice in her head was prevailing as she got a grip of the curtain and pulled it back.

She gasped even though there was nothing there. Her gasp was at the wind as if it had taken shape. But that's all that was behind the curtain: the invisible wind, the window, showerhead, and her brown sugar Soul Purpose shower body gels and scrubs.

After letting out a deep sigh of relief, she closed and locked the window. Next, Paige exited the bathroom and zipped through her bedroom and out into the hall. The hallway bathroom had no windows, so she bypassed it. She went into Norma's room and made sure the windows were locked and the blinds were closed.

"Ouch!" Paige tripped over one of Norma's toys and landed flat on her front side as she hurried to leave and go check Adele's room. Paige stood, brushed herself off, and then looked down at her stinging knee where she'd left pieces of rug-burned skin on her baby girl's bedroom floor.

Paige limped over to Adele's room as tears streamed down her face. Sure her skinned knee hurt, but not enough to draw tears. Her tears were a compilation of that physical pain and the pain her heart was feeling. Tears of anger. Mad at God for allowing the pain. Paige sniffed as she checked to make sure Adele's blinds were closed and windows locked.

She shook her head, wiping tears as new ones followed. She made sure the sliding patio doors were locked, the kitchen windows, the living room windows, and finally the front door. As she turned away from the front door she had a second thought. "The screen," she said, and then turned back to open the front door to make sure the screen was locked.

Paige swung the door open and was certain that as the scream erupted from her mouth, her heart had stopped. She couldn't breathe and she had no idea if she'd ever breathe again.

"Arrrrhhhh. Ahhhhhhh," Mrs. Robinson screamed when she saw her daughter through the screen door. "Oh my God, Paige. What's wrong? What happened? Is he here? What did he do to you?"

Paige's heartbeat had once again skyrocketed as her breath got caught in her throat. "Mom, nothing's wrong with me. What's wrong with you?" Paige asked through the screen door, finally able to catch her breath. "You're the one screaming."

"But I'm only screaming because you screamed."

"I only screamed because you scared the living daylights out of me when I opened up my door and saw you standing there. Why didn't you knock?" Paige still had her hand on her heart. She'd been in such a frenzy, running through the house like a madwoman in a horror movie making sure all the windows and doors were locked. When she flung open the door to check and make sure the screen was locked, all she saw was a figure. The tears in her eyes had already blurred her vision. Just the mere fact that she hadn't expected anyone to be standing there frightened her. The scream escaped before she could even make out the figure to be that of her own mother.

"I was about to knock but you flung the door open like a madwoman," Mrs. Robinson said, removing her hand from her chest and finally able to get her heart rate back to normal.

Paige just shook her head as she opened the door and let her mother in.

"Good, Lord, child. You were almost the death of me."

"Ditto." Paige was walking toward her couch but then she stopped in her tracks and turned toward her mother. "Who?"

Her mother looked at her with a puzzled look on her face. "Who what?"

"Who did you think did something to me? Ryan?" Paige rolled her eyes and shook her head. "Mom, Ryan isn't that type of guy. He's—"

"Blake." Mrs. Robinson swallowed hard as Paige stared at her. "I wasn't talking about Ryan. I was talking about Blake. I mean, yeah, at first I thought Ryan might have done something crazy to you, but then when I got that phone—"

"Mom, you know Blake is in jail. Why would he be here?" Paige couldn't wait for her mother to finish talking in order to get that question out. She had a feeling that her mother knew something that she didn't know. Paige didn't know if she wanted to know.

Mrs. Robinson hated to be the bearer of bad news. She took a step toward Paige. "No, Paige, not anymore. I . . . I . . . got a message." Mrs. Robinson gave off a nervous chuckle and shook her head. "You know me; never checking those voice messages." She let out a laugh that quickly evaporated, eaten up by the serious glare Paige was giving her.

"Mom, come on," Paige said, getting agitated. She just wanted her mom to spit it out. "What's going on?"

"Oh, baby. He's out. Blake's out of jail." Mrs. Robinson immediately walked over and put her arms around Paige who just stood frozen stiff, her eyes staring off into Neverland. "He's been out a week. I'm sorry, baby. The courts called the house and left a message. It was the only working phone number they had on your contact list. You know you've moved a thousand times since Blake went to jail. They called a couple weeks ago. I just got the message. I only checked the messages because I was worried sick about you. We were supposed to take the girls to the park today and then you didn't show up. You didn't call. I thought that maybe something had happened to you and then when I got that message I just thought . . . And then I just raced out the house to come see about you. Your father was calling after me trying to stop me but I just had to come see about my baby." Mrs. Robinson's words just kept going on and on and on. She was near hysterics.

Paige, in a zone she couldn't describe with words, patted her mother on the back. She'd ignored the ringing phones while she wallowed in misery after checking the mail. She'd been in no shape to pretend to be having fun with her girls at the park. She couldn't allow them to see her in this state.

"Mom, calm down. It's okay. I'm all right. Blake isn't here." Paige pulled away from her mother, then turned and walked away in thought. Here she'd been checking all her windows and doors just in case Blake had sicced some private detective on her to watch her every move. All along it could have been Blake himself watching her.

"Baby, are you all right? Do you want to come stay at the house with us for a while?"

Paige shook her head while still dazed. "No, no, Mom. I'm fine. Blake's not going to bother me."

"But how do you know? That man is crazy."

"Because I'm not the one he wants," Paige hated to say as she turned around to face her mother. "He wants Adele. He wants his daughter and I have a feeling that he'll stop at nothing to get her."

Chapter Thirty-three

This wasn't the first time Paige had found herself waiting in an attorney's conference room. The last time she sat in one she'd been on the same team as Blake. The woman he knew as his estranged mother tried to sue him for a ridiculous amount of money. Back then Blake had lost that battle. Paige was hoping for a repeat and that she would be the victor.

Paige thought she'd throw up while in the conference room the receptionist had directed her to in order to wait for the attorneys to arrive. No, maybe she'd die of suffocation from hyperventilation, if that was at all possible. Maybe she'd drown in the sweat she couldn't manage to keep under control. If it weren't for the fact she needed to live for her two daughters, she'd rather just die. But it was her daughters she was fighting for. Her daughters were the reason why she was going through such agony, at least one of them anyway. Adele. She had to protect Adele from the man she now considered a monster at all cost.

First thing Monday morning after receiving that letter from Blake's attorney, Paige had called the attorney and set up an appointment for that Wednesday to meet with him. That Saturday upon finding out about Blake's release and intentions toward Adele, Paige's mother had calmed her down; well, the two had managed to calm each other down, enough to have a conversation with clear minds. The result of the conversation was the two coming to the conclusion that Paige would stop assuming the worst and just hear the attorney out as far as Blake's desires.

"Maybe Blake really doesn't want Adele. Maybe he's just trying to scare you or get back at you for the years he spent in prison. He really probably just wants all his money back from that divorce settlement," Mrs. Robinson had reasoned. "You know how that man was when it came to money and the love of it. It truly was the root of all evil in his case. He put that clause in the divorce decree for a reason. He wasn't going to rest until he found a way to convince the world you'd cheated with Norman, and get his money back in return by doing so."

That had all made sense to Paige. It absolutely was a possibility. Blake knew that proving that she had committed adultery would void their divorce settlement and Paige would owe the monies back to him. That hadn't worried Paige. She'd give up that money in a heartbeat if it meant keeping Blake out of the early years of Adele's life. And that was her goal today. Wednesday could not have gotten here fast enough. Now neither could those darn attorneys.

Keeping hope alive, Paige had abandoned her idea of packing up the girls and leaving the country. But it wasn't something she wouldn't revisit if things didn't go as planned today in her meeting with Blake's attorney. As a matter of fact, it was still an option. She was alone. She could stand up and walk out of that conference room at any moment without anyone stopping her. Without anyone trying to reason with her. Not even her own conscience and certainly not the voice of God. She'd tuned that out for once and for all.

As if having an out-of-body experience, Paige stood. She walked over to the conference room door and placed her hand on the doorknob. She'd kept a couple gifts from Blake, who was now her sworn enemy. She'd keep one from God as well. She'd keep the free will He'd given her. And she'd use it—now.

***

Paige ran into her house without even closing the front door. In her four-inch heels, she made her way straight toward her basement door, flung it open, and barreled down the flight of steps.

"Uggghhh," Paige said as she missed the last step and landed flat on her bottom on the hard concrete. Why hadn't she gotten the basement finished? Had she, she would have at least landed on carpet with some padding underneath it. Her back rammed into the edge of the step, shooting unbearable pain up her spine. In tremendous pain, she wished she could just sit there and wallow in it until it went away . . . until it became at least bearable. But she'd tried that in life before, and each time the pain never seemed to go away, or was replaced by something even more painful. Besides that, she had no time to spare. Once her attorney arrived in that conference room to find that she was no longer waiting, he'd surely put two and two together and come looking for her. But she'd be gone, long gone. Her and her two girls gone forever.

Limping over to the storage area of her basement, Paige proceeded to push, move, and throw boxes and plastic containers filled with out-of-season clothing, Christmas decorations, and other miscellaneous items out of her way. Paige collected the luggage set she'd been digging for. No, it wasn't Louis Vuitton, but it would hold the small pieces of her and her daughters' lives that she could manage to fit in them.

With all her strength and trying to ignore the pain in her back, Paige placed the strap of the carryon on her shoulder while lugging the large and medium suitcases up the basement steps. Right when she got to the top step, the larger one went tumbling back down the steps.

"No!" Paige yelled as she watched it land. Frustrated, her eyes filled with tears of pain, anger, and fear of being caught before she could go to the preschool, scoop up her girls, jump in her SUV, and drive as far away as she could.

She flung the medium-sized suitcase and carryon onto the top landing and went after the large suitcase. With the lone suitcase in hand, she made it back to the top of the steps and threw it down. Paige grabbed the carryon and proceeded to hit the girls' bathroom and her private bathroom, filling it with all the toiletries and necessities she felt they needed to get through the next couple days at least. Once she'd done that, she dragged the larger suitcase into the girls' room and filled it with as many undergarments and outfits of the girls she could. Last but not least, the medium-sized suitcase she filled with as many of her belongings as she could.

She carried the overstuffed suitcases out to the SUV with contents spilling through the parts she was unable to zip closed. Thank God she wasn't flying. She'd have to pay a fortune in overweight and extra baggage fees.

After putting the luggage in the back hatch of her SUV, last but not least Paige went back into the house and randomly gathered some of the girls' toys. Her eyes did a quick sweep of the house. The kitchen doorway prompted her to go and at least get a couple of snacks and juice boxes to tide the girls over until she found a place to lay their heads for the night. With an armful of toys she walked into the kitchen. Every time she grabbed a box of crackers, cookies, fruit cup, or juice box, an item from her hand would fall to the floor. And each time an expletive would fall from Paige's mouth. She didn't care about being a cussin' Christian trying to stay saved. The only thing she cared about right now was saving Adele from Blake.

Eventually she gave up on trying to juggle everything, leaving a trail of items that had fallen from her arms behind her. Whatever got left behind simply got left behind. Paige didn't even bother to close her front door after exiting the house. For one, her arms were full and if she had tried she would have dropped everything. For two, she never planned on returning to that house, that life, ever again anyway. And with that, she threw the contents of everything in her arms into the opened hatch, closed it, and headed for the driver's side.

"My purse!" she shouted, then made a beeline back toward her house. Before she even made it to the steps she remembered she hadn't even carried her purse into the house. It was, hopefully, still sitting in the passenger's seat where she'd left it after frantically leaving the attorney's office building and jumping into her vehicle.

Finally situated in the driver's seat, Paige went to start the car, only the keys weren't in the ignition. "No, no, no!" she yelled, beating her fist against the steering wheel. She dropped her forehead onto the steering wheel, feeling defeated and drained. At this point she just wanted to give up. Forget about fleeing town with her daughters. But she couldn't give up. Giving up would mean giving up on Adele. She couldn't live with herself if she decided to do that. So once again, Paige ran back into her house. She revisited every room she'd been in, looking for the keys to no avail.

"Where could they be?" She found herself standing in the middle of her living room in tears asking herself. That's when she looked to the open basement door. "The basement," she said, snapping her fingers and making her way toward the basement door and then down the stairs. Over in the storage area was where she found the keys lying. She'd thrown them down in her pursuit of digging out the luggage.

Paige breathed in, exhaled, and then headed up the basement steps. She'd done it. She'd managed to pack up as much of her and her girls' life into her SUV in record time. With keys in hand, she powerwalked to the front door, placed her hand on the screen doorknob, and opened the door . . . only to find him standing there.

Chapter Thirty-four

"Jesus Christ you scared me," Paige said once she'd opened the conference room door and found her attorney standing there.

"I'm sorry, Paige," Rudy Fergunstein, Paige's attorney, said as he entered the conference room Paige had been waiting in the last few minutes per the receptionist's instructions. "I'm late as well. My court hearing ran over." Rudy was a small—Kevin Hart small—soft, yet very well-spoken man. He wasn't the least bit intimidating in stature, but his knowledge of the law and the legal system wasn't to be reckoned with. Rudy definitely knew his way around the law the same way a fat kid knew his way around a bakery. Rudy was very intelligent and always played by the rules. He felt one didn't have to play dirty in order to come out clean. Seeing him standing there reminded Paige to play clean and by the rules. Although just seconds ago she envisioned successfully going back to her house, gathering her and her girls' belongings, and fleeing town with them, it wasn't the right thing to do. It would only come back to haunt her. She had to trust in Rudy's skills to get her through this. That's all she had left.

"No problem, Rudy. Thank you for coming through for me last minute. It's great to see you again."

Paige hadn't seen Rudy since he helped her file for divorce from Blake. He was working for legal aid then. Now he had his own family practice firm with his brother and sister as partners. He'd made sure Paige remained on his mailing list, sending out postcards and letters at least once a year. Paige felt indebted to Rudy for his free services and support back in the day. She promised if she ever got in a position where she needed legal representation, Rudy would be her man. She'd patronize him without second thought. The minute she'd gotten off of the phone with Blake's attorney, she'd called up Rudy. Now here he stood ready to help her at perhaps the fight of her life, and unknowingly, arriving just in time to have stopped her from doing something she could have possibly lived to regret.

"I asked Mr. Dickenson's attorney to give me a minute with you to go over some things," Rudy said, taking a file and spreading it out on the conference room table as he sat down next to Paige. "We have several options we can entertain, but first we need to hear exactly what your ex-husband is seeking: custody, partial custody, full custody with child support, or just the return of his money paid to you in the divorce settlement. Who knows? But I do want you to know that you do, in fact, have options. I don't want you to feel weak and powerless in your situation. You have power, Paige," he said sincerely.

"Well that makes me feel a little better." Paige exhaled and allowed her tense shoulders to somewhat relax.

"I'm not saying this just to make you feel better. It's the truth. In all honesty, I don't see any judge taking a child away from its mother and giving it to a felon fresh out of jail, a child who doesn't know the man from Adam."

Paige nodded. That's another thing she hadn't taken into consideration. Thank goodness for Rudy. The five minutes Rudy was able to spend with Paige to go over some possibilities wasn't a lot of time, but it was enough to let Paige know that Blake had major strikes against him. The ball truly was in her court, and Blake couldn't just come onto her home court and try to steal it. And neither did she necessarily have to pass him the ball. Not that she considered this a game or Adele a ball. There was far more at stake.

"Mrs. Vanderdale," Blake's attorney, Randall, started when he entered the room. "We meet again." He was the same attorney who had represented Blake in the suit between Blake and his mother.

"We do." Paige nodded, trying not to be the image of the stereotypical angry black woman Randall had once witnessed her to be. The kind Norman's mother thought all women of color were thanks to those reality shows. She smiled and willed herself to remain cordial versus hold it against the man for having the nerve to represent someone like Blake, a known felon. A known violent felon.

She did hope, though, that she didn't have to kick off her shoes and run across that conference room table and get at the man if he wasn't talking right.

"Rudy, my man." Blake's attorney shook hands with Paige's attorney. "Haven't seen you since the bar association shindig. How's the wife and kids?"

"The wife is fine. Just one kid. Junior is well," Rudy replied.

"Good, good," he said while flipping through a file he carried, showing just how disinterested he truly was in Rudy's wife and kid. "So, first things first, as I'm sure none of us have time to waste. Adele. She wasn't born premature was she?" He stared right at Paige.

"Well, uh . . ." For a split second Paige wanted to lie. She wanted to let out a big, fat "Yes! She was born three months early . . . maybe four." She could tell already which road Blake's no-good attorney was about to travel before he even put the car in drive and his foot on the gas pedal. A lie would have shut him down. Paige could have easily lied and said she'd gotten pregnant later, after her last sexual encounter with Blake, but that she'd had the baby early. But Rudy nodding for Paige to go ahead and tell the truth put a stop to it. *Rudy to the rescue yet again.* "She was pretty much born on her due date."

"You married a Mr. Norman Vanderdale . . . what, the same month your divorce was final?" Randall said it as if that made Paige the lowest of all jezebels.

"I did," Paige said with her head held high. *This man is not going to break me down.*

"Hmmm. Talk about shotgun wedding." Blake's attorney laughed.

"If you don't mind," Rudy interrupted, "can we just get to exactly what it is that your client wants since he chose not to show up himself?"

Blake's attorney smirked at Rudy and then turned his attention to Paige. "Mrs. Vanderdale, during the divorce hearing you were under oath, correct?" It was obvious this man loved to dance around because he certainly had on his dancing shoes and was a master at the two-step.

"Yes. That's correct," Paige replied.

"And during the divorce hearing you were asked several questions under oath? Correct?"

"Come on; what is this? My client isn't on trial here. What's up with the theatrical cross-examination?" Rudy interrupted, just about fed up with his counterpart's dramatic tactics. He was a trial lawyer and it showed.

"No, she's not on trial. Not yet anyway." Blake's attorney let a devilish grin spread across his lips.

"Paige, please just answer the man's question so we can move on," Rudy said, shaking his head.

Paige did as she was instructed. "Yes, I was asked several questions," Paige said. "Like my attorney said, can we please just get on with this?"

Blake's attorney nodded. "Certainly." He scanned a paper and continued. "I actually pulled the transcript from the divorce hearing between you and my client. One of the questions the judge asked you was whether you knew yourself to be pregnant at the time of the divorce. And you answered this question under oath, did you not?" His eyes darted knowingly back and forth between Paige and her attorney.

Right then and there Paige thought she was going to throw up. A pain swept through her gut that felt like she'd made the wrong move on the dance floor with Blake's attorney and he'd stomped her foot. Hard. And she'd been wearing an open-toe shoe.

When Paige looked to Rudy and his face looked as if he'd eaten a rotten apple four weeks ago and now it was filled with maggots, she knew this wasn't looking good.

Blake's attorney didn't hide the fact that he was getting a thrill out of this by his smug expression. "By the look on both of your faces, I can see the two of you know exactly where this is heading." He had victory written all over his face. "Lying under oath is a very serious charge. You do know that if you told the judge you weren't pregnant at the time of the divorce and you really were . . ." He shook his head and let out a tsk.

Paige, in her heart, knew that she had not knowingly lied under oath. She'd absolutely had no idea that she was pregnant when she'd stood before that judge and stated such. But with the whole shotgun marriage to Norman before the ink even dried on the divorce papers, she'd have a hard time proving that to any jury of her peers. No one would believe her. No judge, no jury. She'd end up in jail for sure. By the time she got out, Adele would probably be in the custody of her father, her biological father, Blake! Just that thought put Paige into such a panic that she began to spurt out words without first consulting her attorney.

"What do you want? The money from the divorce settlement back? For me to announce to the world that I cheated on Blake, and therefore he had every right to be upset and beat me and rape me? Huh? Is that what you want?" Paige cried, standing and hitting the table with her fist.

"Paige, please, don't say another word," Rudy tried to warn her.

Paige ignored his plea. "Because if that's what you want, that's what you can have," Paige said. "I don't care. He can have every dime and then some. Just please don't take my daughter from me. Please." Paige wept like a baby as she melted back down into her seat.

Rudy placed his hand on Paige's shoulder to try to calm her down . . . and to remind her that he was there to do the talking for her. Although it was just a tad bit late for that. It was a turnover. Looked like Team Blake now had the ball.

Blake's attorney just sat there stoic. It was killing him not to display his excitement of seeing Paige break down. After a few seconds of having a stare down with Paige he finally spoke. "Are you finished, Mrs. Vanderdale?"

Breathing deeply, Paige realized she'd made a scene. She hadn't taken off her shoes and run across the conference table, nor thrown the pitcher of water that sat in the middle of the table at Blake's attorney. But she wouldn't be telling the truth if she said there wasn't a part of her that wanted to. She swallowed and held her head up high, even though she really wanted to just crawl up under the table.

Blake's attorney stood and took the floor. "Your daughter, Adele. She's an heir to the Vanderdales, as in Norman Vanderdale Sr. who took over his wife's family business?" He looked to Paige. "Hmmm. You hit the jackpot didn't you? You know, I can't blame you one way or the other for getting your deceased husband, God rest his soul, to sign that child's birth certificate. You certainly get to wear the crown of gold diggers." He laughed.

"Okay, that's it!" Paige stood and had bent over to remove her shoe before Rudy stopped her.

"Please, Paige. I think it's a fine time you let me do what you're paying me to do. Let me do all the talking from now on. Please. Okay?" His eyes pleaded with Paige to just be quiet and trust him.

With eyes shooting daggers and steam flushing out her ears, Paige silently agreed as she sat back down.

Rudy exhaled and straightened his tie. He then gave Blake's attorney his full attention. "Look, first of all I didn't come here for you to insult my client," Rudy said in a stern tone, one he didn't even know he had in him. It was a tone that immediately captured the opposing attorney's attention. "Now either you tell us what you want so we can work something out that satisfies both parties, or do what you have to do. Like you said, Mrs. Vanderdale here isn't wanting for money. She hit the jackpot with the Vanderdales who are well-loved and recognized members of the community. They are honest God-fearing people who have an excellent relationship with not only their grandchildren, but the mother of their grandchildren. As a matter of fact"—he turned to Paige—"don't you and Mrs. Vanderdale attend church together?"

Paige nodded as she watched Rudy in astonishment do his thing. This kitten was turning into a roaring lion right in front of her face.

Rudy directed his words back to Blake's attorney. "And don't think for one minute the Vanderdales won't spend every dime of their money seeing to it that by the end of this, both you and your client will make Satan look like Shirley Temple. Your client is a rapist, a woman beater, and a man who slept with his wife's best friend. He's now

HIV-positive. Now I typically don't play dirty, but since you invited me into your pig pen, I might as well sling a little mud."

Paige didn't realize a huge smile was on her face and the voice in her head was cheering Rudy on. *Get him. Get him good!*

Rudy continued, "So you have five seconds to lay it all out on the table or you'll be figuring out how to explain why your client knowingly slept with this woman knowing he was HIV-positive. It was his way of getting back at her. It was attempted murder."

"That's a lie and you know it!" Blake's attorney stood, wagging a finger at Rudy.

"Prove it!" Rudy spat.

Paige sat on the edge of her seat in excitement. Oh how the lion was roaring.

Rudy continued his roaring. "The same way my client will have to prove that she had no idea she was pregnant at the time of the divorce hearing, your client will have to prove that he didn't know he was HIV-positive and had set out to destroy this woman's life by purposely trying to infect her with it. This woman has had to take test after HIV test and has been mentally affected by it tremendously. Oh my, and if at the time your client had sex with my client against her will knowing he was infected with HIV, and she in fact was pregnant at the time, I guess that would make it two counts of attempted murder. Jesus, this could be a huge mess! Isn't that right?" he said to Blake's attorney, who stood speechless with his mouth gaped open.

Well, Rudy had done it. He'd managed to silent Blake's attorney. Looked like the dog's bark had been far worse than his bite. Finally, after what seemed like forever, he tried to speak.

"No, no need to speak now," Rudy said. "Since you didn't take the opportunity when it was given to you, I'm going to keep speaking and be the one to lay my offer on the table."

Hot darn! Paige thought.

Rudy had taken back possession of the ball. "Your client will get every cent back from the divorce settlement."

Blake's attorney swallowed hard. "That's fine because that's all we ever really want—"

"I'm not finished," Rudy stopped him. "And those funds will be put in a trust for his daughter serving as back child support and future child support until the child turns eighteen or graduates college, whichever is the latter."

"But—" Blake's attorney started.

"Shut up! I'm not finished," Rudy spat. "You had your turn to talk and you should have used the time to do something other than try to throw daggers at my client. You wanted to dance around the issue, well, get to dancing to the tune of the fat lady singing because this is about to be over for once and for all."

Paige had to sit on her hands to keep from pumping her fists in the air.

"Now I'm sure you'll want to talk visitation or something," Rudy said, getting no response from his opponent. This alone let Rudy know right then and there that the intention never was to get Adele. It was to get money and to humiliate Paige. "My client will grant your client visitation rights . . ."

Paige went to speak but Rudy's next words halted her.

"Over her dead body!" Now it was Rudy who let out a sinister chuckle. "You and I both know that no judge in their right mind is going to give that man visitation, not with all the dirt the Vanderdales are going to pay the best private detectives in the world to dig up on your client.

Your client can try to dispute whatever he likes, but who do you think society is going to believe? A convict or the pillars of the community?" Rudy shrugged. "But if you want to try us, then do so. But if you ask me, if you close your eyes and even dream about crossing the Vander-dales, when you wake up the next morning, you should call them up and apologize for just dreaming about it." Rudy winked and then began to gather his things. Once he'd collected the entire file that had been spread across the table, he nodded for Paige to stand up. It was time for them to leave.

Rudy still had some final parting words. "Now, you can take everything back to your client that we just discussed. In the meantime, I'll have an agreement drawn up and a courier will deliver it to your office by the end of the week. Until the next bar association shindig, you and your wife and kids take care."

"I'm uh, not married. I have a life partner and a golden retriev—"

"All set?" Rudy said to Paige, displaying the fact that he truly hadn't the slightest concern about the man's family life.

Paige nodded and allowed Rudy to escort her to the door. Paige stopped once she made it to the conference room door. "Can I just ask you one thing?" Paige said before they exited the conference room. "How did you even find out about Adele?"

"From you," Blake's attorney replied.

Paige was confused. She'd never talked to the man or, to her knowledge, anyone who even knew the man.

"Well, you didn't tell me exactly," he clarified. "It was the conversation you had with the prison doctor. You mentioned something about getting an HIV test during your pregnancy. That information was passed on to your ex-husband and the rest, as they say, is history."

Well, there Paige had it. She and her attorney left the conference room cool, calm, and collected. Once Paige and Rudy were on the elevator and the doors closed, Paige threw her arms around Rudy.

"Oh my God. You were wonderful in there. You were great. You saved my baby. You did it." She released him from the tight hug.

"Yeah, well," Rudy said, sounding modest. "But I'm just glad we got out of there when we did."

"Why?" Paige asked.

"Because I was out of control. You saw me. I mean, who was that guy in there? In five more seconds I was either going to turn into Al Pacino and start yelling, 'You're out of order.' Or I was going to get my Jack Nicholson on and shout out, 'You can't handle the truth.'"

On that note, both Paige and Rudy laughed the entire elevator ride all the way down to the lobby. Everything had worked out for Paige's good in the end, even with all her truths being on the table. Blake Dickenson or his attorney would not be picking on her anymore. Game over!

Chapter Thirty-five

"You preach, Pastor Margie," Naomi shouted as she stood to her feet. She looked over at Paige, her eyes willing her to join her in agreement. Paige simply smiled and nodded, not even thinking twice about getting on her feet.

It was only obvious to Paige that she wanted to be anywhere but in church right now. The outside world only saw the smile she wore that peeked out from underneath the brim of her church hat. Or the clapping of her hands to one of the popular church songs the choir sang on a regular basis. Even today as she clapped from the pew instead of the choir stand, no one saw through the mask. No one saw how jaded she was with church and the whole God thing. She didn't even want to lift her voice up in that place, let alone lift her butt up off that pew.

She'd told the choir director she didn't feel well and was trying to nurse away a sore throat. She didn't want to get anyone else sick by being up there in the choir stand breathing all over them. She'd put the nail in the coffin when she added, "Because if I didn't know any better, I'd think I'm coming down with the flu. I seem to have all the symptoms." With the choir scheduled to perform in a local gospel choir competition, the last thing the director wanted was for Paige to be in close quarters with the other choir members and pass on the bug to them. So while everyone else sang praises to God, Paige just sat and quietly countered their every word.

"God has been so good to me," the choir sang.

"Lucky you," Paige groaned under her breath. "Wish I could say the same."

"The struggle is over," they sang next.

"For who?" Paige seethed. "Surely not me." She sucked her teeth and thought, *Even if my struggle does end, you best believe there's one waiting for me right around the corner.*

"Don't give up on God."

"Tah." Paige almost laughed on that one. Even if she had, no one would have heard her. No one could make out what she was saying over the tunes of the music ministry behind the choir's vocals. To them it just looked like she was singing along with the choir. "I should have given up on this whole 'trying to stay saved' thing a long time ago; then maybe the devil would have left me alone."

Finally the choir had made it through its usual three songs: two fast, one slow. Now it was time for Pastor Margie to preach. Any rebuttals that Paige had about the Word that was about to go forth, she'd have to keep in her head. This was going to be hard. She didn't want to hear the Word of God. She didn't want to hear anything He had to say, no matter who He said it through. As a matter of fact, she didn't even want to be here in the church. She'd done nothing but curse God since she got home from her meeting with Blake's attorney this past Wednesday.

Sure she'd gotten the victory that day in the conference room. Rudy had drafted and delivered the two-page document to Blake's attorney personally on Friday. Blake had been in attendance this time. Blake received a cashier's check from Paige in the exact amount she was awarded in their divorce. It was arranged for a third-party accountant to be there to set the fund up for Adele. Everything went off without a hitch. When Rudy left the conference room, the document was signed. Per their signed agreement, Blake would not press the issue of custody of Adele. Informing the child of her biological father's identity would be left to Paige's discretion. Everything had turned out in Paige's favor, but she refused to jinx herself and celebrate. And she also refused to give God the credit. Who cared if things always appeared to turn out well for her? What did it really matter knowing God would see to it that another trial would arise to break her down?

In this instance, she gave the credit to Rudy. It was he who stood up for her against Blake's attorney. It was him Paige saw working it out to get her out of the lion's den. It was God who allowed her to be placed in it. She'd leave it to the rest of the world to give God credit for stuff. She was sure He wouldn't miss her. She was sure He wouldn't have missed her today in church either. But when Naomi had called her last night to confirm dinner after church today, she'd ended the phone conversation with, "See you in church tomorrow."

Well, Paige had already told Naomi she and the girls would be over for dinner, so she felt put on the spot and couldn't come up with a way out of going to church quick enough. What would it have looked like if she made her way over to the Vanderdales' to feed her face but didn't go to church? Paige felt it was much easier to sit through this two-hour torture than explaining her absence from church to Naomi for two hours.

Pastor Margie was already ten minutes into her sermon when Paige had no other option but to tune into the program already in progress. She'd already read through the church bulletin twice. She couldn't find anything else to divert her attention to.

"So, saints, with all that being said," Pastor Margie said, "if I were to give you a title for today's message it would be 'You Ain't Sick; You Just Got the Symptoms.'"

Paige began to cough, and not to play along with her little white lie about being sick. It was a real cough. Her saliva had gone down the wrong pipe. She was swallowing when Pastor Margie spoke the words that convicted her about the lie she'd told about being sick.

"You okay?" Naomi whispered in Paige's ear.

Holding her throat and swallowing to moisten her pipes, Paige was only able to nod.

"Now I usually never preach behind anyone else or recycle someone else's sermon, but today, for the first time in all my years of ministry, I'm led to share a message I received over at Power and Glory Ministries by the house prophetess. Now some of you may say, 'She's preaching somebody else's word.' But at the end of the day, when God's using you as His servant to speak for Him, it's His Word.'"

"Amen," several congregants called out.

"Whose word is it?" Pastor Margie asked.

"God's Word," was the congregation's reply.

"I'm not going to say everything Prophetess said verbatim, but I will speak it however the Lord gives it to me." Pastor Margie smiled and continued, briefly glancing down at her notes that lay next to her open Bible. "Now I don't know about the rest of you, but I've been delivered from some things in my walk with Christ. Even as a pastor, I'm still getting delivered from some stuff." She stopped in her tracks. "Oh yeah, y'all go on and let out y'all's gasps. I know that some folks do what we like to call people pedestal worshipping: making folks out to be more than what they truly are, which is human. But y'all's pastor is human. Can someone say human?"

The congregation obliged. "Human."

"I know there is some big stuff some of you have had to get delivered from, stuff like drugs, alcohol, fornication, pornography, adultery, et cetera. But can I share the number one thing folks who come to the Kingdom have to get delivered from? Well maybe I shouldn't say Kingdom. Maybe I should just say the folks who come to this church. But nonetheless, the number one thing is that old cussing demon."

There was laughter and chuckles throughout the sanctuary.

"Ummm, hmmm. I hear you laughing now, but I know some of you don't even make it out the church parking lot good without letting that tongue rip."

Again there was more laughter.

"You know you right, Pastor!" someone shouted.

"So let's just say you got delivered from the cussing demon and you never said a cuss word for an entire decade. Because as you know, you do choose to cuss. Cuss words don't just slip out. Amen?"

"Amen," a few members replied back.

"So after all these years," Pastor Margie continued, standing behind the podium, looking down at her notes every few seconds or so, "someone gets on that one nerve that's been at the bottom of the barrel for the last ten years and now it's the last and only nerve. That nerve that had been your saving grace gets jumped all on and battered. The next thing you know you choose to let loose all those cuss words that have been suppressed, piling up under that last nerve. I mean you cuss that person out left and right. Even if you don't cuss them out in their face, you are walking the floor of your own home just letting it rip while you talk about them."

Folks couldn't help but laugh because they knew Pastor Margie was telling the truth. A few of them were guilty of what she was speaking about.

"Umm, hmm. I hear y'all laughing because you know I'm telling the truth."

"Speak the truth, Pastor," someone called out.

"So you finish dropping F-bombs and everything else and then all of sudden, you feel awful. All unholy. And you feel . . . empty. Something's missing. It doesn't take long for you to figure out that the Holy Spirit had to get to stepping. He couldn't be a part of that. He couldn't reside in that filthy dwelling. That's not who the Holy Spirit is. I don't care who you are and what you say, the Holy Spirit is never going to tell you to cuss or to cuss someone out. Period, point blank."

Members began to clap.

"I know some of y'all like to use the comparison of Peter cursing in the Bible. 'Well, the Bible said Peter cursed,'" Pastor Margie mocked with a know-it-all expression on her face. "But come on, saints. There is a difference between cursing, cussing and swearing. 'I swear to God,' which we all know we are not supposed to do or say, is swearing. 'God D word,' or sending somebody to hell, if you know what I mean, is cursing. But just outright reading somebody with every profane, vulgar obscenity that exists, to include but not limited to the F-bomb and the B-word, now that's cussing!"

"Teach us, Pastor."

"Help us!"

"Oh, I'm going to help somebody all right. Somebody is going to get set free today," Pastor Margie said, taking a handkerchief that rested on the podium and dabbing the corners of her mouth. "And I know some of you will even try to say when Jesus turned those tables over he was going off. Well even if he cussed, even the Bible didn't print the cuss words for you to say, now did it?"

"You right about that," was heard from the back of the sanctuary.

"Getting back to my message, so now that you done cussed like a sailor, feeling empty and convicted, you start to feel alone . . . like God is no longer with you. Then you start questioning things. You start saying to yourself, 'I know I got delivered from that cussing demon. I remember lying right out on the floor at the altar, kicking and screaming and throwing up in the trashcan . . . running around the church sanctuary. I thought I was delivered because I went ten whole years without cussing.'" She shrugged her shoulders and made a goofy face. "'Guess I didn't get delivered after all.'"

There were some sighs and head nods.

"But I'm here to tell you, saints, don't you question the power of God!" Pastor Margie's voice grew loud as she whipped from around that podium. "When God delivers you, you are delivered. God does not fail at what He does. You are still delivered. You are still saved. What you experienced was just an impression of who you used to be that the devil finally achieved at bringing forth. See, the devil knows he has no power over your future so he has to keep a tight grip on your past, of who you used to be, to mess you all up. But let me hear you shout out 'I ain't me no more.'"

Naomi had recalled Pastor Margie having a sermon about that when she'd first attended New Day. That sermon had helped usher her into the understanding of who she was in God. She was glad to jump to her feet and shout it out like she'd done before. "I ain't me no more."

"You know how you meet someone for the first time, you two go your separate ways but they might leave an impression of themselves on you? Or if you wear a ring for a long time and you take it off, there is an impression of the ring on your finger. Now the person is not there anymore, but the impression they left behind is in your mind. Now the ring is not there anymore, but there is an impression of it left on your finger. But it's not real. It's gone. Just like that demon is gone. That spirit is gone. But there is an impression that Satan has put on your mind. Oh my God, your mind . . . the battlefield!"

"You say that, Pastor. You say it!"

The congregation went crazy while some pumped their fists, did a Holy Ghost dance, and even ran around the church sanctuary. Some just sat with silent tears rolling down their face.

"So what I need you to do is rid yourself of that impression of whatever that thing is right now. Impressions are reminders of a thing even though it's long gone. Declare that thing long gone and to stay gone and to take its impression with it in the name of Jesus. It wasn't real. God saved you. God delivered you. No one can beat Him. He is the most powerful and the most high. Hallelujah! That impression of yourself the devil is placing before you trying to convince you that is who you really are cannot beat who God made you to be. Who God made you to be: a wonderfully made child of the King who is holy and acceptable unto Him . . . and who does not do unholy things and that includes cussing!"

Members began to cry out and some even rebuked the devil. Pastor Margie did a little dance while a couple other members joined her.

Pastor Margie used her handkerchief to wipe her mouth again and then continued. "I don't have to tell y'all that this ain't about no cussing demon. I'm just using that as an example. That's just a thing and we all got something. That thing had some of y'all in a funk because it had you doubting the power of God. Had you doubting who God says He is . . . and even who God says you are. Had some of you backsliding, walking around talking about, 'Well, since I wasn't really delivered, I might as well go on back to my old self, my old ways. Since I cussed, I might as well get drunk. Since I cussed and got drunk, I might as well sleep with old boy from around the way . . . even though he got a wife. Fornication and adultery; might as well kill two birds with one stone.'"

There were a couple chuckles.

"So do you see where I'm going with this, saints? Do you see what just one impression of something can lead to? But I'll say it again. It ain't real. It's a façade. A mirage. An illusion. In other words, it's a lie. Don't you believe it. The devil is a liar!" Pastor Margie shouted. "Don't you let the devil trick you into believing that you didn't get delivered and that you can't stay delivered." The New Day congregation was on their feet. It was rare that Pastor Margie got loud during her sermons, creating such an emotionally charged service. That wasn't her typical style, but she was out of control today. God was in control.

God was in control and anyone in that sanctuary could see it, including Paige. Paige knew that woman who had just preached was not her usual pastor. If it wasn't her usual pastor, then it could have been only one other thing: God. Paige couldn't argue, or come to any other conclusion, than God was now using Pastor Margie to deliver a message with power and unapologetic boldness. And that's when Paige also put two and two together and concluded that she'd witnessed the same actions in Rudy.

"God was there," Paige said under her breath, a tear streaming from her eye. God had, in fact, been there for her. He had been in that conference room that day acting on her behalf, through the appointed person, Rudy. And today He was doing it again through Pastor Margie.

"So once your heart, mind, body, and soul is filled with doubt," Pastor Margie said, now using her regular soft tone, "don't nothing look right anymore. Everything is wrong. Everything looks wrong. All this bad stuff is happening to you and you use that as confirmation that God isn't who He says He is. God doesn't love you. God isn't there to protect you. If He was, then why does all this bad stuff keep happening to you? Why is nothing going right? Why, when it rains, does it pour? And the big one y'all: 'why is more being put on me than I can bear!'"

"Hallelujahhhhhhhh!" That ringing sound pierced Paige's eardrums. It took her a minute to realize she was the one shouting it out. Now standing on her feet with one hand lifted, Paige allowed tears to fall freely from her eyes as she continued to listen to her pastor.

"I hear you, saints, I hear you. 'I just don't understand why God is subjecting me to all this,'" Pastor Margie mocked. "I'm here to tell you today that God is not subjecting you to anything. He's injecting you. It's part of your immunization."

There were some puzzled looks among the congregation.

"Oh, I see I done lost some of you." Pastor Margie chuckled. "Well, let me see if I can help some of you find your way back, not get too deep but make it plain."

"Make it plain, Pastor," someone instructed.

"You know how when you get injected with the flu immunization, after a couple days or so you might wake up feeling like you have the flu? I mean, your head hurts. Your throat hurts. Body is aching in some areas. You have to really stop and say to yourself, 'I know I got the flu immunization, but I think I still done caught that dang on flu anyway. I got that stupid shot and it didn't work. I still caught the flu. I'm sick.'" Pastor Margie was rubbing her head, putting her hands on her throat and bending over as if in pain. "You have all the symptoms of the flu because, basically, you were injected with the flu antibodies. Because of this injection, your body will now know how to fight off the flu. The injection subjected you to the symptoms, of what it might feel like. But because of this immunization, you can now be around someone who actually does have the flu and it will not hurt you. It will not make you sick. You will not die."

"Glory! I will not die," Paige yelled out.

"I know where you're going with this, Pastor, preach!" the lady next to Paige yelled as Paige continued to cry a river.

"You've already experienced the symptoms of the flu through immunization, so when you are subjected to the real thing, baby, you can withstand it. You will survive. But the effects of that immunization make you think you are sick, but you ain't sick; it's just the symptoms."

Applause and praise flooded the sanctuary as Pastor Margie made her way back behind the podium to wrap things up. "As parents we have to make sure our children receive immunization shots so that they are protected against something they might come into contact with that could kill them. That could destroy and tear down their little bodies until death is welcomed versus the pain. We would never want that to happen to our children. Well, our Father feels the same way about us." Pastor Margie pointed up to the heavens and then placed her hands on her Bible that lay open on the podium. "Those shots we subject our children to, they hurt. They are painful. They make them uncomfortable. Grouchy and mean some-times. They give some of them all types of symptoms and side effects that make them think they won't live through it. Again, saints, that's what our Heavenly Father does for us. So, in closing, what I need you to get is that God is not subjecting you to all kinds of bad stuff. He's not turning His face from you in order to let Satan have his way with you. God is injecting you . . . with immunization. He's not subjecting you; He's injecting you. And just like with our babies, there is a series of immunizations, but when all is said and done, the power of the injection is stronger than any infliction that the devil could ever possibly bring upon us. Now give God a hand for His Word," Pastor Margie said as she left the pulpit and a sanctuary full of souls who knew God had injected them with the power to conquer all things, whatever curveballs life had to throw them. And Paige was one of those souls.

Chapter Thirty-six

"Look at you, gorgeous," Ryan said as he hugged Paige and kissed her on the cheek. It didn't matter that when he'd called her two days straight after their date a couple weeks ago she'd ignored him. It didn't matter that she'd ignored his text message on day three, checking in on her to make sure she was okay. It didn't matter that on day four she sent him an "it's not you, it's me" text, followed by a "don't call me, I'll call you when I'm ready" e-mail. None of that apparently mattered to him when now, two weeks later, he had instantly agreed, within minutes, to meet with her to talk; an invite she'd sent him via a Facebook inbox message.

Paige had committed all three impersonal no-no's when it came to communicating in a relationship. She just didn't want to get him on the phone and endure the awkwardness it would surely entail. How could she have verbally asked him out without giving him some type of explanation for going ghost on him, especially after the last time they'd been together they'd shared an amazing time?

After they'd eaten dinner, with a taste for the best cheesecake in the Midwest they went to the Cheesecake Factory for dessert. It was there Paige felt so open that she did just that: opened up to Ryan. She shared every detail and every crevice about every single part of her life. *Everything.*

All Ryan did was listen. He didn't interrupt her with questions. He just listened, detecting Paige was so open that he was sure she'd provide all the answers without him even asking the questions. And that she did. By the time Paige had shared her entire being with him, the cleaning crew was sweeping up the floors in the restaurant. That didn't stop them though. They talked more on the way to the parking lot where their cars were parked. This time it was Ryan who got naked before her, not literally of course. But exposing the vulnerability most men weren't man enough to. He shared details about the times he did past women in his life wrong and how it was his fault. There was no "she wasn't giving me what I needed; she was too big; she was too small; she didn't listen to me; she didn't support me; she didn't laugh at my jokes," blah blah blah. No, it was, "I was a low-down, dirty boy who knew better, but continued to do worse." That was his truth.

He confessed how meeting a woman, who in essence was like meeting his match, changed the game completely for him. Finally being the one who got played instead of being the player made him see what a scoundrel he really had been for not being honest and respecting others' hearts. It didn't feel so good with the shoe being on the other foot. But in denial and insisting the player couldn't be played, he'd stayed with the woman, doing back flips in order to get her to drop all her other zeros so that she could be with him, her hero. He knew he only wanted her because she didn't want him more than he'd wanted her, which was what he'd been used to from women in past relationships. The minute she became putty in his hand he would have dropped her like a hot potato and he knew it. The attraction would have been gone.

Well all rules changed when she invited him over to her house one night and broke the news that she was pregnant. This was the wakeup call she'd needed to settle down. He was the one she wanted to spend the rest of her life with. They'd settle down and raise a family. They'd have the cat, dog, white picket fence, and the whole nine yards. They did, until the baby came out as light as El DeBarge. There was nothing wrong with that but for the fact that both Ryan and the girl were the complexion of Wesley Snipes. The numbers didn't add up. Literally, the 0.09 percent results translated to "you are not the father" on the paternity test didn't add up. Ryan was sick, considering he'd made all the changes he needed to in life to adjust to his new life with her, and the baby. It made it even harder considering they'd had a shotgun wedding because of her pregnancy.

Ryan thought he'd never recover from that situation. His way of coping was turning into a male whore for a lack of better terms. Women were worse than men and couldn't be trusted as far as he was concerned. They would only be good for one thing in his world. Then he'd met his sons' mother and she, too, turned up pregnant. Boy did he make her pay for the sins of the previous woman. When she told him she was pregnant he didn't believe her and admitted he could have been a lot more diplomatic in relaying that to her. When all was said and done, this time—both times—the numbers added up and he was 99 percent his sons' father. No one could deny he wasn't the bomb father to his sons, but he hadn't been the best fiancé to their mother. It took her sudden diagnosis and death of aggressive breast cancer for him to realize that.

He took her death extremely hard. But then a coworker, who happened to be Catholic, invited him to church one day and everything changed after that . . . for the better.

Paige felt like she'd met her match in Ryan, in a good way. They connected on so many levels and had experienced close to some of the same situations in life. They had connected emotionally. They hadn't even realized how much time they'd spent exposing their lives to one another until security drove through the parking lot making sure that they were okay, seeing it was four in the morning and everything around was closed.

"We might as well go to breakfast," Ryan had suggested.

Knowing Paige had promised the girls a day at the park that Saturday, and she'd already be exhausted from staying out way later than she'd anticipated, she had to decline, but had promised to call him the next day. That was the first promise she'd made him . . . and she'd broken it.

But just like now, as Paige stood there feeling the moisture on her cheek from Ryan's kiss and the warmth from his arms that he slowly removed from around her, they'd managed to pick up where they'd left off two weeks ago. It felt like just yesterday she'd stood in the restaurant where he'd greeted her with a kiss on the cheek and a warm hug. And that's just what Paige wanted: she wanted to pick up where they'd left off. She hoped he'd allow her to make many more promises and fulfill them this time.

"You look great too." Paige smiled at Ryan. "Thanks for meeting me here at the park." Meeting at the park had been Ryan's idea. He had a high school senior photo shoot, so when he read Paige's e-mail asking could they get together to talk, he figured it would be convenient for her to just meet him there.

"No problem." There were a few seconds of silence. Ryan lifted his hand toward the walking trail. "Shall we walk and talk?"

"Sure," Paige agreed as the two headed off on the trail. There were a few more seconds of silence and Paige decided that first things were first. "I'm sorry." She owed him that off the bat. "I'm sorry that I just got ghost on you, sent you that tacky informal text and e-mail and stuff, and ignored your calls. You deserved better."

"I agree and apology accepted," Ryan said.

Paige stopped walking. "Wow, that was easy."

"What?"

"You; accepting my apology without making me beg for forgiveness."

"Ahh, no need to torture you," he said. "Unless you're into that kind of thing."

Paige shot him an eye.

He put his hands up in defense. "Just joking. Dang."

Paige smiled and the two started walking again.

"You shared a lot of yourself with me on our date a couple weeks ago. You gave me a big piece of you and it wasn't fair for me to just leave you hanging like that. But I got some disturbing news from my ex that next morning that just really set me back. Completely stole the total bliss I'd experienced the night before with you. I got scared. For a moment I even lost trust in God. And I don't care what anybody says, if you can't trust God, then you can't trust anybody, especially yourself. So I didn't trust me to be with you. I just felt like my life was a huge dark cloud, that I was a walking disease called misery."

"And do you still feel that way?" Ryan asked.

"No." Paige shook her head. "I realized that I wasn't sick. I just had the symptoms."

Ryan scrunched his face up in puzzlement.

"Never mind." Paige chuckled.

"So is this—our little talk—you telling me that we can pick up where we left off?"

Paige exhaled and stopped walking again. She looked downward.

"Uh-oh."

Paige turned and faced Ryan. "Ryan, let me be blunt with you. I dig you. You give me butterflies. I feel connected to you like no other person. Let me really go there and say I don't doubt for a minute that God made you for me and that maybe He even removed people from our lives so that we could ultimately make our way to one another."

"Well, dang," Ryan said. "Go on with your bad, holy bold self."

"I'm serious."

"I know you are," Ryan said in a serious tone, stopping and taking Paige's hands into his. "I feel the same way." He stared into Paige's eyes sensing there was more. "But . . ."

"But even though I'm not sick, I still need to remain in quarantine for a little while longer. I need to just be alone with me . . . work my way through the symptoms."

Ryan, still holding on to Paige's hands, let out a deep breath while he looked up to the sky. He then closed his eyes.

There was silence and it wasn't awkward. It just was. Paige felt an energy flowing about that felt like heaven. It felt like God was right there in their presence. She couldn't explain it. Neither could she explain the tear that slipped from her eye.

"So this is it . . . for now," Ryan said as he opened his eyes and looked at Paige again.

"For now. But, Ryan, I believe with all my heart that when we meet again, just like always, we're going to pick up right where we left off spiritually . . . and emotionally."

"And I believe that. God says you are mine. Which is why you can take your time. Take all the time God will have you to."

"And you."

Ryan looked into Paige's eyes with those sexy eyes of his. "I'll wait. It's going to be unbearable, but I'll wait."

"Oh, it won't be that bad," Paige said. "You'll live through it."

"Oh, yeah, and how do you know?"

"Because God won't put on you more than you can bear. Trust me. I know." Boy oh boy did she know.

Ryan released Paige's hands and gave her his infamous wink and then she watched him walk away. She turned around and continued her journey on the path before her.

Reading Group
Discussion Questions

1. Paige seemed to waiver throughout the book in her trust for God. Do you think that makes her a bad Christian or just human?

2. On the outside it appeared as though Paige and Norman got married for all the wrong reasons. How do you feel about their choice to marry?

3. How did Mrs. Vanderdale's perception of African American women, based on what she'd seen on reality television shows, make you feel?

4. Should Paige have blamed herself for Norman's death since she sent the text he was replying to when he got into the car accident? Should Norman's mother have blamed her?

5. Paige made a decision to withhold the true paternity of Adele's father until she sees fit. How do you feel about that?

6. Mrs. Robinson feels that Paige jumps from one relationship to the next too soon for fear of being alone. She urged Paige to spend some time courting herself so she could get to know herself better. Do you agree or disagree? Explain your choice.

7. Miss Nettie felt Paige started getting to the point where she leaned on Naomi's prayers, trust, and faith in God to make it through rather than her own. Do you agree or do you think Miss Nettie was just being a busybody?

8. Ryan, who has also dealt with some hard blows in life and some tough relationships himself, agrees to give Paige her space, promising to wait for her until God says she's ready. Do you really think a person can have that much obedience and patience?

9. Did you view Paige as a lukewarm Christian or a struggling Christian, in her words, trying to stay saved?

10. Pastor Margie preached about truly being delivered. Do you think when Christians backslide they are no longer delivered?

About The Author

BLESSEDselling author E.N. Joy is the writer behind the *New Day Divas* five-book series, the *Still Divas* three-book series, and the *Always Divas* three-book series, which have been coined "soap operas in print." Formerly writing secular works under the names Joylynn M. Jossel and JOY, this award-winning author has been sharing her literary expertise on conference panels in her hometown of Columbus, Ohio, as well as in cities across the country. In 2000 Joy formed her own publishing company, End of the Rainbow Projects. In 2004 Joy branched out into the business of literary consulting, providing one-on-one consultations and literary services, such as ghostwriting, editing, professional read throughs, and write behinds. Her clients include first-time authors, *Essence* magazine bestselling authors, *New York Times* bestselling authors, and entertainers. Some of Joy's works have received honors, such as being named an *Essence* magazine bestseller, garnering the Borders Bestselling African American Romance Award, appearing in *Newsweek,* and being translated into Japanese. Joy's children's story, *The Secret Olivia Told Me* (written under the name N. Joy), received the American Library Association Coretta Scott King Honor. Scholastic Books acquired the book club rights, and the book has sold almost 100,000 copies. Elementary and middle school children have fallen in love with reading and creative writing as a result of the readings and workshops Joy performs in schools nationwide.

About The Author

Currently, Joy is the acquisitions editor for Urban Christian, an imprint of Urban Books, the titles of which are distributed by Kensington Publishing Corporation. In addition, Joy is the artistic developer for a young girls group named DJHK Gurls. Joy pens original songs for the group that deal with issues that affect today's youth, such as bullying. You can visit Joy at www.enjoywrites. com.

Coming Spring 2015!

You Get What You Pray For:

Always Divas Series Book Three

(Lorain's Story)